ON THE EDGE

Dick Hannah

ISBN: 9781301821419

This book is a work of fiction and any resemblance to persons, living or dead, or places, events or locales is purely coincidental. The characters are productions of the author's imagination and used fictitiously.

I hope you enjoy the story as much
as I enjoyed writing it.

*****

ALSO BY DICK HANNAH

Toe the Line

Vapor Trail

ON THE EDGE

CHAPTER 1

There is a specific fear, a state of panic really, that takes root within most people, parents particularly when they first discover that they've lost track of their child. It's the moment when a father loses sight of his son in a crowded food court, the second or two when a mother realizes that the little hand that belongs to her daughter that was holding her hand is no longer there. A flush of extreme anxiety with undertones of foreboding follows that first moment and is quickly replaced by hope. Hope that as the crowd parts he will see his son, or she will feel the little fingers reach up and wrap around her hand again. When that doesn't happen the panic becomes terror. My terror began halfway into my Monday, six-mile run. It was Georgia I missed first.

"Where are the others?" I said to my small class of fitness enthusiasts who followed me.

They all looked back at me with blank stares. The terror didn't start then. I still had hope that they'd come running up, so we dropped down for some push-ups while we waited.

My father, Luther, started Adventure Fitness Corporation ten years ago. All the clients call it AFC. He will never call it that, and the clients know enough to use the whole title when they are speaking to him. He started it so he could leverage his twenty years of Marine Corps training. The transition from the Marines to civilian life is rough, particularly if you have over twenty years in the Corps like he did. Luther is one of those marines whose very personality revolves around being a Marine. AFC gives him that opportunity to continue to be a

Marine, the opportunity that the Cops took away from him.

I left the starting point, the parking lot in Stonebridge shopping center, with seventeen people; seventeen crazy, wake up too early, obsessive-compulsive athletes led by one tired, slightly burnt out, failed Marine. When we stopped, we had seven. We were on the corner of West Eldorado and Stonebridge. My mind goes straight to how mad Luther will be if he finds out I've lost his clients.

Six men and one woman were still with me. Ten others were somewhere in the dark morning behind us. I continued the push-ups. Luther caters to a wide range of athletes. Some are comfortable sprinting for miles while others have a hard time running at the pace of a fast walk. It was possible that a few were just taking longer to catch up than I wanted. It wasn't till we reached our one-hundredth pushup that the first slight hint of unease sprouted into concern. Worries about Luther took root as well. Not one of the lost clients had come in.

"We've lost a few, Instructor Malone." It was Gentry.

He was our oldest client and the ersatz second in command for whichever instructor showed up that day. Still leading the push-ups, I looked up Stonebridge Drive hoping to see a group of ten clients appear.

As a rule, Luther only hires Marines, and although he's never stated it as a policy, he's never hired an officer till he hired me. Since he is my father, I've heard Luther's views of officers for most of my life. Among his many complaints is that he thinks they lack the competence needed to lead his clients. "It takes an NCO not a manager to do this right," he was fond of saying. I wasn't panicked yet though. The clients are people. They get lost, get turned around. There was still hope that the lost group would come moseying up out of the darkness.

"We started with seventeen, right, Mr. Gentry?"

"Yep, seventeen," Gentry confirmed before the thick, sarcastic voice of Totten, cut him off.

"What are we paying for again?"

This was common for Totten. He has been with AFC for over

three years, but never missed a chance to point out how it was lacking. In my six months, I'd found the best way to counter him was to keep him busy changing from one exercise to another.

This morning, the anxiety growing, I wasn't in the mood for Totten. "Keep doing push-ups, Mr. Totten," I spoke definitively, trying to assert my authority with a soft and no-nonsense commanding voice.

The other clients heard me and I saw the dark silhouettes of their heads slump as they realized they weren't getting up from the pushup position. They kept up the exercises. They looked like a small cluster of oil pump jacks moving up and down, up and down in a West Texas oilfield.

I checked my watch and realized that five minutes of waiting was more than enough time for stragglers to arrive. Somewhere between Eldorado and University, in the suburbs north of Dallas, with ten minutes left before daylight was supposed to break, there were ten lost, and most likely very pissed off clients any of whom might find it worthwhile to call Luther later and complain.

I gave the stragglers another minute and then I got up and looked up the road. It was time to make a decision. Action, any action was better than this. It was well past time that they might show up. Still, a pang of regret, remorse at giving up, hit me and I refused to believe the other ten clients were truly lost. I stayed there and kept my eyes on the road.

"Come on Joe." Totten used my first name, knowing it was not allowed. "They're not coming."

"Just do the exercise like he said." Gentry said.

"If you'd rather do something harder, Mr. Totten, we can do that?" I said.

A chorus of "Shut up, Totten!" came from the other clients.

Even the first slight hints of the Sun were hidden behind the flat, North Texas horizon. Random lights left on in the four-story office building miles away sprinkled the eastern sky like powdered sugar on dark chocolate frosting. I looked back along the path we had just run. The lights from the houses and the street lamps allowed me to see a few blocks down the street. No one. Not a soul running toward us. The few minutes I had given the stragglers sloughed away and nothing changed.

"Mr. Gentry," my voice broke the silence. Everyone, including Gentry, looked up, their eyes waiting, expectant. "You run back to where we started along Ridge Road. I'll take the group and go back the way we came. Keep an eye out for any clients, grab em up, bring em back to the parking lot if you find em."

"Got it," Gentry said.

"Want me to go too?" It was Totten.

I acquiesced with a nod, not caring if he went or not, just hoping to put a buffer between me and his sarcasm. Better to give Gentry a buddy, I reasoned. I waved my hand at him to go along.

For years I'd been drilled to never split the force. It's a time-honored lesson for any Marine made real through stories of MacArthur in the Korean War and the Chosin Breakout. When we were little, my father taught my older brother and me lessons from Marine history. Never splitting the force had been a major theme. With a premonition of doom blossoming in the pit of my stomach, I split the group in the hopes of finding the lost clients.

In the Marines, I spent three months in Ranger training. I still know the fifth stanza of the Ranger Motto, the one that included the words "I will never leave a fallen comrade to fall into the hands of the enemy." I watched Gentry and Totten as they ran down Eldorado toward Ridge, then I turned to the remaining five clients. With a final tug of regret, sure I was doing the wrong thing by leaving; I told the five to get up and led them back up Stonebridge Drive, back the way we had come. I slowed the pace, alert for my lost clients. I split my focus between the missing clients, the two clients I'd just sent off by themselves and on keeping what was left of my group together. Despite it all, Luther was still my chief concern.

AFC is not a regular, go to the gym, and help old ladies get fit type of group. We start at five in the morning and make our clients crawl through mud, run to exhaustion and do push-ups till their arms feel like they're going to fall off. It's a good gig for an instructor. The clients are generally obsessed with physical fitness; they love the challenge and the mass hysteria that seems to follow in its wake. In general, our clients are extremely disciplined. This morning's break was abnormal, and the worry followed with me as we ran.

"What do you think happened?" It was Mr. Rochester, running slowly next to me.

"I don't know." I tried not to let any panic show through in my voice.

"You think they all turned around?" Rochester again.

I knew that they hadn't all just turned around. They know better than that. Images of a client with a twisted ankle, an older client with a heart attack, or worse the thought of someone colliding with a car cascaded through my thoughts. They all ended with Luther.

"You think one of the road guards screwed up?" Rochester continued.

I could feel the guilt taking shape in my gut. When I lead the clients on runs, especially long runs like today's, I leave some of the faster runners behind to direct the slower ones. They act as traffic cops, telling the slow runners where to turn. They are supposed to catch up after the last runner passes them. As we ran back I tried to remember who the four clients were that I had dropped off that morning.

"I guess they're really lost, Instructor." I heard Rochester sigh as we made our final turn before reaching the parking lot.

We had not found a single lost client. No Miss Georgia, no Miss Ridgeway, not even Mr. Chopra, all of them fast, reliable runners. I felt a shot of anger flare within me at Rochester's resignation. Anger at his negativity, anger at the lost clients, at having to split the group, but mostly anger at what I knew Luther would say.

"They're lost cause your clients never listen to instructions,

Mr. Rochester." My teeth clamped down. I felt it and forced my jaw muscles to relax. "Do you think they're hurt?" Rochester said.

I looked at Rochester angrily. Was this Rochester of all people making sarcastic remarks? Totten I could understand, not Rochester. Then I saw his eyes. They were not devious or castigating like Totten's would have been. I had to remind myself that not all the clients were out to embarrass me like Totten. Instead, Rochester looked genuinely worried. Like a sheep desperately trying to keep up with the herd, his eyes casting around for an unseen wolf.

"They'll be fine," I said. Then I spread the group out for some more exercises before they began to mill around the parking lot. I turned and looked as the group dropped to the ground and started push-ups again. The sky was slightly less dark than it had been before. The jaw clenched again. My deadline for finding the missing clients was approaching. The class lasts an hour. We were less than five minutes from hitting that limit. I glanced at my watch then peered through the semi-darkness one last time, hoping to see a small group of runners jogging toward us. No one materialized. Where the heck was everybody? My shoulders slumped, but I caught myself quickly and stood up straight again. No way was I going to show my failure in front of the clients.

"That's it for the day, folks," I said to the small group who stood around me, all of them looking up the road from the pushup position as expectantly as I. "Go home. See ya tomorrow."

"You want us to get our cars and go look for them?" Rochester's worried eyes again.

My voice stern, I said, "Nope, just go home. I'll take care of it."

I looked down at my feet and I shook my head, my morning text to Luther composing itself. Usually, they were quick letters like Seventeen clients, long run, no problems. That's what he would expect. Today's would not be so easy. Once, a few months ago, I had to write him one that said, One client went down with a twisted knee. I advised her to ice and elevate. Something like that usually got him mad.

If those ten clients didn't return, today's status report would make him go nova. Seventeen clients. Six-mile run. Lost ten.

CHAPTER 2

I watched them all wander off slowly to their cars, my concerns growing as the day brightened slowly around us. It wasn't just the loss of the clients, that was, of course, the predominant factor, but I developed a slight unease about open areas during my time in the Marines. An off-shoot of my time in Iraq, but nothing I can't handle. Before workouts, I stake out the more shadowed areas or set up under the darkness beneath the oak trees. I'm less vulnerable in the darkness. I like to have something concealing me, even if it is just darkness. Now, with the tinge of the orange in the eastern sky, I felt an overriding need to get away from the open areas. I checked my watch again. Two minutes overtime.

I looked up and saw movement on the path, still several hundred meters away. I continued to track it till it resolved itself into the form of a line of runners, then eventually became Gentry and Totten with several others behind. I counted them as they came into the parking lot. They had found nine. There was still one missing.

"Where's the other?"

Gentry's voice was despondent. "This was all we found."

"Then we only have sixteen."

"You didn't see anyone else?" Gentry's heavy voice was staid and undeterred, but there was a hint of panic, perhaps accusation somewhere beneath the surface.

"No." I tried to sound authoritative and in control.

Inside fear was beginning to boil over along with the anger and worry.

"Want me to run back again?" Gentry asked.

"No," I said. "I should have made sure we stayed together. This is on me. I'll take care of it."

"I don't mind." He was insistent.

There was a sense of relief with the return of Gentry and Totten and the other runners, I realized it wasn't worth the worry to split the group again.

"No, I'll take care of it, you can leave." I turned and looked at the few clients who remained in the parking lot.

"Does anyone know who's missing?" I yelled at them.

"I can't believe you lost a client." This was Totten. For a moment I thought of making him do push-ups as punishment, but the lost client took priority.

"Was Georgia with you?" It was Bradshaw. He'd come back with Gentry and Totten.

I looked across at the remnants of the group that had come back with me, some still milling by their cars, others in the midst of leaving. I saw the white Volkswagen that belonged to Miss Georgia. I yelled across at the group, "Who saw Miss Georgi last?"

Everyone looked back and forth among themselves and I realized it was a poor way to phrase the question. "Hold on," I thought back quickly. "I left Miss Georgia behind to direct traffic at Glen Oaks, who passed her?"

Seven people raised their hands.

"Okay, and who was the last to pass her."

I watched as people pointed back and forth, but it became evident that Mr. Bradshaw had been the last. She had been the nexus of the problem, the reason we lost the others. With no one on that corner to tell runners which way to go, everyone behind her had gotten off course.

"Fuck," I muttered. "I'll go back and look for her. You guys can take off. At least now we know who's missing."

"Are you going to be out here tomorrow?" Gentry asked as he picked up his water bottle and got ready to leave.

I nodded.

"I'm going to be here for sure," Totten said to him without being asked. "I can't wait to see how you lose someone in a push-ups workout."

I turned to face him. "You got a problem, Mr. Totten?" He smiled as he sauntered away from me and towards his car. "Nope. You're the one with the problem, Joe. You lost the client, not me."

Several clients watched him say this and I knew I should reprimand him, some punishment push-ups, low crawls, or a few minutes doing sit-ups under the water hose. Using an instructor's first name was a glaring show of disrespect; it was something he'd never pull with Luther. He was goading me, but why? What was the purpose? I watched him leaving and felt more and more impotent the further away he walked. I lost the tug of war between reprimanding Totten and finding Georgia as he neared his car. Then, like a wave lapping onshore and retreating to the ocean, he won and the moment where I could do anything passed.

I'm the newest instructor, as well as the youngest. I have the added burden of being the owner's son. I constantly have to prove myself, I am always tested, and Totten was just the loudest of the bunch. I had just lost this test. His car started and drove off and the parking lot was left almost empty. My jaw clenched as I watched him go. What else could this morning bring, I wondered.

I turned back toward the path and looked in vain for the familiar gate of Miss Georgia appearing along the road, a tall figure, loping stride, a ponytail. Instead, all I saw was the dull gray morning coming on inexorably and the brake lights of the clients as they left.

Gentry drove up and rolled down the window of his expensive SUV. "I'm going to go back the way we came to see if I see her."

I sighed and realized that there was no way I was going to beat the morning home. I was going to be stuck out here, in full daylight looking for a lost client whether I liked it or not.

Luther loved to use my fear of the open against me whenever he referred to my taking over the business, I refused to give him more ammunition by just abandoning a client in the hopes she would wander back.

"I'll take care of it." I tried to make it sound final. "I'm going to run back the way we came."

He disregarded my statement. "Okay, I'll go take the car and see what I see."

"You don't need to do that."

"No problem."

He turned and drove down the street. I turned back to the parking lot and saw two or three clients waiting around, not wanting to leave when a member of the team was still out there, obviously ready to get back to their work-a-day worlds, but stuck in a limbo between their regular lives and their workout lives. I envied them and yelled at them to go home. They obeyed quickly and I looked at the last of the morning's darkness slowly drift from the area. I took off at a run down the sidewalk. I craned my head upwards searching for a lonely, solitary, runner coming back to the parking lot.

I ran mad. Mad at the coming day. Mad at the inability of the clients to follow orders. Mad at Totten for insulting me in front of the clients. Mad at Gentry for wanting to help. Mostly mad that I knew Luther would use this against me. The anger lent strength and speed to my legs as I flew along the path. I made the first major turn along the road and squinted as the day grew brighter around me. I picked up my pace, my chest heaving, legs thick with fatigue, running fast not to find Georgia, but to outrun my anger.

Eventually, the anger dropped off and my thoughts turned to Georgia. She is a good runner, one of our best. There are only four clients who could beat her in a race. Some days even I have trouble keeping a comfortable lead on her. She's also one of our most conscientious clients. She would only have left the group if there was trouble. I ran faster, each step carrying me closer to the point where I dropped her off.

She wouldn't have wandered off or gone for a run on her own, the further I went the more I was sure something was wrong. My breath came in loud gasps. I prayed as I ran that my message to Luther would read: "Six-mile run, found Georgia with a twisted ankle." Something, anything that would make the day turn out okay.

Georgia had been the third road guard that I left behind that morning. She had been stationed just beyond the coffee shop. My last words to her were, "Wait here. Have everyone cross the street here, and run that way. Catch up after the last person." No room for confusion. No reason for her not to follow us, eventually.

I rounded a corner and was confronted with a major intersection. The tree-lined section of the sidewalk ended and I was back out in the open again. The sky, a dull blue now, was just a moment from becoming full daylight. This was the spot where I had left the first road guard, Mr. Totten. "Stay here. Make sure the others go straight on. Catch up after the last man," I had said. He had caught quickly, why hadn't Georgia? Where was she? I looked both ways before crossing, not just for traffic but for any signs of her.

I made it to the next intersection in just under a minute, sprinting the whole way. I looked up and could just make out the coffee shop further down the road. My breath was ragged now, heaving. I had left Mr. Gilbert here. He got the same directions, "Stay here. Tell the other clients to keep up the pace. Catch up ASAP." Once Gilbert had stopped, it had been just me and Georgia out front.

Now, with the coffee shop coming closer with each step, worry overcame the fatigue I felt and I forgot about my burning lungs and sore feet. I looked ahead and saw that the sun had broken over the horizon. I dredged my legs for some small bit of reserve strength that I could use to run faster, to find Georgia, to outpace my anger at Gentry and Totten but mostly to beat the coming daylight.

The sun hit my eyes and made me miss a crack in the sidewalk. I tripped and fell, but rolled into the grass that bordered the pavement. I came up quickly with a sharp pain in my knee. A quick loud curse followed. I kept my focus on the coffee shop and grimaced through the pain as I ran. I wondered at the possibility of Georgia having hurt herself. Georgia could have tripped on the path, knocked her head and stumbled somewhere on the side of the road. I should have been more careful on the run to listen for her calling for help. I looked over my shoulder but decided against the idea of going back as quickly as I had considered it.

Just a few paces from the coffee shop a man wearing a bike helmet and biking shoes ran awkwardly out of the vacant lot that bordered Glen Oaks. He ran inside and He shouted at the lone employee and pointed at the lot next door. Something was wrong. Panic and fear were etched across his face. I felt the same unease and panic in the pit of my stomach. It blossomed into something more as I sprinted by the coffee shop, pulled up to the vacant lot, knowing what I'd find there without needing to be told.

There was a path that disappeared into the trees. I plunged head-long through the trees and almost collided with a mountain bike lying in the middle of the trail. The light filtered through the trees and let me make out where the biker had walked, his trail highlighted by the disturbance in the blanket of dew that covered the tall grass. The man had probably stopped to take a leak or maybe wanted to ride down toward the creek.

I found Georgia's body crumpled in the middle of the lot, surrounded by tall grass and trees, just a couple of meters in front of the bike. Her shirt was ripped and cut and running shorts missing. Her stomach, breasts, legs, arms, all covered in cuts and stab wounds. Her skin was covered in blood. The leaves of the plants were splattered and coated in blood as well. The smell made me gag and I stepped back instinctively. I heard the biker coming back, his footsteps and panting breath dominated the stillness around us. Everything around me was alive, as if this moment was making me hypersensitive. I took in the blood, the vacant stare from two open, lifeless eyes. A car passed loudly on the road behind us and somewhere far away a bird chirped and called. The biker was saying something, his lips moved but I couldn't hear him. I bent down and felt Georgia's neck. Her skin was cold beneath my fingers. There was no pulse. For some reason, my mind finished composing my morning text to Luther.

Seventeen clients. Six-mile run. Lost seven. One dead.

CHAPTER 3

The area where we found Georgia was in the process of transformation: spotty, high-end residential construction on one side of the street to intensive mixed-use on the other. Like a teenager trying to sort himself out, the area was unsure of which way it would grow or how it was going to end up. The vacant lot was situated between the coffee shop on one side and an expensive-looking apartment complex on the other. In a month that same lot would probably be a new restaurant.

For now, it was a dumping ground. I wondered, somewhat morbidly, how long Georgia's murder would delay the development. I had been there over an hour, so long that my thoughts had ranged over everything else. From worry to guilt, then anger. Now, I was on the prosaic. I looked out at the overgrown flora through the large windows from the far corner of the coffee shop. I was nestled in the back, my back to the wall so I could see everyone coming and going.

My questioning by Detective Chen of the Addison Police Department had ended fifteen minutes ago with a stern warning not to go anywhere. Since finding Georgia I had been questioned three times by an assortment of police officers in greater and greater roles of responsibility. What had originally been a bit hostile had turned more gracious after I'd asked them to call my brother. Mike is a detective with the Dallas Police Department. Apparently, he knew Chen and was able to convince him that I was less a suspect and more a credible witness. Ten minutes ago Chen had told me my brother Mike was on his way.

"Just wait here, Mr. Malone, I'm sure we'll have more questions for you." I had found the quietest corner of the coffee shop, moved the chair so I could see the door and the window and waited for what would come next, sure that at some point Luther would arrive. My loathing for that moment increased exponentially with each passing minute. It was as if I could feel his coming, like the pressure dropping before a storm.

"Have you thought of anyone who would want to hurt Miss Pelham?" It was Chen, back for more questions.

I shook my head.

"Did she have any enemies?"

I said I didn't know her that well and was forced to re-explain the AFC group and how we operated.

"At this point," Chen continued, "we're not completely confident that this was a random event." A deep thrum roared from down the street, and I knew that large, diesel pickup that made that noise. Luther. I closed my eyes as apprehension crawled over me. Chen went on, "The fact that she was mutilated suggests that whoever killed her was intensely angry at her."

I nodded but the sound of the diesel engine held all my attention. I could hear it coming through the walls of the little shop. How could I be so sure it was him? I thought. Texas is full of diesel trucks. Despite my rationalization, I knew it was Luther.

"Whoever murdered her stabbed her viciously," Chen droned on. In the back of my mind I heard him say that if I knew of anyone who might be angry at her, I should tell them. The coffee shop seemed to tremble and shake from outside as the truck pulled into the adjacent parking lot. My father drives a large, black truck that looks like a cross between a semi-tractor trailer and a Sherman tank. I shook my head in answer to Chen's question as the huge engine rumbled to a stop.

"Our best guess is that she was lured into the lot by someone she knew. Can you think of anyone who might have had the opportunity to do that?" I shook my head as I imagined Luther climbing down from the cab.

I had already explained to them how I ran my workouts, had told them about the runners who had seen her and those who had not seen her, told them as much as I knew.

"You look worried," the detective said. "Is there anything you haven't told us?"

The constricted space of the coffee shop, the constant movement of the police officers in and out of the area, but most of all the idea that Luther, somewhere in the parking lot behind me, was on his way, all of it made me much more anxious. But any other questions the detective might have had behind his slitted, curious eyes were brought to a halt by Luther's arrival.

He came into the coffee shop, striding purposefully, his demeanor, clothes, bearing; all of it exuded military precision and seriousness. Luther dresses like a paramilitary soldier, black cargo pants, undershirts that would not be unusual at a gym and hats that are usually pulled down low, that make the omnipresent sunglasses look like a part of the bill of the hat themselves.

I watched as an officer approached him, obviously intent on asking my father who he was or what he was doing. He spoke abruptly to the officer, pointed toward the coffee shop and the vacant lot, and then strolled past, leaving a questioning glance on the officer's face in his wake. If nothing else Luther commanded respect, when he didn't get it, he pulled rank, if he had no rank he faked it if only because he felt he outranked everyone around him.

As I watched, I realized I had hoped the police officer would call his bluff, tell him he had no business here, tell him to meet me at the station, or at home, anything to insulate me from my father for just a little while longer. Detective Chen followed my gaze.

"That's your father?" he asked. I had already told him about

Luther during our first round of questions.

"That's my boss," I corrected.

The detective stood up and intercepted Luther before he could come across to the back of the shop. I watched them.

Luther hates policemen. I've been around him enough to have heard every crazy conspiracy theory he has about the police. I could sense his disdain in his body language, even if the detective might not. I saw it since I had watched it all my life. It hadn't been lost on me that though Luther may despise police he looks and acts like the very thing he hates.

Chen gestured with his hand and pointed at me. Luther turned his eyes to me. I've seen Luther angry most of my life. When I was a kid, I'd often been the focus of that anger. Since I left the Marines, Luther's anger has been replaced by a look of dismay and disappointment. It's been a while since I had seen anger. His eyes were filled with anger now. Somewhere, I felt a strange sense of relief that at least his look of disappointment that he usually gave me now days was gone.

Luther broke off from the detective and came over to me. "What have you told them?" Luther asked.

"I had to tell them what happened." Immediately I felt like a kid. Luther would have been happier had I told the police nothing.

Luther probably would have given me a raise if I had told them to screw off, and he had found me in the back of their cruiser, handcuffed and facing charges of obstructing an investigation. That's the way Luther's mind works. I betrayed him by providing any information beyond my name and address. Just by sitting passively I was letting him down.

"What the hell happened?" Luther said.

"I don't know."

"Not good enough. Try again." His words are quick, short and staccato.

"I started on a run..."

"Where to?" he interrupted.

"I was going to run to the County Road, cross under at the

highway, then run back."

"How many clients?"

"Seventeen."

"Seventeen for a run," he spoke and looked past me somewhere. "With that many, I would have stayed at the parking lot, but still even you should have been able to handle seventeen. So what the hell happened?"

I sighed as I heard the implied insult in the phrase "even you," but I let it pass, as I have for my whole life and went on.

"Well, we started fine, and I left some of the faster people behind."

Luther's eyes swung up abruptly and his fist slammed down on the table making a clattering sound in the small coffee shop. Several officers looked up. Luther's eyebrows drew down between his eyes in a crisp V.

"What?"

"I left some people behind as I ran to..."

Luther interrupted me by lunging forward across the table, his voice still low, but louder now than before. "You left the clients behind? On purpose?"

"On longer runs I leave some faster runners behind to tell the slower ones where to go," I said.

"Are you fucking kidding me?" he said.

Behind Luther, I saw Chen stand up and warn of a couple of police officers who looked like they were on the brink of intervening.

"Haven't I always told you to keep them all together?" I saw his knuckles growing white as he gripped the table between us.

I knew it was getting out of hand and tried to explain. "Like I said, when the runs are long I like to leave the fast runners at critical intersections to instruct the slower clients where to go. Once the last of our group passes they get to catch up. I told you about this. I told you about this two months ago."

"You never told me you left clients by themselves."

"Yeah, I told you when we were doing that leg workout..."

His fist found the table again. "You never told me this," his voice rose. "If you had, I would have told you to never break up the unit or leave clients alone." He stared across at me icily. There would be no chance of convincing him he was wrong.

As if it took a force of will beyond mortals Luther seemed to collect himself and said, "Go on."

Another sigh on my part. "I left Mr. Totten at the light at the end of the trail where it comes near those condos with the park. I left Mr. Gilbert at the next light beyond that one." I nodded out the window. Luther didn't move. "I left Georgia right out there." I pointed out the coffee shop windows to the spot near the water fountain. He turned to look out the windows at where I was pointing.

When he turned back to face me he led with the back of his fist.

CHAPTER 4

The sun was shining but not yet oppressive. The night had been cool, not cold. The type of night that didn't get cold enough, one where everyone knew the next day would be hot. The cloudless sky too was a harbinger of the mind-numbing heat that would invariably arrive. The desert sand, hard-packed beneath our feet, was not shining up at us as it did in the summers, but it held its own foreshadowing of heat. It held the oncoming heat like a canteen would water, except this would radiate up and into us throughout the day. The only benefit might be that maybe it would keep the hostiles inside where they would cause less trouble.

Despite the foreboding heat an almost imperceptible smile creased my face. So far it had been the best day I'd had since I came to Iraq. The patrol, now almost four hours in, had been quiet. All we had spotted was a pack of dogs traveling in the same direction. The movement, seen as little more than a blur on the horizon, had sent my Marines pinging. Then, identified and studied for long seconds through the reticle of our point man's ACOG sight, all we'd seen was half a dozen dogs, trotting through the desert, disappearing behind scrub brush and hillocks, only to reappear seconds later like dolphins popping up for air before disappearing again beneath the water. The leader, a large, dark-brown mutt with an identifiable spot of mange on his haunch, held his head high as the other, more mottled followers fell in behind him.

We were in Iraq. It was my second deployment to the Middle East, but my first to Iraq. The other deployment I had been sent to Afghanistan to help with setting up forward refueling bases for helicopters. It had been an easy deployment. Lots of hurry up and wait and supporting other units, but my unit saw not a hint of combat. Six months back in the states, then I had been assigned a rifle platoon and I was off to lead them in Iraq. This was a different monster. We were pushed to work in the field constantly, movement to contact missions, ambushes, village pacification. It had been a rough few months in Iraq, to say the least.

"Sir!" one of my Marines, gave a harsh whisper from behind me.

I stopped and crouched automatically. The rest of the platoon paused and did the same, their eyes already alert and scanning. Gunnery Sergeant Lamb, my platoon sergeant, the second in command of the platoon, jogged toward the center or the column, directly to me. Several of the Marines regripped their rifles in their hands, and looked around quickly, as they saw him run up the line of men.

Unlike some of the newer Marines, I've been in theater for almost nine months. I've seen the differences between a Marine running due to enemy contact, and one running to communicate less life-threatening news. I kept myself relaxed and hoped that my Marines would notice and emulate the nonchalance.

I took a knee as he approached and watched as the Marines up and down the line did the same. Without being told the entire unit created an ersatz defensive position, all weapons pointing out.

"What's up?"

"Your radios down," he said. "I've been calling."

"Shit," I looked down at the Motorola on my ammo vest. Before I could do anything my radio telephone operator, RTO, Specialist Wilson was at my side.

"I got it, sir." he pulled it out and began to change the battery. I knelt down next to Lamb.

"Marlberg says the objective is just over that rise." He

pointed up along the line of our march. "About 500 meters."

I nodded. "Good."

I looked back and saw my platoon of Marines, tired, but ready and primed to keep moving. They knew as well as I that the sooner we finished the mission the sooner we would be back inside the wire, resting and relaxing. That was the drive to finish that lead us all forward. I might command them in battle, and set the mission and vision for the platoon, but the drive that pushed them forward was their desire to do well for their brothers in arms, their other Marines, but also that desire to get back to the hooch and relax.

We had three squads, each with two three-man fire teams. Each squad also had a machine gun team attached, that made three squads of three teams of three. We had a mortar section with us, and we had a heavy weapons section that would help if we saw any armor. That was thirty-three marines, privates, corporals, sergeants and higher all reporting up to me. Next to me was also an FO, forward observer, a Platoon Sergeant named Gunny, of course, a medic and a Weapons Leader. Finally, we had an RTO or Radio Telephone Operator. All told thirty-nine and myself. It was enough to take on just about anything we ran into in this AO.

"You okay, Sir?" It was Lamb again, the Gunny.

"I'm good Gunny," I said. "Tell the Marines to gear up and get ready to move into position. Should take us a few hours."

"Roger Sir," Gunny said and he took off at a trot to talk to his squad and section leaders.

CHAPTER 5

Luther has hit me before. My brother and I grew up with Luther hitting us. It isn't something I've come to expect, but whenever it happens, I'm never surprised. This one was a surprise. In all the years of Luther's particular brand of corporal punishment, I've always been safe from it in crowds. I must have thought a crowd that consisted of police officers was safer than most.

The police being there may not have saved me from his outburst, but they converged on him immediately when they saw him hit me. Distance was put between us. I heard him argue, but one word from Luther reverberated above the others, it came across even above the shock and pain of his hit, "Don't tell me how to treat him, he's my son."

It has been years since Luther took ownership of either me or Mike in public. It struck me, and I latched onto it not because it was touching, or because it was something I longed to hear, but because I was shocked by the complete indifference I felt when I heard it.

Chen took over and the crowd of police officers dispersed, all of them with angry, unforgiving eyes directed at Luther. He sat again, confronting me from across the table. This time Chen did not retreat quite so far away as the last and he gave me a look that said if I needed him he was just a second from intervening again.

"How long have you been leaving clients by themselves?" Luther jumped back in as if nothing had happened.

"I'm trying to give all of the clients a good workout, Luther.

If I try to keep everyone together, the fast runners get antsy. If I take off, the slow ones get left behind."

"You think it's better to deliberately leave clients behind, to split the force?" I saw Chen lean forward as Luther spoke.

"It always worked until now."

"This was a pretty big fuck up this morning!" He said.

Chen took a step forward then waited to see what would happen. I was braced for another swipe.

"Did you tell them anything? Did you leave them any instructions?" Luther was picking up more and more military-style speech. The short clipped manner of speaking was the one he used whenever he was reverting back to his time in the Marines.

"I always say the same thing. I tell them to wait for the last person, encourage everyone who passes."

"So what happened this time?"

"That's really it. I got to the County Road and realized something was wrong."

"What the hell does that mean? Something was wrong?"

Chen stood at the table now.

"I was waiting at County Road doing push-ups and was going to catch everyone up there. After about fifteen minutes I realized we had lost everyone."

Luther continued to stare across the little table, and I wondered what else he wanted me to say. It was like being in the center of a spotlight on a dark night, nowhere to hide. His mustache twitched back and forth as he thought. It reminded me of the little light that blinks on my computer, the one that lets me know the processor is working.

I had been a Lieutenant in the Marines, and for the first half of my tour, I was the one that my men alternately feared and looked up to. Luther never got past the rank of Gunnery Sergeant. In the Marines, he would have had to defer to me. Even in my worst counseling sessions with my superiors, Captains, Majors, even Colonels, I never felt as low and out of place as I did when I spoke to the man who sat across the table from me now, the man who, at least in the Marines, never out-ranked me. Sitting across from him I felt like a three-year-old who had been caught in a lie.

"How did you find the others?"

"I figured that they might still be running down Stonebridge, so I sent Mr. Gentry and Mr. Totten down that way, while I ran back the way we had come."

"So you split the force even more, even after you knew there was a problem?" His voice was firm and level. "You deliberately provoked a second break in contact."

"Look, Luther...," I started, my hands coming up to make a supplicating gesture. I didn't get a chance to finish.

"Hold it!" he shouted. He pointed at me as he interrupted. Chen almost jumped in front of him. Luther looked up sharply.

"We'll call if we need you." He jerked his thumb at Chen.

The detective looked at me to see what I wanted him to do. I nodded. He reluctantly backed a step or two away. Luther leaned forward and spoke under his breath.

"How much of this did you tell these jack asses?"

It was a tricky question. Luther is secretive about his business. He doesn't advertise, doesn't promote it beyond owning a website, and doesn't do anything except run it quietly, efficiently and productively. Like every other part of this conversation, I knew he wasn't going to be happy with my answers.

"Pretty much what I just told you," I spoke slowly, my mind racing to remember everything I told the police, hoping I was right. "I called Mike, he's on his way here, plus there are seven clients who can give me an alibi."

Luther's eyes shot open and for a moment I thought his fist would follow. Chen came forward again. I wasn't sure why Mike would provoke a smack. Then I realized what I had said. It wasn't Mike. It was what I'd said about the clients. I watched anger spread across Luther's face and realized what I had done.

"You didn't give them any of the clients' names, did you?"

His hands were back on the table now, his face moving in close to mine, his voice low. Chen inched closer again, his eyes glued to Luther and his actions.

I knew that I'd just lost any ounce of defensive cover I might have had. I had given the police a few of the names of our clients. Sure, I did it to provide my alibi, but giving out a client list was sure to send Luther into orbit. It was like throwing jet fuel on a bonfire.

"Crap, I'm sorry."

"Do you know if they started calling them yet?" His voice was quick and I noticed for the first time a glint of panic in his eyes.

"I don't know. I doubt it."

Luther got up, his eyes vacant, lost in thought. He brushed past Chen and strode to the counter. He spoke to the barista behind the counter and began to look for money to buy a coffee. I noticed he only ordered for himself, he didn't ask if I wanted anything. The last thing Luther needed to be saddled with was the clients getting the news of the murder from the police before he could do any damage control. New clients might reconsider when the news that one of our clients had been brutally murdered on a workout. Veteran clients might find a reason in this to try something new.

Luther walked back to the table, as tense as I had ever seen him. His gait was clipped, his arms were so rigid they hardly moved. He sat down silently and took a small sip of coffee. His eyes fell on mine like a rifle sight settling on a target.

"First, you're fired." He spoke with no emotion, almost as if it was something I should have expected. "Second, you are not to speak to the police again regarding my business, if you do I'll sue you."

I smiled. "You're kidding, right?"

"No," his voice boomed off the walls. He jabbed his index finger at me. Chen moved up next to the table smoothly and his hand came up defensively.

Luther stood, his finger still jabbing. "Had I known that you were leaving clients by themselves like this I would have fired you sooner. I'm going to go clean up your mess. Me, not you.

You need to get out of my sight."

I stood up next to him and he turned to confront me, his eyes alive. "What about our agreement?"

"That's over." His hand leveled between us in a flat sweeping motion, almost hitting Chen. "

You've seriously compromised my business and my livelihood. Your actions have had a direct and negative impact on me and the clients. You're gone."

CHAPTER 6

The morning didn't get better after I got home. My mind had been a turmoil of thoughts as I ran home. Usually running helps me forget my problems. In today's case, the problems were still too fresh and real. For those rare times when running doesn't help me, I turn to my work. I sat down at my desk. I looked at my latest project. My mind continued to swirl. No matter what I did my mind kept returning to the clients, to Luther, but mostly to Georgia.

What had happened? Why would she have gone down into that lot? Who killed her and why? But mostly, could I have done anything different to prevent it? This was an easy question to answer, and it left me feeling impotent and hollow inside. There was so much I could have done.

If I could go back in time, I wouldn't have left her there alone. Was Luther right? Was I too cavalier with the client's safety?

Eventually, I gave up on my work and retreated to the shower to try to rinse it all away. It was a few minutes into that shower when I heard a muffled yell and someone pounding on my apartment door. The pounding brought all the problems crashing back. I knew before I turned off the water that it was Mike. Only my older brother would announce himself with such a distinctive and obnoxious manner. I made him wait.

The pounding continued.

I got out of the shower, threw on a t-shirt and shorts and moseyed back into the little living room. Now he was pounding and yelling my name.

I opened the door and there was Mike. Despite the attitude, he entered the apartment with a smile. My brother, as predictable as Luther was random.

"So, I heard you're looking for a job?" He tried and failed to stifle a laugh at his own joke. Mike has always been his own best audience.

Typical for Mike he wore starched khaki pants, boots, and a starched powder blue shirt. The Dallas Police require their detectives to look professional. Mike adhered to this mandate through the liberal use of starch. Had he been off duty Mike would have been wearing the same uniform, minus a mote or two of starch. His hair was cut short, like Luther's and mine, but his eyes were bright and fun-loving. He slugged me on the shoulder good-naturedly as he stomped across the living room into the kitchen, his boots and his heavy frame making his movements echo through the thin floor of my little second-floor apartment. It always bothered me that no matter where he was, he entered a room as if he owned it. My apartment received no special dispensation.

People always said we didn't look like brothers, where he is large and barrel-chested, I am lean. He is loud, I am quiet. We get along because we've known one another all our lives. We also have a common enemy in Luther.

"Seriously," he continued, "I have a job that's perfect for someone like you."

"What?"

"I arrested a hooker this morning at Abrams and Lovers. Get your ass down there. You can have your own corner."

"Up yours," I told him as he made himself a cup of my coffee.

He didn't turn as he changed subjects and got serious.

"I got a look at your crime scene," he said. "Pretty gruesome."

"I saw it too," I dropped into the large work chair at my desk. "I don't need to be reminded."

My cluttered living room doubled as my workspace. Three

large tables lined the walls and made my apartment seem much smaller than it actually was. My projects are models of products. That is my full-time job. Models of airplanes, oil rigs, new buildings that were being designed, all of them lined each table. Scattered around were various tools and other detritus of modeling; paints, dental picks, magnifying glasses, tweezers and glues of all types. No couch, no table, no TV. My only sop to comfort was the large, far too expensive, work chair.

Mike, his coffee finished, leaned against the wall. "I know they asked you already," he said. "Any thoughts on who did it?"

I shook my head. I hate when Mike interrogates me. I can feel his eyes watching me as if he's reading my gestures. I think he realizes it makes me uncomfortable and levels his gaze on me with extra weight.

"No one?"

"She was just a regular client."

"Was she liked by the others?" Heavy gaze.

"As far as I know."

"Would Luther say the same?" A sideways glance.

I shrugged. "Who knows what Luther would say?"

He smiled at that.

"She was in good shape," He turned to face me as he spoke. "Are you surprised?"

"By what?"

"That she was murdered, Ass," Mike's brow lowered as if I should have guessed when he was serious and when he wasn't.

"Of course, I was surprised. But shit happens. She was a girl alone in the dark, I mean any weirdo could have overpowered her, dragged her into the woods and killed her."

"Nope, she was lured down there." He took a sip of the coffee; ostensibly I believe to make me wait for more. "There were no signs of her being dragged or of a fight."

"Then maybe it was a bum," I said. "Some homeless nut lured her into the woods."

"You think she was stupid?" He asked. "What kind of girl allows herself to be lured into the woods by a bum in the dark?"

A shrug was the only answer he got from me.

"Plus... a transient in McKinney? Take a look around next time you're in that neighborhood, very few transients. They even have a bunch of rent-a-cops to keep em out." He paused and I wondered if he practiced his knowing glances in front of the mirror at night. "Nope, it was someone she knew."

I sighed and leaned my head back, eyes closed. "Can we talk about something else? I'm trying not to think about it."

He shook his head as if I'd just disappointed him. He'd given me that same look for years when I gave up on a game of basketball where he was trouncing me when he tackled me too hard in football and I decided I'd had enough when he'd break into my room with his friends just for the fun of wrestling me to the ground to make me say uncle or worse. I've known that look for years.

"Holy shit," he let the words fall slowly out of his mouth. "Guess I should have known you wouldn't have the stomach for this type of thing."

"I just don't want to talk about this, Mike." It came out more plaintive than I had intended.

"Okay, okay," his hands came up defensively. "One last thing."

"What?"

"Mom says hi." He winked.

"Great," I said. "That makes it all better."

He laughed under his breath and looked around the room, his eyes roving over each model until they fell on the oil rig.

Mike walked over to stand over it. "What's going on here?"

I jumped up to stand between him and the model. "It's not dry yet."

"I know, I know." Mike threw up his hands and edged by me to get a closer look at the model. "No touching, I get it."

"I mean it, Mike," I said. "I have to have that done for Friday morning. It's fragile."

Mike leaned down close to the model and inspected it as if

he knew what to look for. It was a three-foot model of a floating jack-up oil drilling rig. Six other models in various stages of completion were placed around the living room. The oil rig was the largest of the bunch and it was natural that Mike's eyes would find it first.

He stood back and looked at it from several angles. He peered at it quizzically but eventually shrugged and stood back. He turned to another project on the same table. This one was boxed up and wrapped in plastic, ready for pick up.

"And this is what?" He pointed at the box as he looked through the clear plastic at the model beneath.

"That's a new strip mall some architect needed."

"Really?"

This is typical whenever Mike comes over. His visits are rare thankfully. I've lived and worked here for almost six months, this was only the third time he had been in my apartment.

I looked toward my bedroom and hoped he wouldn't think to go in there. I craned my neck to see if I had I had shut the bedroom door when I came out of the shower. It was open. I cringed. If he had to use the restroom, he would be able to see in. Mike picked up the box with the strip mall and held it closer to his face. I stepped forward tentatively. He must have seen the worry on my face since he offered another quick apology and put the strip mall back on the table.

"Expensive?"

Another shrug. "Not really, but they need it today, and if it breaks, it will take a couple of days to re-do." I re-checked it to make sure everything looked okay but kept my eyes peeled to see if he started toward the bedroom.

"You free-lancing this architect one?" he looked at me, his eyebrows raised. "Seems like a small fry. Not what I would expect from one of Kathy's clients."

He knew my boss Kathy better than I since he had spent some time dating her in high school. He liked to ask about her whenever he came over. It was only a matter of time before he started to dig for intel on her.

"He probably would have done it himself," I explained. "But he needed it fast. I'm sure Kathy's charging a premium for the quick turnaround."

"How quick? How much of a premium?"

"I started it yesterday afternoon."

"How much you think she's charging him?" He looked at me conspiratorially.

I've never understood everyone's interest in my models. I've never gone to Mike's office and asked him about his job. "Hey Mike, what's this file? Homicide? A murder seems kinda small for you. No Multiple Homicide cases this week?"

I shrugged as an answer for him.

With the bedroom door open, the fragility of the models he kept grabbing plus everything that had happened that morning, I was anxious for my brother to stop with the questions and leave.

"And these?" He looked around my little apartment. "How much?"

Another shrug. "I don't know, Mike." The plaintive tone in my voice escaped by accident.

"Maybe it's a good thing you got fired."

"What the hell does that mean?" Now the tone was clearly angry.

"You look busy," he explained. "I just mean maybe it's time you and Dad called it quits."

Mike loved to call Luther, Dad or Pops whenever Luther couldn't hear. I guess he finds it humorous or brazen when really it just highlighted the fact that neither of us is close enough to Luther to actually call him Dad to his face. I wished he'd stick to one name and quit trying to be funny or sarcastic or ironic or whatever he thought he was being.

I responded with another shrug.

He ambled over to the third work table. He inspected some of my tools as if he were in a buffet line and he was trying to decide between the prime rib and the chicken. "Pretty neat."

I cringed. I hate when people call my work "neat." I thought for a moment of what Mike might say if I called his work "Pretty neat." I looked up at him and saw a grin plastered across his face, a sure sign he'd gotten the reaction he wanted.

"Why'd you come over here?" I asked. "To rub in the fact that Luther fired me today?"

Mike's smile dropped. "No," he said. "I was worried about you."

"Whatever."

"Seriously," Mike said. "Mom called. She said Luther was furious. Then when I was at the crime scene, I heard from Chen what our dear old Dad said at the coffee shop. I thought you might need to talk to someone a bit more understanding than Pops."

"I'm fine."

"I see that," he replied.

He looked like he was going to say more, but a knock at the door stopped him. Without asking, Mike stepped to the door and opened it. I knew it was Kathy, knew from her knock. I also knew she would not be happy that she came early. As soon as she saw Mike her smiling face became a deep frown. A large grin spread across Mike's face as he saw Kathy.

CHAPTER 7

Kathy, blonde, petite, usually a whirlwind of ideas and energy, walked slowly into the apartment like a death row inmate being led to the gas chamber. She didn't even try to camouflage her annoyance at seeing Mike. She shot a glance at me that said she blamed me for her situation. Standing next to the much larger Mike, Kathy looked preternaturally thin, and the hair that she commonly tucked behind her ears made her look even more mousey. I guessed that the only person she would have liked less to see in my apartment than my brother was Luther.

"How the hell are you, K?" Mike held the door open wide for his old friend and my boss.

She stopped in front of Mike and a palpable unease settled into the room. It was an unease that germinated years ago when Luther retired from the Marines and moved back to Dallas. I was a freshman in high school, Mike a junior. Kathy and her family lived one street over. Kathy and Mike were classmates and dated for the last two years of high school. It had not ended well.

"Maybe I'll come back?"

There was a war going on behind Kathy's eyes, anger at Mike latent and fresh, but also a desire to get her hands on the strip mall project, her need to get updates on the other projects, her desire to manage her projects and her business. I knew that she would have trudged on with business had it been anyone else, it was only Mike whoever caused her to stumble. It was a rare event, Kathy unsure of herself.

Kathy started her business while she was in college. It started as a business school assignment, nothing more than a theory really. She proved it out and decided to keep in going after college. Her company, All Information, AI for short, provides technical writers and designers to companies working in the oil field industry, a gargantuan market to tap into in Texas. Three years after she founded the company, just a year and a half out of college, AI was firmly in the black. It had grown with each passing year.

"I'll come back later," she repeated.

"What? Cause of me?" Mike said. "We're all adults. We're all friends right?"

I saw her cringe but succumb, nonetheless.

Kathy and I are a lot alike. We are most comfortable when we work by and for ourselves. Instead of acting like a boss or a project manager she tends to be my agent and assistant. For the other services she has, the writing, the editing, the project management, she runs those services strictly. For me, she meets the clients and translates their needs to me. After that, she leaves me alone to get my work done. If I want to take all night to place a heat exchanger into a model of a refinery, then I can do that. No one breathes down my neck or makes demands that might increase the cost of a model. She provides an easy-going environment and in return, she gets a dedicated, somewhat cheap modeler who can turn projects around quickly. It's symbiosis in its most basic form.

Kathy moved around Mike, ignoring him as best she could and targeted the model behind me. "Looks great!" Kathy bent down to examine the strip mall model more closely. Unlike Mike, she took it in with a practiced eye.

"So do you, K." It was from Mike. Kathy rolled her eyes. "No, I mean it, you do."

She made her lips form a smile that anyone but Mike would have known was forced and tried to get back to ignoring him.

Usually, when Kathy visits, she takes a seat and we discuss upcoming projects, the status of my existing projects, and we spend a few minutes talking about business and anything else that might come to mind. I think she does this to try to get me used to dealing with people in business. She's aware of my problem with crowds. I think she means her visits as part of a therapy regimen. It doesn't work, but I don't say anything. Today, she was eager to leave. Her movements were more abrupt than usual, she made no move toward the chair, she glanced at me with furtive eyes that still held accusations.

Mike continued to talk without either of us listening.

"Have you seen this stuff, Kath?" Mike said as he swept his arm around the apartment. "I mean, I don't know how much you're paying this loser, but whatever it is, it isn't enough."

I repressed a smile. Mike has rarely praised anything I have done in my life. Most of our lives have been an exercise in discovering new ways to run me down. Hearing him praise my work, even when he inserted the word "loser" into it, was rare praise. I saw Kathy force another grin that showed she wasn't comfortable talking about business with Mike.

"I keep telling him he's the best in the business," Kathy said.

"Seriously, K," Mike continued. "How much do you pay him for this? Like this one here, the strip mall. The dork says you need it quick, that the client's paying a premium. What's the price for something like that, and how much do you give him?"

Kathy's eyes blazed.

"Shut up Mike," I tried to cut him off. It's one thing to piss Luther off by giving out too much information. It's another thing entirely to lose my job with Kathy.

"No, I'm serious. I'm looking out for your bro," he refused to be silent. "I mean I don't know the industry, but this is great stuff. This is as good as the stuff you see in museums. I just want to know that she's treating you fairly."

"She is," I said.

Kathy, eyes still on fire, tried to sound calm as she said, "I pay him better than the going rate."

Mike picked up the strip mall project and held it out in front of him. "I don't know Kathy, this looks pretty good for a rushed job."

Kathy and I both lunged for the model at the same time as Mike picked it up. Kathy beat me to it and snagged it from him.

"Trust me, Mike." I could hear the rage she was holding back. "I know how important Joe is and how good he is at his job."

It's rare to hear Kathy's compliments, and even though it was forced on her by Mike, it felt nice to hear it. If it wasn't for the tension in the room and Mike's interference, I might have been able to enjoy hearing them.

Finally, the strip mall secured in her hands, Kathy retreated toward the door. "I'll be by tomorrow for the oil rig. We might get some more business from this firm." She nodded toward the model in her hand.

"How much do you give him when he brings in new business?" Mike tried a flaccid joke. Kathy ignored him.

"I've got some other meetings to get to," she brushed by Mike.

I know that Mike can be a pain. I'm his little brother if anyone knows this it would be me. I could teach a master's class in how to deal with jerky older brothers. When we're together, he's okay when someone else is around he's a jackass when that someone is Kathy, he's insufferable, genuinely pompous, spectacularly aloof, and an unapologetic bore. He's a lot like Luther.

"Let me help you with that." Mike took the model from Kathy.

"I'm fine." Kathy stepped back to fend him off.

"I insist." He might have thought his smile was winning. Even I could tell it was losing. For a moment, they looked like they were preparing for a game of tug-o-war, Kathy holding half the model, Mike the other half. Kathy's eyes found mine, and I saw the hardness soften for just a second. A smile appeared, false, full of hostility.

"Sure Mike," she said as she released the model and made way for him. "That'd be great."

I could almost see the strain she held in check as she struggled to be civil to my brother.

Mike took the model like it was a trophy and headed off down the hallway to the stairs. He gave me a parting smile and I heard him yell, "Call me later, B."

Kathy hung back and looked back into the apartment.

"Next time," she said. "Give me some warning he's here." I thought for a moment she might be making light of the situation so I smiled in response. She did not return the smile.

"I'll be back for the oil rig tomorrow."

"You said I have until the end of the week."

"Tomorrow," she cut me off. "And make sure the bastard's not here." She tilted her head down the hallway.

I shut the door behind her and looked at the oil rig. It would take all night to finish. At least I had no more employers to piss off.

CHAPTER 8

With the objective only five hundred meters out, it meant that we would be able to see it soon. Then again, they would be able to see us as well. "Was he able to get eyes on?"

"Roger, sir. He left a two men security team in an overwatch position. He's on his way back now." "Good."

Wilson came up next to me and handed my Motorola back. I slipped it back into my pouch. He stayed there, at my side, looking up at me like a hungry dog at the end of a long day who knew he was about to get his supper. Wilson had that type of enthusiasm that never flagged, no matter the task.

"Raise the CO," I said. "Let him know that we're moving our guns into position." He nodded and began to work his headset to transmit the message.

Lamb helped me unfold my map from the over-sized pocket on my thigh. Marlberg ran up and knelt to us. He smacked Lamb on the head good naturedly.

"We're here," Lamb pointed on the map with a rifle round. He, as protocol merits, used the end of a round from the extra magazines on his chest to point out our position on the map. It had taken me weeks to get used to this particular SOP. Lamb, a fifteen-year Marine, never failed to remind me those first few weeks that a finger, usually gloved and dirty, makes a poor pointing tool for maps. Now, pointing using a stick, a rifle round, a pen, anything, was second nature to me as it was to everyone else in the platoon's leadership.

"Right," I said.

"The objective..." Marlberg took the bullet and used the

end, a lead tip encased in a deep golden copper, to point at a red grease mark dot on the map. "Here!"

"And the security team?" I asked.

"Right on that ridge, Sir." He moved the bullet up and down a ridge depicted on the map.

I studied the map then stood up slowly to look at the surrounding terrain. I noticed several of the Marines around me had changed from pulling security on their knees to the prone position. The entire platoon should have been in the prone. I hated laziness in my Marines. I gestured to my Squad Leaders who were looking at me for direction. I used the flat of my hand and gestured down to let them know that all of their men should be in the prone position now. We'd been stopped long enough and we weren't going to be moving soon. In less than ten seconds there wasn't a Marine, other than me, Lamb and the RTO who were kneeling.

"Okay," I said more to myself than to Lamb. "Move up to the front of the formation, Marlberg and I will bring the guns up to you. You take them to your security position and help Marlberg set them up."

"Roger, Sir." Lamb swiveled on his knee and ran in a crouch toward the front of the formation. I turned and did the same thing the other way, Wilson following along happily. Marlberg followed and split off towards two of his machine gun teams. I went to get the one at the back of the formation.

When I reached the end of the line, sweat covered my face. I could feel it, heavy on my back, sticking to my shirt under my armor. My body armor, thirty-five pounds, hung heavy. My rucksack, plastered on top of the armor, felt like a bloated tick sucking not blood but energy, directly out of me. This was the time when we needed our energy most. This was the time when the mission could get dangerous, instead of being fresh and ready we were strung out and nearing if not exhaustion, then something just short of it.

I could sense the nerves and anxiety of my Marines around me. This is the part of the job we all hate, the uncertain times. There were more things we didn't know than we did. Was there an enemy emplacement in the village? If so, how big? How hostile? S-3, the intelligence arm of the Battalion had no idea. "That's for you to determine, Lieutenant." Master Sergeant Livery had told me last night. "You go figure that out so that the next time a Platoon Leader asks me that, I can say more than "I have no idea."

It was a typical recon operation. Nothing flashy, no true objective, just lots of uncertainty. It was something, despite almost an entire year, I had not gotten used to. It wasn't until Iraq that I truly knew how deep confusion and ambiguity can run. At home, under Luther, the house ran with a precision that only a life-time in the military can hone, but at home, the only ambiguity was Luther.

The only time I had felt marginally safe in the past few months was inside the wire at the temporary staging base by the airfield. Only there, behind several rows of barbed wire-topped fences, with constant and entrenched security emplacements, only there did I feel some safety creep back into my psyche. Nine long months of worry. Two-hundred, sixty-nine days and nights where the most secure area in my life was still under threat of mortar or rocket attack, and that didn't count the days we were outside the wire.

Then, in just the past few weeks, I'd been able to find some contentment in the desert. No sweeping sand dunes with camels, but hard-packed, almost white soil, rocky terrain with hills, spurs, and wadis that stretched for miles. There was anonymity out in the desert, alone with the platoon, particularly at night. The movements, nature, flora and fauna, it all moved in its own way. It was easy to see when something moved the wrong way or was out of the ordinary in the desert.

"What's up, Sir," Sergeant Marlberg came back, running in a crouch.

"You ready?"

As the weapons squad leader, Marlberg was in charge of the three, crew-served machine guns.

"Yep," he said.

"Get the mortar teams as well. I'm setting the FO in place with you and the guns." I watched Marlberg's eyes shoot up in surprise.

I had been expecting it. Marlberg and I had a running disagreement about the use of our Forward Observer. As a Radio Operator with a direct link to the artillery and close air support, I thought the FO should be placed in overwatch positions and be used to call in indirect fire like artillery or mortars from afar. Marlberg, a former FO, felt that the FO should be in the Platoon Leader's hip pocket, much like my RTO.

There were times when Marlberg was right. There were missions when I thought having the FO with me was the best use of his skillset. One thing I hated was juggling the squads, bringing in or shifting fire from the machine guns, reporting back to the CO through the RTO and coordinating indirect fire capabilities through the FO. It was too much, particularly on this mission when so much was still up in the air. Leaving the FO at Marlberg's command might have been a bit unorthodox, but it would provide me a greater degree of focus. It was that focus, not a greater number of weapons systems that I thought I'd need in the little village that we knew nothing about.

I watched as Marlberg went around and checked each of the gun teams to ensure that they had their ammunition at the ready, briefing them about the next phase of our mission, ensuring tripods and other equipment was out and ready.

At that moment I was jealous of the gun teams. All of them were privates with a corporal or two manning the triggers. They were told what to do almost every moment of their lives. I watched the ammo bearer and assistant gunner as they made their final checks of their gear. It looked nice, to always be told what to do by Corporal Duffy. They were all eager and bright, particularly Duffy. DeLeo checked his ammo pouches again then took hold of the tripod and threw it on his shoulder. PFC Lazlo took out a belt of the large 7.62 mm rounds out of his ruck and draped it across his shoulder. Next, he positioned two more chains of ammunition in the pouches on his body armor. They all moved gracefully and easily as if he'd been storing and arranging chain, machine gun ammunition all his life. Positioned as they were those three Marines could have their machine gun set up on the tripod and throwing rounds down range in seconds.

I liked to watch my Marines. Watching them do even the most ordinary tasks makes me thrilled to be a part of their lives. Once each team was prepped and kneeling in the center of the line, I jogged toward the front of the formation with them. Lamb saw us coming and intercepted us.

"I can take it from here, Sir."

"I'm coming to take a look at the objective," I said.

I saw the flinch, but he was too good a Marine to argue.

As the Platoon Leader, I had every right to move up with the machine guns and watch as they were put in place and get another look at the objective. Usually, I left this to Lamb, the older Platoon Sergeant who had over three years of time in Iraq. I might have had the seniority and the rank, but he had the experience.

Over the past year, Lamb and I had come to a silent agreement about our roles in the platoon, and I was bending not breaking those rules by going forward with him and the guns. I knew his argument. He hated to leave the platoon without a senior officer or a non-commissioned officer. By moving up with him and Marlberg, we were taking the top three ranking members of the platoon away from the line squads who were still lying in the prone, pulling security while we set up the guns. Had we been taking fire, he would have had a point. We weren't even sure if we were going to take fire. There might be nothing in the village but sleepy, poor villagers, children looking for handouts, village elders with nothing to do but smile and pretend to be cordial; all of this setup could be overkill for what would most likely be nothing more than a walk and talk. My decision earned me a reproachful glare from my platoon sergeant, but not an argument.

I looked back at the platoon as we left the front of the formation. I caught the eye of the next most senior NCO, first squad's leader Sergeant Johnson; hard jawed, confident, imminently capable after over a year in the theater and dozens of engagements. I spoke into the radio attached to my collar and did a radio check with him to ensure we had an open line of communication. I heard a scratchy transmission from him, not great, but fair. I pointed at him and tugged at my collar to let him know he was in charge until I got back. He nodded and gave me a thumbs up. I stepped out of the formation with the RTO right behind me and followed the three machine-gun teams and the platoon sergeant toward the village of Sakhar.

CHAPTER 9

Fired by my father on Monday. Why did it almost two full weeks to hear from Mom? That might seem odd or unjustifiable to an outside observer, for me it was expected, normal even.

I was in my bedroom working. The oil rig was gone, and I had other projects waiting on me, but I needed some time to myself. Kathy's next visit had been tense. She had come in and left as quickly as possible as if staying too long might influence Mike to visit. Since that visit I had been in my bedroom a lot more than usual, catching up on sleep, but working much more. It was a relief to lose myself in something that wasn't work-related.

I had gotten two packages over the past week and had been eager to get back to the bedroom and get those new features involved in the scene. I was making the final tweaks to my bedroom closet when Mom called and ripped me from that little bit of solace that I had been enjoying.

"How are you, Dear?" Mom called us that. I hated it. It was so saccharine and false.

"Fine Mom," I said.

"Everything okay?"

"Are you kidding?" I asked. "I was fired by my father."

"You know he's really upset about that, Dear."

I rolled my eyes and actually had to stop myself from hanging up the phone. I let the comfortable sarcasm take over. "I'm sure he's broken up."

"He is, Dear." She never allowed herself to notice my sarcasm, but I never stopped using it. I don't know if it was a defense mechanism, avoidance, or what. Still, it came out of me naturally whenever I spoke to my mother. I gave up trying to figure it out several years back. It wasn't worth the effort.

"He wanted me to call and tell you that you can have your job back." Mom's voice was as innocent as ever.

"Tell him no."

I heard my mother's heavy sigh. "Now, Dear," she said. "He was just upset. He's had some time to think about it, and he says he really needs you to come back. Those are his words, not mine. He says he needs you."

It didn't sound like Luther. "What did you do? Threaten to leave him?" It was a joke. She missed it. I wasn't surprised.

"I didn't do anything," she said. "He came to the decision on his own. You know I don't get involved in the business."

Mom doesn't have to pretend to be a wallflower, she's a natural at it. To an outsider, my mom would look like the world's greatest patsy but we all knew that she was just desperate for peace.

My parents' marriage has lasted twenty- seven years and survived two wars and countless deployments. During that time, I've never seen Mom change Luther's mind about anything. She's emotionally supportive, but always in the background, reacting to stimuli but never actually influencing outcomes.

My mom raised two sons surrounded by the sometimes violent temper, unapologetic attitude and always bullying demeanor of an old school Devil Dog Marine. Her upbringing never let her consider divorce. A true silent sufferer, she walked the tightrope between her husband and her sons effortlessly and seemingly with no regrets. I'd given up trying to understand either of my parents, much less how they stayed together.

If Luther wanted me back, it wouldn't have been because of Mom, nor because he had reconsidered what he'd said. There was an ulterior motive out there. This call was Luther's opening move, a pawn advancing into the center of the board.

"Don't you like working with your father?"

Whenever Mom tried to play on my sympathies, I was stunned that she wasn't able to see that it never worked when Luther was a part of the equation.

"I like the clients," I said. "I like being paid to work out." This ostensibly was true. The clients were the only reason I went to work. Working directly for Luther was just short of hell. Other than Kathy, the clients were the only social interaction I got.

Last year, fresh out of the Marines, when I started working for Luther he was full of predictions for the future. This will work out perfectly. I've been looking for someone to sell the business to. How often had he told me that? When I first started he said stuff like that often. I knew it was mostly a front, that he was just trying to make up for years of rotten parenting, but it was fun to think he might mean it. Tuesday morning's dismissal had been coming for months. The enthusiasm Luther had felt when I started had waned over the weeks and months. Now, since he had let me go, I doubted that anything could go back to normal.

"Dear?" My mother's voice interrupted my thoughts. "You are going to work with him again, aren't you? You'll forget this whole thing, right?"

"Actually, no," I paused to let the words sink in. "Tell Dad that if he wants me back he needs to come over to my place and hire me again."

"Well," she said. "I was thinking about that. Wouldn't it be nice if you came over for dinner? Then you two could talk."

Surprisingly, feeling as though I had the moral high ground, it didn't pain me to say "no". "He needs to come here," I said. "It's up to him to take the first step."

"He is taking the first step, dear." Her voice was innocent and yet cajoling at the same time. "He had me call," I repeated my last statement, enunciating for her. "He needs to come here, Mom. Tell him that."

I hung up the phone. This time the moral high ground didn't

insulate me from the shame. What kind of son hangs up on their mom? I consoled myself with the knowledge that it was Luther I was mad at, not Mom. Still, she should try a bit harder to be on my side.

CHAPTER 10

At half-past eight, the crickets chirping loud enough to be heard through my bedroom walls while I worked, Luther knocked on the door. I knew his knock better than Kathy's or Mike's. It was one, solitary, solid "whump" that reverberated through the living room, past the kitchen, around the little hall, and into my ears. I looked up and cursed myself for not having expected it and come up with a game plan.

Truthfully, I thought he'd come the next day at the earliest if he came at all. Maybe I was underestimating the position and power I had over Luther at this moment.

I made sure to shut the bedroom door and lock it, then forced myself to sound at ease as I opened the front door. "What's up?"

I realized quickly that if I had I planned out this situation, I would have missed the target. Luther's eyes looked hard in the weak fluorescent light in the hallway, but there was something different about him. I studied him at that moment and guessed that the difference must have come about from some shift in our relationship, something small and subtle, but imminently palpable between us. He stood in front of me, waiting to be let in and I saw something in his eyes, a pained look.

There was definitely something different in his eyes. I felt out of place, unsure of myself like I'd just walk into a strange neighborhood and was not sure how to get home. I could see Luther felt the same. His lips were pursed behind the whiskers of his mustache, and I could sense him struggling with himself, straining to regain his ordinary, dominant position, but also needing to stay calm. Why? What could he possibly need? My mind raced to try to imagine different possibilities but none came.

"We need to talk. I have something to ask you and..." He paused. His speech was uncharacteristically unsure. "Your mother said I need to apologize."

Ordinarily, I would have accepted this second-hand admission, rationalizing that it would be as close as I would get to an actual apology. This time, I told myself, it wasn't enough. I was a wronged employee, as well as his son.

"So you're apologizing?"

He shrugged and stepped into the apartment. I shut the door behind him and watched him limp into the apartment. At that moment, that moment when I saw the limp, I knew I had been wrong. I had deluded myself into thinking that he was there due to an overwhelming sense of self-reproach. His slumped posture wasn't from guilt, it was due to an injury in his leg or knee. His softened eyes were dull from pain killers, not regret.

I struggled to keep my shoulders straight. I watched him and wondered why I'd let myself be fooled.

In those couple of steps, it was obvious that Luther could barely walk, much less run. Luther was in my apartment to rehire an employee not to find absolution for a transgression against his son. He wasn't here to make things right between us.

"Fuck," I thought there was no "right" between us, and I realized again that there never would be. I heard a grinding sound and realized I was grinding my back teeth. I stopped before Luther could hear it.

Luther looked around the room critically. He stared at the bare walls that I had not bothered to paint since I'd moved in, nail holes still visible from the previous tenant's wall hangings.

I watched as he studied the kitchen through the weak light that came from the 70s era chandelier, most likely taking in the fact that all I had on the counter was a coffee pot. Had he looked in the fridge he would have seen little more than a gallon of milk, some fruit that I kept in there to keep safe from the flies, and a mote of bread and cheese which besides the gross of Ramen in my cupboard was the only staple in my diet.

The starkness of my apartment is shocking to my guests, it's one of the reasons so many gravitate to the models. There's so little else to see. It hadn't changed since the last time he had been there, six months before.

"Still working with models?" I heard the disdain, thick in the back of his voice. Someone else, someone who hadn't lived with him all their life might have missed it. I couldn't. He said it as if the models were a waste of time and money.

He leaned down to look closely at a tractor-trailer I had started that morning. This was Luther stalling. The last time he was in my apartment he treated my work like a person who hates dogs would treat a lovable family pet, he ignored them completely.

"Still with Kathy?" He stalled some more.

"Yep." I stood by the still open door and waited, my arms folded across my chest.

"Good," he said. "She's a hard worker." It was the same compliment he gave whenever he talked about her. Luther, I knew, thought that saying someone was hard working was the highest compliment he could give.

He limped over to another table to look at the next model. "I would have thought they would do this stuff in-house. Maybe hire a firm or something for the complex ones." He nodded at an almost finished model of a garbage truck that a large corporation wanted for the lobby of their new headquarters. I decided it wasn't worth the argument to tell him that Kathy was the firm. He wouldn't want to understand anyway.

"So, what's up? Why are you here?" I was tired of the stall tactics.

I could tell by the lift of his eyebrows he thought my question was abrupt, borderline rude. Let him think about it. I was past caring.

He paused as if considering whether he wanted to reply. Finally, he eked out, "I need some help."

I didn't say anything and eventually, Luther turned, still limping, to look at me. His mouth worked back and forth as if he were chewing on something. It looked like he gave up and thought of a different approach.

"Look." He sighed. "Can we get some coffee or something, it's on me." He started for the door as if his word made it so.

My spine stiffened as I realized he was trying to manipulate me. I spoke quickly and shut the door. "How about we stay here?"

I wasn't used to countermanding Luther's orders and I wasn't sure how it sounded. I hoped my voice didn't sound as wavering as my thoughts. I knew Luther knew about my problems outside my apartment and was trying to get me into a more vulnerable position. Even an injured Luther could be formidable. He turned, and for a moment vexation streaked across his face. I had a distinct feeling that he was contemplating leaving. He pursed his lips, and his fist clenched. I took a step back without thinking. He began hitting his fist against his thigh in an impatient gesture. He needed a favor and it was eating him up that I was making him ask for my help instead of me offering it. I let him stew. He dropped his eyes and turned to look at the room again.

"Do you mind if I sit?" He nodded at my chair.

"Yeah, sure."

He sat heavily. "I guess you've noticed my leg." I nodded.

"Happened this morning. Doc says it's a possible ACL tear I'm out for at least three months." I looked at him and thought it might be a lie or an exaggeration. An ACL tear would require a crutch or at the very least a cane.

Luther didn't let me think long about that but went on. "I need you to come back out and work the clients the next couple of days."

Other than me and Luther, there was only one other instructor, Cochlin. Cochlin was in Mexico for the rest of the month, another two weeks. Luther and I were supposed to handle all the workouts until he came back. Three months ago Luther fired Horne, the fourth instructor. Filling all the slots had been tough with only three instructors, tougher still with Cochlin gone. With a gimpy leg, I imagined it would be embarrassing for Luther as well as bad for business to have just one lone, lame instructor show up.

"So you're here because you have no one else to turn to?" I asked. "Maybe you should have thought about this before you fired me."

His eyes met mine and anger flashed across them. "Fuck the clients," he said. "I could give them as good a workout on one leg as I could on two."

"Then what is it?"

"First, are you coming back or not?" There was no grace in his eyes.

"Why?"

Luther's voice lowered. "Yes, or no?"

I decided I wasn't ready to relinquish the upper hand.

"Why the big switch? Three days ago what I did warranted a firing. What's the deal, now?"

Luther leaned forward aggressively. He looked as though he was about to stand, then he sat back again. "No big switch," he sighed. "It's just that you might not have been as wrong as I initially thought."

"Not as wrong as you initially thought?" I almost laughed but caught myself as I saw his face roil. "How about not wrong at all? What I did had nothing to do with Georgia being murdered."

"Okay, okay." Luther held up his hands. "I might have been wrong, I probably shouldn't have fired you. What you were doing..." He pointed at me as he spoke. "While I still don't condone it, I may not have been as reckless as I initially thought."

I didn't respond immediately but finally said, "Okay."

He hadn't actually apologized. There was no, "I'm sorry,"

no, "I made a mistake." He did say that he had been wrong, but there hadn't been an apology. I thought about making him apologize, but realized that I had just gotten as close to a formal apology as I would ever get from Luther.

"So, we're good now? You're coming back out in the mornings?" Luther sounded excited, almost as if unsure of how I was going to respond.

"Not yet," I said. "I want a contract."

"A contract?" There was bemusement and a back throated guffaw in his response.

"Yeah," I said. "I want a contract. I want something on paper that says you'll sell me AFC within twelve months for a price we agree upon tonight."

"I can tell you it will be three hundred grand to buy me out." He snapped. "And if my handshake and word aren't good enough for you, well....I don't know what we're doing here."

"Written contract." I held my ground. "And you have no inventory, no production, no nothing. How can you think I'll pay three hundred thousand?"

"I have the best name recognition for this style of fitness in Dallas," he said. "Plus loyal customers. You'll make three hundred grand in ten years. Three hundred is a bargain." His voice growled as if I was insulting him. "Plus, there's no way I'm selling in twelve months. Try three years."

"A loyal customer base that is disintegrating as we speak," I countered. "I'll go for two years and we can discuss a price with an arbitrator in six months."

"If I say yes to two years and the contract," he said. "You'll be back out in the morning?" He stared at me. "Tomorrow morning. We're back to normal."

It took a moment of reflection but eventually, I nodded. "Yeah, I'll be out first thing day after tomorrow. Not tomorrow."

"Okay," He held out his hand for me to shake.

I took it and pumped his hand, feeling as though I'd missed something.

"But you have to work next weekend too." My mind raced as I tried to think about what was happening this weekend. I felt as though he'd outmaneuvered me somehow, but I couldn't figure out how. A smile played on the ends of Luther's mouth. I released his hand and realized that although I hadn't seen it, the trap had just shut around me and I had no idea what it was.

CHAPTER 11

"What is this, a joke? You can't run a race in the desert." Kathy's response was more vehement than I expected. It was more than my own had been when I found out.

She showed up that evening, about a half-hour after Luther left. She came in without saying a word. Her first objective, the project she was there to pick up. She inspected it diligently, a one-sixteenth scale water filtration system. No word of greeting, just a wave of her hand to tell me hello. She might not be as brusque as Luther, but she is just as driven. I sat down and waited. I thought about what a field day a therapist might have trying to determine why I tended to glom onto such overbearing employers.

Despite only working for Kathy for half a year we've known one another for the majority of our lives. I guess she figured me out long ago and just used that to get the best work out of me. I was never the type who bought into a group philosophy. I had a difficult time during my first few months in the Marines, a hotbed of groupthink. It wasn't until I got to my regular unit that my CO, Captain DeNova recognized my personality type and found a way to use it to the Corps advantage. Gradually, without my recognizing it, the Marines got easier for me under his leadership. I completed tasks quicker, I found that I understood orders and operations better, I enjoyed being around my Marines more. Captain DeNova realized I performed best when I was left alone.

"I've seen soldiers like you before," he told me one day as he provided me my monthly counseling report. "It's just a matter of figuring people out and using them effectively. Marines like you fall apart when you're confronted with tasks that involve a group. But ask you to perform the same task alone, you excel."

"Oorah Sir," came the standard reply. I wasn't really listening at that point, I was just replying to reply.

"What were your favorite sports in high school?" "I played football, tennis, track, and soccer, Sir."

"You liked tennis and track more than the other two didn't you?"

I considered before giving my pat answer that time. "Roger Sir."

"And you probably like singles tennis more than doubles tennis."

That's when it had clicked for me. It's a lesson I have taken with me ever since and I'm sure Kathy recognized this aspect of my character and used to her benefit. All of our meetings are just the two of us and all except one have been in my apartment. She knows where I feel safest. She acts as a gatekeeper and primary contact for all my projects. Beyond all that, beyond finding the work and picking it up, she leaves me alone to complete the projects. Three days on making sure the gray paint is the perfect shade for a parking lot, why not? As long as the projects are completed on time. Redoing an entire landscape project so that I could make the water feature look more realistic, that's been known to happen too. As long as she gets the work by the deadline and it meets the customer's requirements, she leaves me alone. It's a symbiotic relationship with very little contact. She gets a dedicated, modeler who can turn projects around quickly, I get a paycheck that is enough to pay for my apartment and a bit more.

"Looks great!" She had taken her time, had gone around the model three times looking at details.

Still looking at the model, she held out a folder for me.

"These are the final detail drawings for the garbage truck. It needs to be done by Monday."

I had taken the folder but said, "I'm not going to be able to make that."

She had turned at that point. Her face was a mixture of concern and fear. "What's the problem?"

"I'm taking a week off and can't finish it by then."

"Are you looking for a raise?" Kathy's voice was a whisper. In the past year, Kathy had lost two other employees to a rival contracting company and was desperate to stem the flow of talent from her business.

"This isn't about money."

"What then." The concern remained written on her face. "Are you interviewing with someone else?"

I shook my head. "It's not that. It's for Luther. He needs me to compete in a race next week. I leave Thursday and won't be back until Monday. So..." I held up the folder and let the fact that the garbage truck was impossible to land heavily without saying anything more. It was the first project I'd ever refused.

She stood there, stock-still, stunned, in the middle of my living room.

I had expected this. Kathy always had another job ready for me when she came by to pick one up. I probably could have taken the garbage truck job and worked on it all day and night and gotten it done. I had three projects in various states of completion, could I fit another in? Possibly. Still, the race had a host of complexities and the more I'd thought about it, the more I realized I'd need to concentrate on it.

"A race?"

I nodded.

I saw relief spread across her face. Then like a riptide sweeping into the beach then back out again, another emotion came over her, this time it looked like confusion. "Why so sudden? You didn't even file a vacation request."

"I know."

She looked at me, waiting for more. When I didn't offer one she went on.

"It may be none of my business, but what kind of race is this?" She stood with her arms crossed and stared across the room as if preparing for an argument. It was a mixture of pseudo-parental concern, managerial confusion, and curiosity all in a five-foot-two package.

I walked across the room and grabbed a couple of pages I'd printed out a few minutes after Luther left. I handed her the print outs, information from the race's website. She took them and skimmed the pages quickly. She looked up with a face written with even more confusion, a bit of underlying mirth as if she thought I was joking.

That's when she had said it. "What is this, a joke? You can't run a race in the desert."

I tried not to smile, but when she smiled, I couldn't help myself.

When she saw my smile, her's vanished. "Big Bend?" She held the paper up between us. "You're kidding right?"

I shook my head.

"This is in three days!" Her voice was filled with disbelief.

"I know."

She looked at me steadily, again waiting for more. She gave up after just a moment.

She repositioned her feet and re-crossed her arms, the papers getting stuck in the process. "Tell you what," she said finally. "Let's go down the street. There's a new café, we'll get a coffee and a dessert, we can talk about this. It will be on me."

It felt like she was pulling the same stunt Luther had tried, getting me outside the apartment so she'd have the upper hand. For a moment I felt betrayed. I expected that type of tactic from Luther, from Kathy, it was a different matter.

"That's alright," I turned away from her. "There's not much to discuss."

"Look, Joe, do you think you're ready for this?" she gestured with the papers. "I mean, this is the desert. There's going to be a ton of people there. We both know you can barely make it a couple of hours outside your house, how in the hell are you going to survive three days in the desert?"

"I'm going." This was my last resort argument. Just saying "I'm going" was going to be what I said when all else failed. All the arguments I had thought up had vanished when I confronted Kathy. I tried not to worry that I was already on my last-ditch argument.

Kathy has never brought up my problem before. I knew she was aware of it, but it was a guarded secret between us, something we both acknowledged but we never mentioned.

"You can't even go to get coffee with me." She pointed to the door accusingly. "How the hell do you think you're going to survive the desert?"

I pursed my lips as I tried to think of something to say, but nothing came to mind, not even the last-ditch argument came out.

"There are closer races," she continued. "Shorter races, if you want to work on getting outside more. There are easier ways to get out than going to West Texas for a week." I cringed as she said work on getting outside more."

"You're having trouble just talking about it!" She waved her hand at me as if this concluded the argument. "This is ridiculous."

"Luther needs me to go." I never anticipated using that as an argument.

"Your dad?" The incredulous smile turned into a smirk. "When have you ever cow-towed to your father?"

"He hurt himself and he needs me to go." I made my voice firmer.

I'd expected Kathy to argue about the projects and my taking a vacation, but now she was getting too personal. Was it any of her business why I was going? I knew that Kathy disliked Luther and I also knew that she treated working out as a lifestyle choice for people with too much time on their hands. She hated the fact that I didn't dedicate all of my time to her work. Whenever the subject of Luther had come up, she made it sound as if my working for Luther was a phase I would grow out of.

Her voice rose as she said, "I'm amazed he thinks you can go!" She waved her hand at me as if my problems with open areas could be localized to some part of my body. She paused when she saw the skin tighten around my eyes and my lips curled under. Just a moment's pause though, because she gathered herself and plowed on. "Seriously Joe, you can't do this, we all know you have a problem?"

My back teeth ground down when she called it a problem. "I'm fine."

She let the statement hang for a moment before she spoke again. "Okay, if you're so fine, let's go get a drink." She started for the door.

"No," I said.

She stopped and looked at me. "Have you given any thought to how you're going to survive." She shook her head.

"Again, you can't even go down the block for a drink with me, how are you going to survive in the desert?"

"I think I can do it. Usually, if I have something to focus on, I can kinda block everything else out." It sounded weak, even to me. Kathy shook her head as I spoke. Her face was locked in permanent skepticism now.

"I don't buy it. You're going to West Texas, to run this race, cause Luther asked you? I asked you to go to Kansas City last June, you wouldn't go on that trip."

"There's more than just Luther." I realized that she would need an actual reason. I pointed to the paper that was still in her hand.

"What?" she followed my finger and glance down at the paper again.

"The train," I said. We were in super uncharted territory now. I never thought in my wildest dreams of going down this path, particularly with Kathy. My eyes instinctually drifted to my bedroom door.

"What train?" She skimmed the papers. "This? The fact that you go to Big Bend on a train?" She looked up more confused than before, the sheet flapping in her hands as she pointed at it. "So what?"

"That's one of the reasons I want to do this." I knew sounded like a child asking his mother for permission and I tried to think of some way to redirect our conversation. I felt caught, almost stuck between Luther and Kathy, a ping-pong ball bouncing between them; both of them far stronger personalities than mine.

"The train?" Kathy's voice dripped with cynicism.

"I like trains."

"Lots of people like trains, Joe?" Kathy didn't sound convinced. "They usually grow out of it."

My eyes involuntarily leaped toward the door to my bedroom. Kathy's gaze followed and at that moment I knew I'd have to show her what was there for her to understand completely.

CHAPTER 12

Despite all the advantages that satellite images provide, it still skews the perception of the objective as much or more than old-world reconnaissance. There is nothing like getting a real pair of eyes on the objective. The village of Sakhar was much more spread out and far smaller than the impression I'd gotten from both the S3 intel group and from my own study of the satellite image. What from 20 miles up looked like several buildings arranged in a mass around two main streets, looked like little more than a few farmhouses and huts when I looked at them through the FO's 40X binoculars.

"Do you see it, Sir?" It was Lamb. There was still unresolved tension in his voice. I knew he was worried about the rest of the platoon and didn't want me here.

I rolled away from the berm that was concealing me and pulled out my map again. "Hold on," I said.

I studied the map and the grease pencil notations I'd made on it earlier, then rolled back up to the berm for another look through the binoculars.

"You can just make out the roof, sir." Lamb again. Was it condescension in his voice this time?"

"Yeah yeah," I said. "Hold on, I'm trying to determine the best way in."

I saw the roof, or at least thought I did. I'd found quite early on that the longer I studied things through binoculars the more my eyes played tricks on me. What I thought was a roof could very well end up being nothing but the road behind the next building. The dusky, sandy, tones of the brown walls camouflaged and masked so much that there were times I came away from a reconnaissance with a worse understanding of terrain and the makeup of the objective than when I'd started.

I cursed under my breath then panned to the right.

"I see four different roads in," I said. "And several game trails."

"Yep," this time it was Marlberg. I hadn't heard him come back from setting up the perimeter. His silent way of moving was always startling.

"I'm thinking that we should take the road that enters the town from the South, just like we planned," I said. "That way we can cover the back of the town, you and the guns can focus on this side and the North."

"Roger, sir."

"We have movement." It was Marlberg, calm and conditioned, not at all worried or apprehensive. Lamb and I rolled and looked over the berm together.

Marlberg guided us in on what he saw. "One o'clock, about fifty meters from the first building on the right. Can't make it out."

I trained my eyes on the spot using the binoculars and scanned them for movement.

"I got it," Lamb said. "It's a bunch of dogs."

As he said the words, my binoculars found the same target. There they were, the same dogs that we'd seen before, the lead dog, black and scruffy, still out in front, but now his tail was down, he was limping on his hind leg, and the entire pack was in full retreat from whatever had scared them away from the village.

"We saw them earlier," I said. There was little else to say about the small pack of dogs. Lamb and I rolled back away from the berm and looked over at Marlberg in our little huddle. "Where were we?"

"The FO," Lamb gave voice to the sore that had been bothering him since we left the platoon. "I still think that the FO should be with you, sir."

"Nope," I said. "I'll have enough to contend with three squads. I want the FO here to cover the whole town. From here he can see our approach from the south, the north, and the west. The only thing we can't see from here is the eastern side of the town. As long as he gets good pre-mission coordinates on that AO, we should be able to take care of it." Lamb was unconvinced, and I saw him about to interrupt.

"I don't want to lose the advantage that this little bit of high ground provides, Sergeant," I said finally.

"Roger, sir," he relented. Lamb knew when arguing was pointless.

"We'll go in with first squad leading, then third and use second as the rear guard. I'm going to use them the most once we're in the village. Third, I'm going to use it to cover the east side of the town. They have the newest Marines in the platoon."

"Sounds good," Lamb acknowledged.

"I'll give you updates as each squad leaves cover and begins to approach the village."

Marlberg cut me off before I could finish. "Movement from the North," he said. "This time it's not just dogs."

CHAPTER 13

I sighed heavily and felt my shoulders slump. "Over here," I said finally. "I need to show you something." My eyes lowered as I sighed. I motioned for her to follow me toward the bedroom.

She smiled as if I was joking. "I know we've been friends for a long time, but I don't know if our HR department is going to like me hanging out in your bedroom." Her joke broke the tension, but not much. She followed just the same.

I turned down the hallway and held the door open. She tried to enter with her usual aplomb but stopped when I turned on the lights, one foot hung in limbo just across the threshold.

I'm able to churn out some decent work for Kathy on a quick basis, but the speed with which she usually needs the projects generally precludes any fine detail work. The project in my bedroom was the exact opposite.

Kathy stared at the model train layout that filled my bedroom. All four walls were covered in a model that incorporated over three hundred feet of track one-hundred and sixtieth the size of the real thing. A long two-tiered table filled all four walls and left only a few feet of spare room in the very center of the room. All of the tables were covered in cityscapes, mountain scenes, rural villages, and paper-mâché mountains.

Kathy, silenced by the size and scope, reacted like a pilgrim entering Notre Dame. Her mouth slightly open, her eyes bright with interest, she turned to look at the quarry immediately at her elbow that dipped down from the upper table to the floor. I finished modeling the quarry just a few weeks before. It was my best work yet. Filled with styrene blocks that looked as though there were in the process of being excavated, it was meant to be impactful. It worked with Kathy. She squatted down to get a better look just as she had with the projects in the living room. She looked at each block, she studied the quarter-inch tall man who stood on a block, frozen in position, yelling at his buddy operating the crane above to haul it up.

"This is incredible," she said as she looked over her shoulder at me. She didn't look at me long. She returned her attention to the layout and followed the tracks from the quarry along the rest of the layout. "This is much better than the stuff you give me."

I shrugged not sure if that was a compliment or a critique.

I've never allowed anyone to see this side of my life. I wasn't sure how much I liked having Kathy look at it.

Before, out in the living room, I'd hoped it would provide a compelling argument for why I wanted to go on the trip. Now, watching her, I felt a knot of nervousness in my stomach, but more than that I felt exposed, the type of feeling that invariably comes when sitting in a doctor's office with nothing but a flimsy gown on. I felt like she was searching through my wardrobe, seeing a side of me that she shouldn't, a personal side, a side that might skew our relationship from that point on.

Kathy clasped her hands behind her back and leaned forward, combing through the details of the layout. She followed the transition of the scene from mountains to foothills then to farmland and finally to a small cityscape and eventually on the far wall where there was a mixture of 50s and 60s era eastern industrial cityscape. She worked her way around the model tentatively, almost reverently, making sure of each movement before she made it. She stopped and looked back at me when she hit the wall that led to my closet.

"Joe," she looked back at me and pointed to the modeled

city. "Are these kits that you put together?"

"Most of it is custom," I answered. "Wood frames, plaster molds."

"It's incredible."

"Thanks," I said, still not sure how to react.

"How long have you been working on this?"

"Since I moved in."

"Have you been going out to get all the materials?"

I shook my head. "I have it all shipped to me. Order it online."

"And the landlord doesn't mind?"

"He doesn't know."

She raised her eyebrows conspiratorially. "This is great, Joe," she said again. "I mean if I knew you were able to produce this level of work..." she paused and looked at me. "We can start marketing you in new ways; museums, office lobbies, trade shows." Kathy worked to find a way to leverage this potential for new business lines.

"Wait," Kathy looked confused. "Where's your bed?" "I have a Futon in there." I pointed to my closet. Kathy opened the closet door and looked inside. A large hole was cut into the wall of the closet so that the layout could move through a tunnel and continue inside the closet. She looked back at me and pointed to the unfinished plywood that I'd just installed. I could see her mind working. She looked back along the layout then her eyes settled on me.

"Let me guess, this is going to show a desert scene." She pointed at the bare wood of the shelf.

"West Texas to be exact," I clarified. "Canyon country." "And that's why you're going?"

I nodded.

"Even after seeing this," she motioned around the room with her arms. "I still don't know if it's a good idea, Joe." "I'm going," I said.

She leaned back against the layout and crossed her arms again. I could feel her ready herself to continue the argument we had started in the living room, but now, she was less critical, as if having seen my secret layout, she had seen the entire scope of the puzzle that was being built.

"We're old friends," she said. "I may be your boss, but we're friends first, and this race thing worries me. First, I'm worried that you're going to have a nervous breakdown of some sort and not be able to work for me." She ticked off her finger.

I turned away from her without thinking. "I'm not going to have a nervous breakdown," I said.

She went on as if not hearing and followed me out of the bedroom. "Secondly, I'm worried cause I'm your friend. I mean I knew you before the war before you had this problem. I'd hate to see you regress to a point that is worse than where you are now." Another cringe I couldn't control as she said problem.

"How bout this." She stepped forward and stood as if she was about to give a business presentation. "Obviously this trip to Big Bend has some meaning to you. I can see that."

She motioned toward the bedroom and raised her eyebrows. "How about if I send you on a train trip? You get to see the sights you want to see, you can take some vacation days, or heck bill it all to the company and call it research. I'll even go with you, I have a minor in psychology. I can talk you down if you start getting overwhelmed by the open spaces." She tried to smile to soften her words.

I moved forward to provide some counter arguments, but she held up her hand again.

"Seriously," she said. "I want you to think about it. This desert thing could seriously mess you up, I don't want to see that."

Her eyes showed a sympathy that I hadn't seen from her since before we started working together.

I swallowed and thought about what I was going to say before speaking. "I appreciate the offer, Kathy." A pause to think that didn't help when the words eventually tumbled out. "There's more to it than just wanting to see some canyon country."

She leaned back and waited, arms crossed, her back against the wall. "Let's hear it."

Another pause, again no help. "Luther said he'd sell me the business."

"And you trust him?"

"He's my father."

"And you want that business?" Again that slightly incredulous tone from Kathy.

"Of course."

She shook her head. "It's still too soon," she said. "You should go slower, I'm worried about you."

"Did you read about that runner who was murdered on Stonebridge Drive a few weeks ago?" I asked. "Sure, why?"

"She was in my group."

"Really?" Kathy looked surprised.

"I was leading the group the morning she was murdered. She was killed on the run I was leading."

The confusion she'd kept on her face stayed. "So? I still don't know how that has anything to do with Big Bend."

"She was supposed to go on this trip with Luther. He's injured, he's worried bout the client's safety, how they'll perceive his not being there. He wants me there in his place." She smiled as she said, "And you really think you're the best choice?" I could see that she was struggling not to laugh.

"I feel responsible, Kathy." My voice rose in the little bedroom and I saw the smile disappear from Kathy's face. "She was killed because of me," I said, not sure now where this argument would lead. "She was in my care and she was killed because of what I did."

Kathy's tone dropped. "You didn't kill her."

"No, but I left her alone, by herself. She'd still be alive if I'd been there."

"Or you'd be the one that was dead," Kathy said.

"I'm going." I tried to impart the finality to my statement.

Kathy's eyes narrowed.

"Well," her voice was low, and the words slipped out with agonizing slowness. "I guess this is one of those pivotal moments. I mean, I've contracted with Messerman for this project. I've told them that the model will be finished Monday." She nodded at the folder I still held in my hand.

She paused as if waiting for me to speak when I didn't respond she continued. "I mean, I have to have faith in my employees, and you're kinda undermining me here."

I leaned back and against the side of the bedroom door and realized that my arms were crossed. A coldness, a resolve reverberated through Kathy's eyes as she watched me.

"If you can't finish this project by Monday, then I'll be forced to find someone else," her voice was hard again.

"Are you firing me?"

"I need someone I can count on, Joe," Her voice rose. "You're running off for a race, I can't work with this."

I tried to interrupt, but she held up her hand and her patient voice returned. "When I found out you were doing your little exercise thing in the park you said it wouldn't interfere with your work." She spread her hands out in front of her as if not finishing the statement made the point for her.

"You're actually letting me go?"

"Do the project and you can stay with AI. Go on the race and we're through." She brushed past me and walked out of the room. I heard the front door slam behind her.

CHAPTER 14

Bridget was murdered on Thursday morning. I didn't even bother to send Luther a text this time. I let the police handle it. I figured he didn't need another message from me about my letting his clients get killed on my runs.

That morning, before she was killed, at five-thirty, as the gray gleam of morning crept into the Eastern sky, I marched out of the parking lot and onto the grassy area where the clients waited. Kathy's visit had been the night before and I was tired still. The clients were lined up in uniform rows, all wearing dark blue or black so that they looked like ephemeral, silhouettes in the field. As Luther demands, the clients yelled out my name as I walked up, a loud bark that everyone yelled in unison. It ripped through the surrounding silence.

The most experienced, most fit clients stood at attention in the first row; Mr. Gentry, Bates, Miss Kay, and Totten. All of them were fanatics, eager and ready despite the early hour. They reminded me of racehorses in a starting gate. I could feel their expectations and excitement.

As I got closer, I saw that I'd been mistaken. I was used to seeing Miss Kay and Totten together, now, I saw it wasn't Totten, but someone else, a new client, one I'd never seen before who was the same size and height as Totten. Behind them, the second row was made up of people not quite as athletically inclined or who were aspiring to one day make it to the first row: Vandemeir, Telge, Christie. Their stances betrayed the fact that they weren't as enthusiastic about this morning's workout. I imagined they were worried that they might not keep up. They were not the thoroughbreds who occupied the first row, but not plow horses like the last row. That last row hosted only six people. These were the clients who struggled with the workouts.

Many of them I imagined were here to prove something not to themselves, but to someone else. They were wives trying to keep up with their husbands, men trying to keep old age from encroaching as quickly as it did. Among this group, I saw Gentry's wife, Sophia, Miss Granderson, and Mr. Schaub.

I didn't know the names of the others. They hadn't been in the group long enough for me to get to know them. All told there were twenty-four people out that morning. Not too large, not too small, imminently manageable. I tried to read their faces behind the dark gray morning curtain. Did they blame me for Georgia's death as Luther had? What rumors had they heard about my being fired? Did they even know about it? Their faces, what I could see of them, were impassive and offered no clues as to their private thoughts.

Seeing the clients helped me come to terms with the argument I had with Kathy. There was a familiarity in the ritual, comfort in knowing what to expect, the realization that I'd made the right decision. I hadn't slept much, and I didn't feel like working out that morning. My body felt slow and stiff. Duty had won out though, a sense of duty to Luther and the clients; a feeling that I was doing this for the end game, to one day, be the president and owner of AFC. This, working when I wasn't feeling up to it, was just a part of the road I had to take to get there. Beyond that was the sense that I had to get back into the saddle.

Kathy had been correct. This was a pivotal moment in my life. Not only did I need to get back out with the clients, but it was past time for me to address my agoraphobia. I needed a return to that normalcy.

"Let's go." I turned away from the clients and ran through the parking lot to the jogging trail that paralleled the road, trusting that they would follow along behind me. I heard the footfalls of the clients and sensed rather than saw them form up into a file behind me. I picked up the pace and heard the thumps of their footsteps turn into tight, quick, clips as they spread out and increased their own speed to keep up.

"Holy crap," Gentry said as he ran up next to me. "You going to go this fast all morning?"

"Probably." It had been two weeks since the last time I had been out since Georgia had been killed. That was a lot of time pent up and wanting to get back into the saddle.

Despite his complaint, his long strides ensured he would keep up. He was older but spry, at least for the first mile or two. I knew him well enough to know that he would be in the middle of the pack after that, his pride and the fact that we had a large number of last row folks would ensure he was never among the last.

"We thought you'd been fired." Gentry again, his voice coming through with slight gasps of fatigue.

"Nope." I tried to sound blasé but cringed inwardly with the thought that they might know more than I'd hoped.

A few strides then he broke the silence again with, "Feels kinda strange. Running like this, right?"

I knew what he was getting at. Just beneath the blanket of comfort, I felt from running with the group was a burrowing unease. A reminder that things had gone horribly wrong the last time I went for a run. This morning was the first time I had truly felt Georgia's absence. There was an emptiness that was pervasive. I'd never really known her, but she was a fast enough runner to be missed on a fast run like this one. Something uncoiled within me and I felt perspiration lace quickly across my brow that came from more than just the run.

The nerves were natural, I reminded myself. Prior to the workout, while I watched the clients from the safety of the tree line, I had wondered how I would feel to be leading the group after the murder. I'd settled on a run, thinking that it provided the best chance to keep my mind off last Monday. A situp or pushup workout offered too many chances for interaction with the clients. At least with a run, I'd only have to deal with the clients on a one-on-one basis, and even then only the ones who could keep up.

Now, just a half-mile into the run, I began to question my decision. A run might offer me some solace from the clients, but it was too much like the last Friday we ran. Too late I realized I should have picked a different routine. I turned and looked at the line behind me, a slight germ of panic deep in my gut as I tried to count the clients. They snaked behind me for almost a quarter of a mile. For a moment I debated whether or not to finish my count. What if I came up short? Without coming to an answer, instinct winning out, I counted. I could still just make out the twenty-fourth runner. I slowed down to ensure we didn't lose her.

"Are you avoiding a run that takes us by the coffee shop?" Again, Gentry, now even more winded.

"Just thought this would be a better route." In truth, I hadn't planned the route at all. Avoiding the area where Georgia had been murdered hadn't been intentional. I wondered just how much my subconscious was chewing on.

"You were missed the last couple of weeks." It sounded like he was more curious than concerned. I knew the clients had a strong and active grapevine.

"I was busy," I lied. "Had a big project."

"Really? What's the project? What's Luther gotcha doing?" It was a new voice this time, one I didn't know. I looked over my shoulder and saw the client I'd mistaken for Totten earlier.

"Not for Luther," I said. "I have a real job." Still running slowly, allowing the others to catch up, we turned down the running path that paralleled the highway.

"What do you do, Malone?"

"It's Instructor Malone." Gentry reprimanded him for me.

"Sorry," he said. "What do you do, Instructor Malone."

"Who are you?"

"Bradly Clark," his voice, unlike Gentry's, hardly winded.

"He started last week," Gentry inserted. I saw Gentry drop

back a little. Even though we were jogging, we'd reached his limit. Now it was just me, Bates, the new client and a silent Miss Kay in the front.

This time it was Bates who spoke. "Yeah, Instructor Malone, what do you do when you aren't yelling at us to run faster?" He edged Clark out of the way, but I saw out of my peripheral vision that Clark's head remained cocked to listen to our conversation.

Bates is the opposite of Gentry. Where Gentry is long and sinewy and looks his age, Bates is short and quick. Spiritually they differed too, Gentry, solemn and secure; Bates, more light-hearted. He might look twenty years younger than his forty years, but Bates is a determined, fast runner. Usually, I counted on him as much as Gentry to help me keep the clients together.

"Nothing that's relevant to this workout, Mr. Bates." I tried to sound as professionally detached as I imagined Luther would want me to sound.

"You might as well tell us," Bates replied, his voice as bright as his smirk, needling the instructors came easily to him. "It won't be hard for us to find out on our own."

"You can try, Mr. Bates," I said. "But you'll fail."

"Are you going to be this closed-mouthed and formal on the trip?" he asked. "It's going to be pretty boring if you are."

"What trip?"

"This weekend's race. Luther told us you were his replacement."

This was a surprise. I wouldn't have expected that from Luther, at least not so soon. "Really?" I asked.

"No, but it's not hard to guess." Without prompting he went on. I glanced back and saw Clark still listening. "Luther's out here yesterday limping around, not running. You show up the next day. It doesn't take much brainpower to figure out your re-appearance means you're going to take his place."

"You're right, and you don't have much brainpower." I cautioned myself to remember that Bates' playful nature didn't mean he couldn't be curious too. My mind jumped back to Monday. Had he been with us? Had I left him behind? Had he been out that morning? I didn't think he had been, but I wasn't sure. Like trying to remember a dream, the more I thought about it the less sure I became.

Bates is a consistent client, usually a part of the workout, but I didn't remember leaving him at a corner to direct the slower runners. I was on the point of asking him if he'd been there when I realized it didn't matter, that the thought had just popped into my head without any foundation or preamble and if I asked him, it would only make Georgia's loss more prescient.

"What about you guys?" I asked. "Are you on the team Mr. Bates?"

"Hell yeah!" Bates possessed an infectious and interminable enthusiasm. "Wouldn't miss it for the world."

"Who else?" I asked.

"Gentry, naturally," he started. "Clark, Rochester, Kay, and Totten."

He ticked each person off on his fingers as he spoke.

"That's only seven," I said. "I thought it was two teams of four."

Bate's voice became soft and conciliatory, "We still need to find a replacement for Georgia."

I felt my teeth grind down as he mentioned Georgia.

CHAPTER 15

Neither of us said anything for a moment. Just as I thought, the mention of Georgia threw a damper on our conversation, the exact thing I'd been trying to avoid. The silence reigned, awkwardly, for the next quarter mile. I found myself hoping that he'd say something, wishing even that Totten was there so he could say something flippant or snide, anything so that we could move past the memory.

At the intersection, I stopped. The instructor Malone of three weeks ago would have left a strong runner at the corner to direct the slower runners, but the seed of insecurity had germinated in my gut and I wasn't comfortable with that tactic anymore. I stopped and I had the faster runners who were with me join me in push-ups. The slower runners all jogged up and joined us.

Once we were whole, I jumped up and the run continued. I expected to lose the same number of clients on this next leg of the run, but I kept my pace between a run and a jog to ensure I didn't get too far out in front. I wasn't happy with it if only because it provided Bates the opportunity for more conversation.

"So, do you think you're ready?" Bates asked immediately as we got up.

I countered, "Think you are?"

"Doubt it, but I at least have been training, have you?"

I shook my head. "Just found out about the race the other day."

I heard a groan from Kay who up to that point had been

silent.

"Uh oh," Bates said. "We were hoping to be competitive."

I couldn't tell if he was being serious or flippant, but answered with a stoic, "I'll be fine."

"Have you raced much before?" Bates said. "Ever done this one?"

"I've raced some."

"This is my third time to do this race." This time it was Clark. "Gets harder each year." He made the statement sound like a question as if he was asking if I'd be up for it.

"I'll be fine," I said again.

Before joining the Marines, I'd raced in fun runs and triathlons. Being the son of a Marine and a workout enthusiast meant that Mike and I were recruited to run or bike with our father whenever he needed company at a race. I never took it seriously, but always enjoyed the workout. Once I was in the Marines, our platoon competed in Battalion wide challenges that were similar to adventure races. This would be my first race since coming home, but thanks to the workouts with the clients over the past six months I was confident I could at least keep up.

We had been running for almost a mile since our last stop to let folks catch up to the pack. I looked back along our route and could see the sluggish form of Bridget as she chugged along on the sidewalk, moving in and out of the glow of street lights as her heavy feet churned. The rest of the group was spread out between her at the back and me at the front.

Slow runners, the type who refuse to engage, the type who accepts their slowness as a part of life, are a constant irritant. I can't understand that type of antipathy. Why did she keep coming out to workouts? She had no drive, no intensity, no desire to improve, my face scrunched up involuntarily as I watched her and the other runners slowly making their way around the bend behind us.

Irritated, I picked up the pace and quickly found my breath turned ragged. Bates and Clark stayed with me, their breathing as choppy as my own. I concentrated on each step; focused on driving my knees, pulling my legs, moving my feet as fast as possible. Finally, as the three of us flew across another intersection, I felt the zeal of running fast and forgetting problems. Then, just as quickly, I felt the need to outpace them, the desire to compete, a pull to stay in front of other fast runners, Bates, Kay and Clark, the only clients still with me.

Petite, and as short as Bates, Kay is lithe and quick. Like Georgia had been, she was one of the group's faster female runners. I knew that she was reaching the breaking point and was only a few hundred meters from falling out. It's something that I've learned to read in the clients. Their breathing grows labored, then weak; footsteps get heavier and shoulders slump; it isn't long before they veer off like something thrown overboard from a speeding boat, caught in the wake to disappear silently.

Most of the clients in the fast group are type A. They hate to lose, even if it's just a Thursday morning run to the highway. Kay acted as if she could take on the world and come back a winner. It was a type of cool overwhelming confidence that I had to pretend to have when I worked with the clients. The same type of trait I constantly had to fake in the Marines. With Kay, it seemed natural and flowed out of her like a never-ending stream. I felt a moment of relief and pride when I realized she was close to giving up as if I'd finally broken a mustang.

At the next intersection she was gone, nothing more than a breathless, sibilant "Shit!" to mark her dropping out.

Clark and Bates continued on, heads down like sled dogs, legs churning, struggling and racing one another as well as me. Their competitiveness was contagious and inspired me. I felt invigorated as we blew through a four-way intersection, heedless of any cross traffic and realized that they were still a long way from falling out.

"Who are the biggest liabilities?" I asked as we sprinted along the sidewalk. I knew they were concentrating on their running as much as I was, but I hoped by making them talk they'd weaken faster or at least believe that I was still a long way from breaking.

Bates spoke quickly, "You."

I turned my head to see if he was serious. "Me?"

"Yeah." He huffed as he looked over at me, his brow furrowed in determination to keep the pace.

"You're kidding?"

"Nope." His voice was flat despite the fact that he had to speak as we ran. "First, you're an unknown." He paused to get another few breaths. "Always difficult to have someone new on a team in these races."

"Second, you're tall and built. Better to be tough and wiry like me, not tall." He nodded toward me.

"I can pull my weight."

"Plus," he cut me off. "You have issues."

"What's that mean?"

"You're just a bit off," he said quickly. "We all know it."

A bit off. I didn't know which I liked less, my boss saying I have a problem or the clients thinking I was a bit off. I looked back at him and waited for more, the three of us dodging cracks in the sidewalk and driveway curbs as we ran.

He saw me waiting for more and said, "You work out with us all the time, but you're different from the other instructors." It was a long sentence and his breathing became rougher.

He looked at me as if expecting an answer, or perhaps expecting me to pick up our speed again. Instead, I listened to the sound of our footsteps and waited, hoping he had more to say.

"I'm not that worried about you," Clark spoke this time.

"Yeah?" I answered. "Who are you worried about?"

He answered quickly, "Kay."

I saw Bates flinch out of the corner of my eye.

"Why's that? She's a pretty strong runner," I said.

"We have a lot of gear to carry. That's a lot the team is going to have to carry for her because she's so small."

I found it somewhat ironic that he said that in front of Bates who was all of five-foot-two inches tall.

"Don't worry about, Kay. She'll be fine." Bates said.

Besides, I'm more worried about myself." Another pause to get his breath. "Running pretty fast, aren't we?"

We hit another intersection and the day was light enough by now for us to see the road that stretched, long, and uphill, in front of us to disappear as it fell over the brow of a lazy hill. The sides of the roadway sloped down into drainage ditches along either side. With so little traffic we ran along the crown of the road, right down the middle. I looked up the road to the crest of the hill and decided that would be our finish line. I picked up the tempo of my already tired legs.

"You're going to kill us before the race." Bates strained to keep up. I could no longer see Clark but could still hear his footsteps.

I kept up the acceleration as we started to climb the hill. I knew where I would end the run. They didn't. That gave me an advantage. I doubted if Bates and Clark would keep up.

We were moving at a speed just shy of a sprint, each of us feeding off the energy of the others, none of us willing to show weakness, each wondering who would be the first to bow out. I felt effervescent, relaxed for the first time in days. I was outrunning my concern and anxiety, outrunning my problems with Luther and Kathy, alone and happy to be running as fast as I could. The only thing that refused to slough away was the memory of Georgia.

Halfway up the hill, I felt more than saw Bates fall off. I could hear Clark still there on my heels so I kept accelerating, inspired by Bates' faltering. Finally, just two hundred meters from the crest of the hill, I heard Clark fall away. It was just a momentary sound, like the deflation of a sail in the wind, but I knew he'd given up. I made myself finish and stopped at the top.

I felt heavy the moment I stopped. All of the lightness and energy drained out of me in an instant and I was sorry I had not kept running. Hands-on hips, gasping for breath I looked back and saw Clark and Bates churning their way up the hill. They stopped next to me, sneakers pounding to a halt.

"What are you trying to do, kill us?" It was Clark again. He bent over at the waist, torso down, head forward.

He looked up at me as if I had betrayed him by running so fast. I turned to walk back down the road toward the dark silhouettes of the running figures who were trying to catch up to us. From on top of the hill, I could see all the runners and took a quick count. I breathed a sigh of relief when I counted the last one, Bridget, just a few minutes jog from reaching the stoplight at the intersection I'd passed a few moments before.

"You're going to ruin us for the race." This time it was Bates.

"Got to train sometime," I said.

I heard them grunt as I started a slow jog back the way we'd come, allowing the gravity to help me down the hill.

We caught each runner as we ran back. There was no premonition, no thought that anything might go wrong as the large red pickup truck came down the hill behind us. The flash of white light from its headlights that presaged its passing us encouraged us to get over to the side of the road, but none of us could miss seeing what happened next.

Lined up on the road, like an audience seated on a rise to watch a summer concert, we all saw the truck swerve drastically as it passed the intersection and pound squarely into the slow running form of Bridget.

Even from several hundred meters away we all heard the sickening crunch of the impact. Later, I decided it reminded me of the sound I had heard as a child when I had watched that box turtle crushed by a car on the highway. I never had any love for Bridget, and prior to her being hit, I would have had few nice things to say, but as we ran down toward her, the truck already gone, I felt a deeper remorse for having watched her die than I felt when I had found Georgia.

CHAPTER 16

Lamb and I both looked toward where Marlberg pointed and saw the plume of dust that he had seen. There was too much sand to make out exactly what it was, so I focused the binoculars on the leading edge of the moving dust cloud.

"Three trucks," I said. "Lightweight. Looks like there are only a couple men in each truck. I don't see any weapons."

"Could be they have an idea we're coming," Lamb said.

"I don't know." Marlberg now. "I don't see any weapons. If they knew we were on the way I think they'd have some technicals, probably with mounted guns." Marlberg described the poor man's gun jeeps that had been so pernicious during the early months of the war. "These look more like a caravan of food or supplies. Maybe setting up a weekly street market."

"It wouldn't take much to turn those into technicals," Lamb again.

While they spoke I watched the trucks. One by one all three disappeared into the buildings. We saw flashes of them as they drove through the village, just a brief glimpse then nothing, as they passed between buildings, like sharks dorsal fins popping up then down in the surf. Eventually, there was nothing left to see and we had to assume they stopped somewhere near the center of the village. The dust cloud stopped moving and the flashes of movement disappeared.

"We got some movement toward the center." It was Marlberg again, by then Lamb and I had already seen it. "I still don't see any weapons."

Lamb grunted. "I still don't like it."

This was the platoon sergeant's job, to alternate between remaining near the back of the platoon to push the men while constantly assessing for dangers and problems. The men called Lamb the Seagull, but never to his face. The first few times I'd overheard them use the nickname I hadn't realized what it meant. Eventually, I'd heard a new private ask what it meant and overheard the explanation through the thin walls of my office.

"He's a seagull, Marine, cause he hovers overhead and complains when we don't give him enough." Then I heard a long pause and the team leader had continued. "If he still isn't happy he swoops in and shits all over everything."

It might have been a more harsh description than I felt Lamb was due, but it was apt. To Lamb's credit, he was as good as, or as bad, as every other platoon sergeant.

"It's not enough to scrub the mission or to make me think we need to change our plans," I said. "We've built this mission around the chance of contact with the hope that there won't be any. I think caution is called for, but I don't see that this changes anything." I saw Lamb suck in a breath as if to argue but cut him off for the second time. "As long as we all follow the plan, we'll be good. If things get too hairy, we pull back under the cover of the guns and whatever arty the FO can scare up for us."

Lamb's breath escaped in a sibilant hiss but was not used for a counterpoint.

"All good?" I asked Marlberg and Lamb.

They both nodded.

"I'm going to head back to the platoon. You two stay here with the guns. I'll make radio checks via my RTO and my handheld as we move back to the platoon."

"Roger, sir."

Corporal Duffy had started a tradition in our platoon of clanging the front part of the Kevlar helmets like football players did with their helmets. High fives or handshakes were hard when we carried so much gear and our weapons. Lamb had tried to put a stop to it early on but had failed when the First Sergeant had noticed it and made a play on Lamb's name. The First Sergeant said he was happy to see First Platoon was acting more like rams than like lambs. From then on there was nothing Lamb could do.

Marlberg banged the front of his helmet against mine.

"Go get em, sir," he said. "We got your back."

Lamb eschewed the head butt but looked me steadily in the eye for a moment. "Last chance," he said. "You sure you don’t want the FO?"

"I’ll relay any instructions through my RTO."

"Be safe, sir."

"We’ll call when we enter and again when we pull back. I’m not expecting to bring any of you down to the village."

They both nodded. I stood up and still crouching jogged over to where my RTO, Wilson waited.

CHAPTER 17

My brother announced his arrival by dropping a bicycle in the back of my truck. I checked my watch, five till six, he was five minutes early. The parking garage was in downtown Dallas, a few blocks from the train station. I looked over the steering wheel and could see the Dallas Post office and the train tracks. As I watched Mike through the mirror I wondered, for the hundredth time that morning, why he wanted to meet up here. Why didn't he want to meet at the train station? Some flare for the theatrical? Worry about Luther showing up? Worse, maybe he was worried I'd have a panic attack before getting on the train? Painfully, he wasn't the only one worried about that.

It was worse earlier when I had arrived. This position, five floors up, allowed me the opportunity to prepare for the train trip, like stepping into the shallow end of a pool instead of jumping into the deep end.

Another loud bang and I returned to watching the mirror. I saw Mike reposition his road bike in the bed then heft a mountain bike in as well. There were two bike rides as part of the race. The first was on the afternoon of day one, a twenty-mile road bike. A second, slightly shorter, mountain bike leg took place at the end of day two. It had taken just one call to Mike to procure his bikes. A second call had come from him to arrange this meeting.

I spent most of yesterday packing my backpack and seething about the ultimatum that Kathy had delivered. For a brief time, right after she left I tried to dream up a way to finish her model in one night and still do the race. It hadn't taken long to realize it was impossible. The folder with the specification had been thrown across the living room in frustration, a mess of papers near the kitchen, a reminder of what had become of our relationship.

Once the mountain bike had been positioned and arranged in the back of the truck, Mike walked around and opened the passenger side door. He heaved himself in and I saw a look of excitement and eagerness on his face as if he as looking forward to the race.

"Heard from Luther?" Mike had shown up Thursday morning later than the local police but in time to see what was left in the wake of Bridget's death.

"No, have you?" I knew the answer but felt like it wouldn't be right not to needle him. All I got in reply was a grunt. Not even a murder investigation would drive Mike and Luther to talk again. I knew he got his fair share of coaxing and pleading phone calls from Mom.

"What did he say?"

"He didn't," I said. "I'm serious, he never came by. He texted. That's it."

"What did he text?"

"He said; You're still going on the trip. Watch out for Horne." I held up my phone so he could see the text.

"Wow, lots of sympathy."

"That's Luther for you."

I got out of the truck and Mike did the same on the passenger side. I took a look at the two bicycles and saw an olive drab, military issue rucksack next to them. "What's the ruck for?" He shrugged. "Just some stuff I thought you might need. I know you haven't been camping in a while; some rappelling ropes, a harness, carabineers, some other stuff I had lying around. You can go through it when you get there." He spoke nonchalantly and smiled his I'm a big brother looking out for my kid brother smile. I've always hated that smile.

Despite the smile, I was glad for the gear. There was a packing list online, but I was missing all sorts of equipment. My plan had been to scrounge what I could from my team and make up the rest. Mike's pack would help. He came around the truck and watched me, regarding me up and down.

"You ready for this?" He slapped me on the back of the shoulder with a hand that felt as thick and heavy as a bear's paw. I turned back toward the front of the truck and studied the train station some more. We could see it over the parking garage retaining wall. His tone turned serious with his next question.

"Seriously, are you going to be okay?"

"I'll be fine."

He nodded but went on with more big brother advice.

"Just focus on each thing as it comes up, then worry about nothing else. Focus like a laser, that's the key." He looked at me severely, like a mentor instructing a student. I decided that I would rather deal with the smile than the mentoring.

"The race is only half the problem," I said.

"What's the other half?" he asked. "The desert?"

"Well, yeah, that, but you saw his text. Luther thinks he's being targeted." I sounded like a fool but knew if anyone could understand Luther's paranoia it would be Mike. " He thinks someone is out to ruin him. He's almost convinced me that the murders aren't random."

"I never thought it was random."

I turned to face him. "But Chen said Georgia was just in the wrong place at the wrong time."

"Chen, sure," Mike kept looking out the windshield at the station below. "I've always thought she was lured down there by someone she knew."

His eyes were focused intently on something down at the station. I followed his glance. He was watching several cars as they pulled up to the station and dropped racers off for the train.

"You think it was someone in the group?" I asked.

"Good possibility," he said. "I don't believe in coincidence and neither should you. If Luther's convinced it's someone in the group or former client, you should take it seriously. I think he's right."

"He called you?"

He shook his head but kept staring at the station. "Mom."

Several more cars had pulled up to the front of the station. People got out and started packing their gear and bikes to different areas of the platform that looked to be roped off and labeled. The racers looked like ants that had found a juicy morsel and were beginning to swarm. First ones and twos, then several at a time as more and more cars pulled up.

"He's crazy," I said. "You know that. It's gone beyond paranoia."

"Yep, but he might be right this time." His eyes continued to stare down at the gathering crowd of people in the parking lot. The beginning stages of barely organized chaos were starting to take form.

Mike went on, "This guy in the text he sent you. This guy Horne."

"I know him," I said. "Jeff Horne."

"Former Marine, no priors, at least nothing major. I was thinking of placing him under surveillance just in case Luther is right."

"Does he have any connection to Georgia or Bridget?"

"Luther says no, but I had Chen question him." Mike paused. "He was seeing Georgia."

"Seeing how?"

"They dated last year," he stopped me before I could ask my next question by giving me a stern look and continuing. "They broke up six months ago. According to her friends, it was a rough breakup. Her choice, not his."

His eyes went back to the crowd and I finally realized why. "He's in the race?"

Mike nodded.

"You want me to watch him?"

"Nope," Mike said. "I just want you to know what Luther's thinking. Want you to know what's going on."

I shook my head and studied the crowd as well. "I doubt if you'll be able to pick him out from up here."

Mike nodded. "Yeah, I know." He turned to face me, his voice and face as serious as I've ever seen. "There's more. We found out something else, but I'm not sure I should tell you till I've done some more checking."

"Now you have to tell me."

"The interview with Georgia's roommate," he said. "She said one of the people Georgia had dated in the past couple of weeks was the owner of the exercise group."

"Horne," I said. "No mystery there."

"Him or Luther," he said. "The roommate couldn't be more specific."

"Shut up."

"She said it was an older guy who owned a fitness group."

"That's Horne."

"I hope so, but we have to keep checking on every lead." Then he turned more light-hearted, his face broke out into a smile. "Don't let it bother you, just be aware. And the best part is if you can get past your problem, it should be a fun race."

"My problem?"

He glared again, but this time good-naturedly. His paw came down again and smacked my shoulder. "Yeah, if you can stop being a freaking perve, maybe you'll enjoy yourself. If anything happens, or if you need anything, give me a call. I'll have my cell phone on the whole weekend."

I nodded, not sure what he'd be able to do, but felt that it was important to let him think that he could help. One more smack to the shoulder and he stepped out of the door, the slam of the car door heralding his exit as much as the bikes crashing into the bed ushered him in.

CHAPTER 18

I started my engine and with my truck following his, the two of us drove down the ramps of the garage to the surface streets. At McKinney, he went left, while I turned right toward the station. I looked for a parting wave, but saw nothing from him, just his taillights fluttering at the next intersection. The plan I'd developed while I waited in the garage was to park on the street across from the platform. If I parked in the parking lot, I'd feel immediately surrounded, trapped. Crowds were to be avoided this early in the mission, I felt. If the exposed feelings did come, and I knew eventually they would, I didn't want it to come immediately.

If I was going to become a part of the crowd, I wanted to enter it on my terms, tangentially not head-on.

Sticking to the plan I parked midway between the parking garage and the main building of the train station. There was a large live oak tree that extended out over the street. I parked beneath it and felt as if it was embracing me. It was comfortable and familiar, like waiting in the wood line for the workout to start in the mornings. I sat in the truck, the hollow echo of cars chugging by on the road next to me, a loud thumping of their wheels on the street all sank in and eventually it too became okay. Over those few moments, it became a part of the scenery, second nature, if not comfortable, then at least bearable.

The sky that had become a hue lighter in the past hour, but it only served to accentuate the darkness of the shadow produced by the tree. Again a slight feeling of confidence settled over me. I could stay here all morning, ensconced in the cab of the truck, and be perfectly okay. That would progress, right?

Even as I thought it, I knew it was a cop-out. I came for the trip, for the clients, to help ensure that no one else would get hurt, but most of all to prove to Luther that I could function as his second in command and eventual heir. It demanded action. I stepped out of the truck and grabbed the two backpacks and the two bikes from the truck bed before my brain could process the fact that I was out in the open. With all the gear, I felt like an overloaded turtle.

I paused to consider my route before leaving the perceived safety of the truck. The pause was a mistake and I knew it as soon as I looked up. A deep shudder ran down my spine, like the cranking of a diesel engine in the bowels of a ship. From the safety of the truck, even up in the parking lot looking down, the plan had been simple. Move quickly through the crowds, don't let any of it have time to become an issue. Move smoothly and quickly through the throng and into the train where I imagined the cramped spaces would offer some solace.

Now, the shudder still resounding, I wondered how I could have expected so much of myself. Was it all the worries of the last day and a half, the anticipation of the train trip, the worrying about packing, the meeting with Luther, my problems with Kathy, had all these things crowded out my fears about being exposed?

Seeing the open path in front of me, the broad street I'd have to cross, the people I'd have to mingle with, opened the floodgates for all of those suppressed fears. The truck was at my left and my hand crept toward it, ready to lift the handle so I could crawl back inside. The urge to retreat was just shy of overwhelming.

A wave from the crowd in the parking lot caught my attention. Mr. Gentry arms in the air, waved back and forth frantically, his smile and gesturing arms good-natured and welcoming. Directly behind him stood Bates, Clark, Totten, all of them huddled together like a large covey of quail, all of them watching me, all expectant and waiting.

I felt the brushed chrome of the door handle, cold in my hand. I turned automatically, surprised by the feel of it, not realizing my hand had grabbed it. I could jump in, lock the door, go back to the apartment and tell Luther and his plans for the future to go to hell. I would finish the model, expand the service as Kathy wanted, become an expert, completely abandon my other responsibilities and only go out on my terms. Become something similar to a hoarder, but instead of hoarding things I would hoard myself.

"You okay?" a soft voice hit my ear from behind me on my right. I felt a hand brush up against my back. I cringed and closed my eyes as I thought of the embarrassment that would inevitably go along with any of my team seeing me stuck by the side of the road needing a stranger to come to my assistance. I turned to face the Good Samaritan and realized how familiar the voice sounded.

"I don't think anyone has noticed that you're having trouble walking out there, but you better do something soon before they decide that you're a nut."

It was from Kathy. She grinned broadly, reveling in having surprised me, clearly satisfied.

"What are you doing here?"

"Let's get you moving first." Kathy grabbed the road bike from my right hand. She motioned me toward the station with her head, away from the crowd and the open expanse of asphalt.

"But, the team is over there?" I motioned toward Mr. Gentry and the others.

"I did some reading after you told me about this plan of yours," she said. "We're going to take the baby steps approach for this sucker. Baby step one, keep things above your head." She nodded toward the awning that paralleled the tracks, a long canopy that was designed to shelter passengers from the rain while they boarded. Then Kathy pointed to the trees that ran along the street. I saw that we would be able to walk to the awning without being too far away from the shelter of the oaks.

I looked at my teammates. "Won't they think it's weird that I don't go say hello?"

"They'll think it's weirder if you break down in a psychotic episode in front of them." Kathy forced a smile to help the joke along.

"I won't have a psychotic episode."

She gestured grandly with her arm. "Then, by all means, go that way."

Knowing now that an alternative with an overhead cover was available was immediately preferable to the roadway.

"No, I guess you're right," I said.

Kathy turned and walked toward the awning and compelled me to follow in her wake with her confidence. It might have been the fact that we stayed under the trees, it might have been that we stayed under the cover of the awning, or it might have been that Kathy provided an impetus, a mission, gave me orders that I could follow, whatever the factors I felt the panic subside slowly with each step I took toward the train. We pulled up near the tracks and she was the first to speak.

"See, it's all a matter of taking baby steps." Her voice sounded triumphant.

"Where'd you come up with that?"

"I told you," she said, "I was a psychology minor. I also have a friend who's a psychiatrist. I told her about your race. It was her idea."

"Not that I'm complaining, but why are you here?"

"Would you believe I came to see you off?"

"Does that mean I still have a job?"

"Let's stick with I'm still mad, but I'm reconsidering letting you go." she followed this with a slow sustained smile that let me know we were back to normal.

If only to stop looking at her, to break the awkward stare,

I looked off to my left and saw a man wearing a bright orange and green shirt with the words Race Official emblazoned on it in yellow. He was directing racers down the platform to where they were depositing bikes and backpacks in a large pile of equipment.

"That must be where the baggage car will be," I said.

"Then that's baby step two," Kathy said. "Let's make it to the end of the platform with no psychotic breaks." I glared. "Let's stop calling it psychotic."

"You're right." Her voice was serious. "Let's make it to the end of the platform with no panic attacks." She emphasized the last two words.

I motioned toward the teams across the parking lot. "What about them?"

"Screw them." Her voice was solid and commanding as if she'd been entering adventure races every day of her life. "You're not on the clock right now. Come on."

She marched off toward the baggage area pushing my bike next to her. Again, feeling like a duckling following his mother duck, I hefted the backpack higher up on my shoulder, got a better handle on the bike and Mike's smaller pack, and followed her.

In front of us, all the way at the end of the platform were three piles of backpacks and other camping gear all waiting to be loaded on the train. A mound of gear, more than anything I'd seen outside the Marines, was all being dropped off in the roped-off area. Scores of volunteers, all wearing bright Orange shirts, helped corral racers and tried to keep things somewhat organized. Expensive looking backpacks were everywhere, stuffed, overwhelmed with gear, equipment strapped to the outside, they made mine and Mike's recycled military ALICE packs look antiquated and sub-standard.

The road bikes and mountain bikes that stood in rows on makeshift bike racks looked crisp and sterling as well. Most were sleek and speedy, some looked like they cost as much as my annual salary. White tags, with race numbers and owner's names, fluttered like dry leaves in a stiff wind from each bike. Heedless of the volunteer's protestations that everything would be fine with their bikes, a couple dozen racers hovered over the bicycles protectively like mother hens over irreplaceable eggs.

We came to the end of the covered area and I saw that I wouldn't have to come out from underneath the roof to drop off my gear. My lungs loosened in relief.

Kathy snapped her fingers in my face. "Hey, you got race numbers. I'm talking to you."

"What?"

"Did you get a race number?"

I stammered and pulled my eyes from the mountain of gear. "No."

"That guy, the one I just met, the one with the beard directing traffic, he's the race organizer, Tony Stacks," Kathy spoke as if she was narrating a story to a struggling two-year-old. "He says you need a race number."

"Okay." I hadn't realized she'd walked away and decided it would be best to keep that to myself. I looked around and felt suddenly lost. My eyes lit on my truck that I could just make out parked down the street. Not a far run.

"You need this?" Gentry's voice broke through. He strolled in among us and held out a race number for me to take. Kathy stepped up and took it from him.

"Thanks," Kathy said to him. "Are you on the team?"

I watched as they introduced themselves, but didn't hear anything. My mind drifted as they spoke. People crowded around, ebbed and flowed like waves around me. I had a hard time keeping my thoughts straight with so much movement around me. It helped if I kept my eyes focused on Kathy.

Eventually, she came over and whispered. "I said I'll help you do baby steps, not do everything for you. Wake up!"

I blinked and tried to look more relaxed.

"Gentry says you need to secure your race numbers to all of your gear then park them over there with the rest."

She nodded to the race number that was in my hand. When had I taken that? "Those race numbers." She pivoted her head toward Mike's bikes. "Those bikes. Go!"

Her simple, straight forward commands were exactly what I needed. I felt myself nod slightly then I turned and walked over to the bikes. It was like I was watching myself perform the functions she had asked, but that was okay. Even performing on autopilot was better than not performing at all.

I secured the number to the bikes then looked for Kathy again. She was with Gentry. She came over to me again as I stood up.

"Come on, baby step three. What's next? Board the train?" Kathy's voice was in my ear again, but if she meant to say more she didn't.

A much louder voice, booming among the small crowd by the luggage cut her off.

"Get the fuck out of my way asshole." A solid shoulder that landed like a steel rod smacked into the center of my back and knocked me to the concrete. I knew without having to be told or even needing to look up that it was Horne.

CHAPTER 19

I only met Horne once, we worked together one morning before Luther let him go. He was memorable though. Beyond that one time, after Luther fired him, I heard a multitude of stories, warnings, and admonitions from the clients. Even Luther had warned me away from him. His firing came so close to my being hired that it went without saying that he would blame me, his replacement, for his being let go.

Once he was released from AFC he hadn't gone far. He started his own workout group, Marine PT, and set up shop in a community park just three miles from AFC. Whenever we ran toward the old state highway, we would see him working out with his own group, many of whom were former members of Luther's group. He is a hulk of a person, far larger than a person would expect a fitness instructor to be. A gym rat, the type of person who hung out in weight rooms for hours and hours, Horne's muscles were so swollen it looked like he'd have trouble straightening his arms or touching his toes. Where I am generally called stringy and wiry Horne is gargantuan.

I straightened myself out and stood up. Horne was already gone, many steps ahead of me, by the baggage, outside the safety of the overhead protection I needed.

He looked over his shoulder at me, he might have even winked. It was the type of look that told me he knew who I was as much as I knew him. The shove had been on purpose but something that might have looked accidental to anyone who saw it. His look also intonated that there would be more to come. The question was why? Was it just to get back at Luther? Was it because of my taking his place at AFC? It felt like there was more behind it. A gentle, friendly hand on my chest stopped me from going after him.

"You okay Instructor?" A pat on my shoulder made me turn. It was from Max. He was a tall, dark-haired man with a complexion that implied a Hispanic heritage. Still, I knew him well enough to know that that impression was wrong, most of what Max sported was manufactured. He tanned often, dyed his brown hair black, and I suspected he used contacts to darken his eye color.

His broad smile never broke and was followed by an outstretched hand that he refused to let drop. A mixture of friendship and lightheartedness played across his face. A former client, I hadn't seen Max in over three months. There was a pack over one shoulder, his left hand steadied an expensive-looking bike by his side.

He turned the handshake into a quick hug, more a chest bump than anything with feeling. "I saw him push you. Putting you in your place I guess." He chuckled as if everything in life was a joke, his white teeth were offset by his dark complexion.

"I suppose." I tried to return his chuckle but failed.

"How've you been?"

"I'm alright." His words slurred together effortlessly. Max was the type who never had a care in the world. The entire group knew that he had left our group to train with Horne, what no one knew was why. I always thought he had been a genuinely good-natured person, eminently likable even if there was a less than substantial veneer. I, more than anyone, had been shocked by his leaving.

"I didn't know you were racing," I said.

"Sure, anything for a bit of fun. Plus, I want to check this out." He nodded down at his bike. Except for the form and the fact that it had two wheels, pedals, and handlebars, it was unlike any bike I had ever seen. "It's a prototype, kinda a hybrid road and mountain bike."

I nodded and he went on like a proud father.

"Yep, my brother and I engineered and built it. We're marketing it as the only bike that can handle all the elements, environments and road conditions as well or better than a mountain bike or road bike."

"Best of both worlds?"

"Best of all worlds," He countered. "What about you? What are you doing here? You never came to races when I invited you."

"Luther ordered me to come."

Max reared back and laughed like a man who'd had too much to drink at dinner and was enjoying the final bonhomie of a party. "You mean I asked you to race with me for four months and it turns out all I had to do was order you to do it."

"No, you would have had to have Luther order me. He's the one with the rank."

This produced even more laughs from Max, too many laughs I thought.

"Where is he? Or is his knee keeping him at home?"

"How'd you know about that?" I asked.

"I hear the news, we all talk, you know that," he leaned in conspiratorially, "I would have enjoyed screwing with him had he come."

"Yeah, when I think of Luther, I think of how fun it is to mess with him." It was an odd thing to say. No one who knew Luther would say that. Max always seemed to think that everyone was in on the joke even when there wasn't a joke.

"But at least you got a free ticket to the race." He let his bike lean against his waist long enough to slap me on the shoulder good-naturedly.

"Tell you what," he continued, "let me go throw my stuff into the pile over there, and I'll find you once we board the train, I can give you all the intel on your competition." He winked.

"I'll find you later."

Max brushed by me and started to work his way to the front

of the line of people with his load. The crowd swarmed around me, but somewhere beneath it all I heard, actually, I sensed a dull rumble. It emanated up from the platform. For a moment I thought it was a miss-balanced air conditioning unit kicking in, or a large truck driving by, but when several people turned their heads to look behind me I knew that something was coming up the railroad tracks. A distinct blast from an air horn that could only come from a locomotive pierced the area. I turned and saw a single bright yellow light far down the tracks. Transfixed like it was an Angler Fish lure, I watched as it gradually grew in size and intensity.

Without thinking about the crowd around me, I trotted down the platform towards the far end of the tracks, away from the station and the other racers. I didn't even notice when the roof over my head disappeared.

CHAPTER 20

Wilson was pulling security, in the prone, one hand on his weapon, his handset on his ear, the perfect Marine. I tapped him on the shoulder and he jumped up without a word.

"Get a radio check with the FO," I said. He bent to the task as he followed me away from the overwatch position where I had left Lamb and Marlberg to set up the machine guns and mortars. It was a good plan and a great position for the guns. The entire village could be seen from here. We were on a slight rise and because of that, the FO would be more than capable of providing support for the platoon if it came to it.

Wilson grabbed my arm to get my attention and gave me a thumbs-up sign. I tried my own radio with my handheld and heard the reassuring voice of Lamb say, "Good copy."

I tried Johnson as well, just as I tried for the past thirty minutes, but didn't expect to get him. I didn't. I wasn't surprised. We had lost contact with Johnson after we'd gone just five hundred meters away from the main body of the platoon. We wouldn't be able to get him again for another few minutes once we came in range for the little "line of sight" platoon internal radios.

The route we'd taken to the gun position had been circuitous and excruciatingly slow. When we'd first set off from the platoon all of us had thought the gun emplacement would be less than three hundred meters to the west. We had been wrong. The gunners and their crews, all 9 Marines, moved slowly. As we moved, Marlberg had continued to suggest moving further, to get a better vantage point, to be able to provide a better field of fire, to support the platoon's movements, or to get more high-ground. They were all good reasons, but what had started out as a simple gun emplacement that should have taken no more than twenty minutes had become an hour-long recon as well.

Marlberg might have been the best scout we had, but he was also meticulous. He had been adamant that the gun teams keep silent and kept our pace slow to ensure that they both remained quiet, but also weren't winded when they were set into position.

Given another couple of months and Marlberg would be off to be a platoon sergeant for another platoon. I would be sorry to lose him. All Marines were good, some better than others, Marlberg was the best I'd ever seen. The last report we'd gotten from Johnson was that all was well back on our original line of march with the rest of the platoon. Johnson and the other squad leaders were all extremely capable leaders, but we'd been too long away and I was anxious to get back and get moving on the objective.

An hour wasted, now at least thirty minutes to get back. Probably another twenty minutes before I'd be able to check-in with Johnson. It was not a good place to be.

My thoughts were broken by Wilson's iron grip on my arm. Not a simple attention-getting grip, this time it was a grip of warning. "Marlberg has movement!" he hissed.

Together we dropped to the prone position. I looked up, but we were in a bowl, all sides sloping up, our line of sight was obscured in all directions. I reached out and Wilson handed me the headset. "Bravo one-four this is one-zero actual, what do you have." I looked back and saw Wilson's rifle was up as he scanned around us, his senses alert, the spinal cord from the handset bridging between us like an umbilical.

"One-zero, two of those trucks are moving south from the village, how copy over?"

A curtain of fear fell across my thoughts as I heard him say "moving south." Johnson and the platoon were near the road just south of the village. They'd be in contact if those trucks continued to move south. I strained to think of what Johnson might have done since we last contacted him.

Our platoon SOP called for him getting away from danger areas and setting up a patrol base. It's what I would have done in the same situation. I was sure it was what Johnson would have done as well, except that Johnson has always been a more aggressive, outside the box thinker than the typical Marine. I could easily see him setting up a hasty ambush and over-watching the road. How would he react to the two trucks? Would he stop them? Search them and the drivers? Would he let them pass? All the worries confirmed that I'd been too long away from the platoon and needed to get back fast.

"I copy two trucks moving south," I said.

"Be advised we have pax in the truck with weapons."

"Shit!" I switched to the platoon radio without answering Marlberg and tried to raise Johnson and the platoon. "Bravo one-two this is one-zero actual, how copy over?"

I listened for a moment but heard nothing but static in response. Had he heard me but I couldn't receive his reply? Were we still too far away for any communications?

"I say again, one-zero," Marlberg transmitted. "There are weapons in the trucks, how copy over?"

"Roger, good copy," I said to him quickly and tried Johnson on the platoon radio again.

"One-two this is one-zero, you have two trucks moving toward your position, do not engage, I say again, do not engage."

I listened intently to the static that came back. It was broken by Lamb.

"One-zero, the trucks are entering into defilade from our position," Lamb told me that the guns would no longer be able to provide cover from the approaching trucks. "Suggest you get in contact with Johnson A-S-A-P." He spelled out the acronym, his words calm and detached, but I could hear his disappointment and frustration.

"Roger, we're moving," I threw the handset back to Wilson,

pulled myself off the ground and ran in a crouch back toward where I hoped the platoon was located. I checked my small compass on my watch band to get a quick bearing and hustled through the brush with Wilson a few steps behind.

I knew before he said anything that things had gotten worse before he ran up and grabbed my arm for the third time. If it had been good news, he would have just whispered it. This grab had taken on a special meaning in the last few moments, I wondered if from then on I'd always associate bad news with someone grabbing my arm from behind.

Wilson hissed into my ear as we jogged. "Marlberg says three more trucks are approaching the village from the North, all armed."

CHAPTER 21

By the time I got to the end of the platform the light had become two distinct circles; the train diesel engine's headlights. I jumped down from the platform onto the rocks that made up the roadbed and pulled two coins and two nails out of my pocket. The nails were taped into a cross and they joined the coins on the rails, balanced on the interior lip where I was sure the engine's wheels would hit them. I looked up and watched the engine as it broke through the last remnants of morning haze. I climbed back up onto the platform and grabbed my camera from the outside pocket of my pack. I stepped back and raised the camera to my eye to snap pictures.

Amtrak used a pair of GE Genesis diesel locomotives to pull the Sunset Express through Dallas to San Antonio. The train for the race was a promotional event and I had thought the race would warrant only a couple of older generation freight locomotives. Instead what I saw were the Sunset Express' engines. The horn sounded again. This time it screamed across downtown Dallas. For that one second, the horn overpowered the thrum of the cars as they passed on the highway, muffled out the noise of the racers moving their gear behind me, and stopped everything in the area. A quick crescendo of rumbling from the large diesel engines followed the horn blast. The engines revved their motors and my heartbeat jumped with the increased RPMs.

The engines boiled with potential energy and the large wheels squealed as the steel rails led the huge locomotives towards us. Light blue and silver two-tone noses sloped down toward the angled front window screen. My camera clicked away. My eyes focused on the features I wanted to remember and intricacies that might be hard to model in my apartment.

I tracked the train as it passed by me and braked to a stop, the halt almost imperceptible. Kathy was there, watching me. She grinned as she caught my eye.

"So this is the research?" she asked.

I nodded and went back to taking pictures. I zoomed in on as many details as possible. The large, worn wheels, that had a silver sheet from their constant impact with the rails; the double-decker cars with corrugated steel and tinted windows, the rusty, tough-looking couplers that joined the cars to the engine, hardware that looked like something from another era.

"Did you jump down onto the tracks?" She pointed down toward the roadbed that was now occupied by a large passenger car.

"Oh yeah," I looked down. Beneath us was a piece of metal on the ballast. I jumped between the car and platform to grab it. The passenger car loomed above me, a hulk of steel and glass, its presence and weight feeling dangerous for some reason. Despite it, for a moment, in the close confines, with the chest-high platform to my right, I felt at ease; covered, completely confident. I felt as if I should stay there in that ersatz foxhole for the rest of the day, crouched down below the level of the concrete platform. I shook my head to clear my thoughts and placed a hand on the side of the railcar as I bent beneath it to retrieve the coins and nails.

With some regret, I vaulted back onto the platform and looked up again to reassure myself that the small awning was still above me.

"What's that?" Kathy came forward.

I held the quarters in the palm of my hand so that she could see. The metal was flat and smooth on both sides, slightly warped one way like a potato chip. I placed the two nails that were now welded into the cross next to them.

"Those were nails?" she asked.

"Yep."

"And these are nickels, aren't they?" She looked up.

"Actually ninety percent Copper and ten percent Nickel."

She looked at me, her face clearly saying she didn't understand. "So, it's not a nickel?" she asked.

"Two quarters."

She held the warped quarters close to her face and studied them. "Hmmm, yeah," she said. "You can still make out some of Washington and a little bit of an eagle."

"You've never put coins on the track before?" I asked.

"Nope." She shook her head. "Can I have em?"

"One, sure."

"How bout the nails."

I nodded as Mr. Gentry, Totten, and several people I didn't know walked up and huddled around. I felt the familiar yet panicky sense of exposure overtake me. Perhaps it was that the sun had risen more, could have been having just come from the roadbed where I felt momentarily safe, or perhaps the thrill of seeing the engine had worn off. I could feel my heart rate ratcheting up as I was introduced to several people whose names flitted out of my memory as quickly as they were introduced. I was saved a full-on panic attack by Mr. Totten's paranoia about his equipment.

Bates came up quickly and spoke to the assembled group hovering around my quarters and nails. "They're beginning to load the gear," he said.

Totten responded, "They better not be hurting my bike." He took off toward the bikes.

There was a massive exodus toward the baggage. I stopped next to Kathy. The others walked on toward the baggage car to oversee the loading of their equipment.

"You okay?" she asked.

I nodded. "You think we can get on the train?" It was better on the platform but with the passenger car standing next to me, I felt a pull to get indoors quickly. If it was going to be either the station or the train, I preferred the train.

"Come on, let's see." We walked down the length of the train to where we saw a porter standing next to the steps leading up to the train car, his bright orange shirt shouting that he was a race volunteer. He saw us approach and spoke before we got all the way to him.

"You want on?" Behind his slight veil of authority, there was a note of ambiguity, as if he wasn't sure what the answer to his own question should be.

"I want to get off of the platform," I gave him my ticket.

"I don't think we're letting anyone on yet."

He looked over my head down toward the front of the train. We turned and saw several people getting on and off the train.

"Looks like they are down there," Kathy said.

"Yeah, but we were supposed to wait for the conductor to pass the word to let people on." He motioned toward the small radio that was clipped to his belt.

"I tell you what," Kathy said. She leaned in close to him, conspiratorially. "How bout you let him on for the moment. He'll stand right there." She pointed to a vacant area in the passage behind him. "If you want him to get off, again, he will, but for the moment, he just wants off this platform."

He threw me a quizzical look that gradually brightened into understanding. "You hiding from someone?" The question was directed at me but Kathy fielded it.

"My husband," she said. "I'd rather he didn't see me with my friend here." She winked at the porter.

As if this gave the argument validity, the porter swept his hand back to let me in. "You want on too, Lady?" he asked.

She ignored him. "I'm going to make sure your gear is okay." She paused as if unsure of what to say next. "I'll be back."

I nodded and she walked away. For my part, I was just happy to be on the train, a roof over my head, walls all around. Cold, solid, stable and small, it was just what I needed.

"Your girl's got spunk." The porter looked into the little entryway space, but I noticed he followed Kathy with his eyes.

"But, do me a favor, don't go nowhere till I get the word?"

I read his nametag. "Thanks, Ahmed. I won't forget this."

"It ain't nothin." He went back to looking down the train, probably still watching Kathy walk away. I went and stood behind him. It had taken only a second for the panic that had remained just beneath the pit of my stomach to be replaced by contentment. He smiled at me when he saw me watching Kathy's ass, not ashamed, just sharing a joke. I didn't return the smile.

Ahmed turned back. "So why you here, man?"

"I have no idea."

He laughed. "No, I mean, why are you doing this crazy race?"

I shrugged. "Mostly to see this train," I said. "I like trains, but I've never been on one."

"Yeah?" It was asked in a manner that encouraged me to say more.

"I build models for a living and I'm making a model," I said. "This is my chance to see what I want to model before I do it."

He nodded as I spoke. "Yeah, we get a lot of folks like you. You can't believe the number of layouts I've seen pictures of from people like you."

"What about you?" I asked. "You like trains?"

"Naw, this is just a way to make some scratch. This race is just me making some overtime. Doesn't matter to me where we go, I always end up doing pretty much the same thing, you know. At least this time we can make some money watching you suckers sweat."

He went on for a while about the places he'd been and things he'd seen then he came back to the race.

"So you guys are taking the train to Big Bend to do this race?" His radio crackled on his belt and he ducked his head to listen.

"They're letting folks on, now. You can go to your seat," Ahmed said.

"Which way?" I held out my ticket.

"You're in car seven, that way." He pointed toward the end

of the train. "A coach seat."

"Are there any sleeper cabins on this trip?" I knew the answer but wanted to get him talking about it.

"Oh, yeah." he pointed down the corridor, an invitation to take a look. I walked down the hallway and peeked into the doorways on either side. All of them were only a few square feet with close walls and ceilings, large couches that dominated the room and an expansive window. I walked into a vacant one and felt immediately more at ease.

"Think they'll be any extras?" I thought about how much more comfortable I'd feel if I could ensconce myself in a tight, close sleeper unit. "I'll make it worth your while if you let me know about any vacancies."

"I bet we can work something out." He looked down at my ticket. "You stay in your seat, I'll come to find you once we get moving."

I gave him a twenty. "Down payment," I said.

He pocketed the money quickly and went back to standing outside. "Uh oh, here comes the rush." I looked passed him and saw dozens of people moving in our direction.

"Thanks again, Ahmed." He gave a perfunctory wave. I thought about waiting to say goodbye to Kathy, but decided I'd feel better getting in my seat. A texted thank you would probably be plenty for Kathy. She'd probably prefer it. With the phone in my hand, I turned and walked up the stairwell to the upper level. My mind working on the best way to thank Kathy without sounding too sappy.

I stopped a moment at the top of the stairs. Row after row of seats spaced evenly across the car like a short airplane fuselage. The aisle stretched down the middle of the seats and as I looked down it, back toward the front of the train, I could see through the porthole of the connecting door that the aisle stretched down the length of the train till it diminished in the distance.

I started to turn to look toward the back of the train and I sensed rather than knew that someone was behind me. Phone still in my hand, thoughts still on my text, a momentary alarm went off in my head about why I hadn’t heard anyone approach. I didn't have time to complete the thought. A fist the size of a Christmas ham knocked me off my feet and the back of my head hit the floor of the train car, bouncing like a mallet on a drum head.

Momentary blackness followed, confusion and anger came next, finally, pain showed up. On the ground, on all fours, the pain radiated through my face from my nose. I squeezed my eyes shut and tried to force my thoughts to come together.

Someone grabbed my shirt collar and pulled my head up. I opened my eyes and saw Horne. I pushed away defensively, but he already had the upper hand. His hand held my shirt and neck in a vice grip.

"That’s for not looking after my girl on the run."

Horne’s voice was little more than a whisper, but he enunciated each word distinctly. "And this, this is cause you're still Luther’s bitch."

I saw his hand rear back, a flash of motion, then the world went black.

CHAPTER 22

My face hurt. Then again it was probably that pain that woke me up. It wasn't the pain in my nose, although that did hurt. Instead, there was a sharp pinch on the side of my face, my cheek. I felt sharp edges of small rocks from the roadbed digging into my face. I pulled my head up off the ground. I was on the roadbed next to the rails. There was a loud squeal of metal on metal, the distinctive sound of a rail car moving down the tracks right next to me. I was at the end of the train, laying on the roadbed, the slowly accelerating train leaving me behind. I stood up shakily and looked behind me. Two cars left.

I ran. My bag was on the ground in front of me and I scooped it up. The train started to speed up, I ran to stay up with it. I knew I wasn't running just to get out of the open, what was foremost in my mind was that Horne was somewhere on the train and I couldn't let him throw me off a train so easily.

The roadbed made for an uneven running surface, but the train was still slow enough that I reached the doorway and stumbled along beside it, my pace stymied by the railroad ties. The train sped up just as I started to pound on the bottom half of the door, the only part of the door I could reach. I hoped like hell that someone was nearby to hear me. The door opened immediately. Ahmed looked out.

"What the hell are you doing out there?" he yelled. I thrust my arm out to him. He grabbed it and he pulled me in.

"What in the world happened to your face. You fall or something?"

I nodded and tried to look less miserable than I felt.

"Seriously, man, what happened?"

I struggled to think of something to say but felt overwhelmed both by the pain in my nose and the relief at making the train. I thought of everything I had already told Ahmed and tried, "He found me."

"Who?"

"The husband."

"Aw shit, man." The skepticism left Ahmed's face. "I'm sorry."

"Guess we weren't as sneaky as we thought."

"Come on, let's get you to that sleeper I found for ya."

He bent down and grabbed my upper arm to help me stand up. "Let's get you cleaned up."

We stayed in the same car which was lucky. I didn't want to have to walk through a crowded train car full of people. There was blood on my hands and I imagined my face was worse. Ahmed led me through the downstairs passageway to the other end of the sleeper car just on the other end of the car. He ducked in then held the door for me.

The sleeping compartment was compact, tight, close; just what I needed. I stepped in and fell onto the couch. Ahmed went into the little restroom and turned on the faucet. A text to Luther sprung to mind; All's well so far, except Horne kicked my ass within the first half-hour. That would inspire confidence.

"Here, use this." He handed me a wet towel and we shifted positions so I was in the restroom. "You want me to go find a doctor or something?" he asked.

I shook my head thinking that he was overreacting. I looked up and saw my reflection in the mirror and realized why he was so worried. Three thin streams of blood ran down my face, passed my neck and disappeared like a necklace beneath my shirt. My nose, the focal point of the blood was swollen and bruised. It looked like I had spent the last thirty minutes in a boxing ring. My nose, which I'd avoided having broken all my life, looked like it had given up the ghost after just one of Horne's punches. Two were obviously too much for it.

I pushed it gingerly with my fingers. It didn't feel broken. My cheek was swollen and my teeth were all intact so all told there was nothing that was too bad.

"I'm going to get a doctor."

"I'll be okay." I pulled out my wallet and handed Ahmed four more twenties. "For the room." He hesitated for just a moment before taking the bills.

"Thanks, man. I got to go check my stations." He began to move out of the compartment. "I tell you what, I'll find some ice and bring it back to you in a few, okay?"

"I'll survive," I waved him away. It was embarrassing to have been waylaid by Horne so easily. The sooner Ahmed left, the sooner I could figure out what I needed to do next.

"Yeah, but it'll help," he said. "I'll be back in a little bit." He shut the door.

I went back to figuring out what happened to my face. I took a few swipes at it with the washcloth. There were several problems, as I saw it. First, what to do about Horne. He was obviously upset about Georgia and blamed me. I guess he had a point. I wasn't directly responsible, but I had been the one to leave her out there alone. I would have to confront him, eventually. Luther may have wanted me here to look after the clients but that didn't mean I'd have to be beaten up while I did it.

Secondly, seeing my teammates with this disfigured hood ornament decorating my face would be tough. I wondered if the ice would help with the swelling. Maybe I should have been more enthusiastic about Ahmed's offer of the ice.

Thirdly, how would this affect my racing? It hurt a ton. I cringed as I thought about how much it was going to hurt in the morning when the race started. It wouldn't slow me down as much as a broken leg, or a sprained ankle, but it wouldn't help me either.

My cell phone buzzed inside my pocket. There had been three missed calls since the last time I checked it. Three calls while I lay sprawled on the sharp rocks of the train track road-bed. I flipped it open recognizing the number as I did.

"Hey Kathy," I answered.

"I've been calling. Where in the hell are you?"

"I'm on the train."

"I figured that," she said. "I mean I don't see you in your seat."

"I found a compartment."

"A compartment?"

"Wait, what do you mean you don't see me in my seat? Where are you?"

"I'm sitting in the seat across from yours."

"What? On the train? What are you doing on the train?"

I squinted and pressed my fingers to the bridge of my nose as I tried to clear my thoughts. All I felt was the ache in my nose and in my temples.

"Where are you?" she asked again.

"Bottom floor of the last car."

"Okay." A trace of frustration tinged her voice. "But, which compartment?"

I stood and looked at the door. "3A. Compartment 3A."

"I'll be right there." She hung up.

CHAPTER 23

I had time to wipe my face and change into a spare shirt from my bag before there was a knock on the door.

"You there?" It was from Kathy. The same knock she used on my apartment door.

"Hold on."

I checked my nose one last time in the mirror and braced myself for the interrogation that was sure to come.

"What's the deal?" Kathy stopped as she saw my face. "What happened to you!"

"I fell, and if Ahmed asks be sure you tell him it was your husband."

I watched her face as she tried to figure out what I'd just said. Revelation spread in milliseconds. "And if I ask?" she said finally.

"Then I fell."

"Fell face first into someone's fist. I had three older brothers Joe, I know a broken nose from a punch when I see one."

"Can we drop it, please?"

She studied me then must have decided it wasn't worth it. "Okay, okay, I was just asking."

A pause followed. She sat down on the couch and looked up at me expectantly as if forcing me to come up with the next subject, daring me too.

"Okay," I said. "So, what are you doing here?"

She threw a backpack on the seat and reclined heavily as if she meant to stay.

"I talked to the race director, he's agreed to let me come if I help him with some marketing for his races this spring."

I leaned in and considered her slowly. "You're drumming up business?"

"I'm here to support you," she said.

"I don't need it."

"Like you didn't need it this morning?" she said. "You almost didn't make it past the parking lot. How do you expect to make it through the desert if you can't even make it through a parking lot?"

"Where'd you get that?" I pointed at the backpack.

"Had it in my car."

I closed my eyes and tilted my head back and sighed. She was right, but I didn't feel like telling her how right she was. The problems with Horne, the immediate difficulty of getting on the train, the experience itself had forced all the worries about racing through the desert out of my mind.

"Look, we're friends right?" I opened my eyes and saw that she was studying me. "Plus, you're a good employee. I'm looking after my investment. I don't want you coming back to Dallas depressed and upset and unable to work. The way I figure it, I help you through this thing then I'm going to have a healthier, happier, employee."

I grunted and shut my eyes again. I've never been comfortable working in a team, what Kathy said made me sound like a co-dependent type. I wasn't thrilled to think of myself like that.

"Seriously, Joe," she continued. "I just found out more about you by seeing that damn train in your apartment than I have over the fifteen years I've known you. You're finally beginning to make some sense to me. I thought you were just some crazy weirdo for years."

I must have scrunched up my brow because I heard her change tactics and my nose suddenly felt tight and painful.

"I mean, I don't blame you. Anyone who had to grow up with your father would have the cards stacked against them, but you're beginning to make sense to me. I want to see you overcome your problems and not be a slave to them. I think I can help."

I sighed again and opened my eyes. I looked at her doubtfully. Kathy is all business, and although what she was saying would ring true with someone who had just met her, I knew her well enough to know that there had to be an underlying reason for what she was saying. There are hundreds of other people who could do the job I do, looking after an employee might be a part of her rationale, but there had to be a money-making opportunity as well.

I studied her as she sat back and watched me. I hadn't expected to need a crutch for the race. One of the aspects of this trip that I had looked forward to was finally confronting my fears; going toe to toe against my problems, fighting them down by myself, and on my own. Wouldn't there be a sense of pride and self-esteem, not to mention the confidence that would inevitably follow that sort of thing? What would happen to that sense of accomplishment if Kathy was there as an usher? Then again would I have made it this far without her?

By that same token, I had been attracted to Kathy for years and years. Like Ahmed, I had taken every chance to watch her walk away, or to steal sidelong glances, but the chance to be more had never been there. Maybe this was that chance? She was gorgeous and sexy. Maybe this was the opportunity to see another side of her and see if there could be more between us than just an employee, employer relationship.

Once I make a plan, I plunge into it with both feet. I'd rather face the quick chill that comes from diving into a cold pool, then slowly wade in and feel the cold inch up my body. That's how I'd imagined this race. It was the deep end of the pool that I'd have to dive into. I'd have to sink or swim. Get it over with quickly.

"Well?" Kathy asked.

"You're a small business owner," I said. "I mean, what more can you provide than giving me some help across the street?"

"If you'd tell me what happened I can help watch your

back," she nodded toward my nose.

"Not good enough."

"I have this." She dug into her bag and pulled out a sheaf of papers. She spread them on the floor between us, then paused. "Is this where we're staying?" She looked around at the room. "I mean, we've got this room for the whole ride, right?"

"We?" I asked. I had just gotten used to the idea of the solitude the room afforded.

"Sure, you don't expect me to stay up there in those cattle cars do you?"

"Look, Kathy..." I began but was cut short by her hand.

"I know what you're going to say. Don't worry, I won't try any funny stuff." She winked and followed it up with a smile. "Seriously, consider me your pit crew. You saw all of those other racers out there, they have people to help them out. That's all I'm here to do. And like I said, I have these," she held up the papers. "I think it could really help."

"What are those?"

"These are notes from my friend," she paused and looked serious. "Doctor Elaine Hermann, a psychiatrist."

"And?"

"Specifically," She cut me off. "These will help you deal with what you will face when we get to the race." She looked eager and excited at the prospect of helping. I cringed inwardly at the thought of being her project.

"Look," I started. "I appreciate it, but I think I can deal with the race just fine."

"Really?" She glanced down at her notes. "What do you know about your problem?"

"It's not a problem."

"Fine, call it a condition."

I could hear the tenseness in her voice and realized it was following the path that my own voice laid out. Despite it, I couldn't find a way to not sound frustrated and exasperated with each successive argument.

"I don't know Kathy. I don't know what it's called or whatever. All I know is that I can beat it. This race can help me do that."

"What you have," she interrupted me loudly, "is agoraphobia. A fear of open spaces."

"Thanks, Captain Obvious," I said sarcastically.

"And," she continued. "It's really a series of panic attacks that are a result of being isolated."

"I could have read that too." I pointed at the paper as she read.

"Being isolated both in groups or in an environment. In reality, you don't have a fear of open places as much as you have a fear of having a panic attack."

I shook my head not understanding and not sure I cared anymore. The pain in my nose intensified.

"What?" She said watching me. "You don't believe it?"

"It's not that," I said. "I just don't know how that is supposed to help me race."

She looked at me sternly. "Joe, the key to confronting an issue is to identify it first. To boil it down to its component parts. There's a lot to be gained by first defining the terms before trying to fix it."

She leaned back as she talked. She was wearing a t-shirt and blue jeans, but ever since seeing Ahmed check her out, I had been trying to decide just what exactly she would look like under the clothes. It made it hard to concentrate on what she said.

"It's like a business. Whenever I write a proposal for a new project, I always define the project in its basest form. I'm attacking this race and you're overcoming your condition in the same way."

"Can we not call it a condition either?" I asked.

"What do you want to call it?" Her sympathy sounded genuine, the idea of being a project came back.

"I don't know."

"Well, how bout we call it what it is; agoraphobia."

I sighed and leaned back heavily into the couch. "Okay, but

again how is this going to help?"

She came over and sat next to me. I couldn't help but look at her thigh next to mine. She grabbed my hand which for a split second felt exhilarating. Then I realized she was comforting me, like a doctor holding the hand of a patient. The exhilaration faded quickly.

"First of all, we've learned quite a bit. All of which is helpful. We've learned that you aren't afraid of traveling." She ticked off a point on her finger. "That fact, according to my friend is a big deal. She said that in most cases agoraphobes are not just afraid of open spaces, or the panic attacks that come with them but are also afraid of changes in scenery. That doesn't seem like a problem with you."

"Great, so?"

"So?" She turned and leaned toward me excitedly. "So we've already made progress in attacking this."

Kathy stood up and moved toward the window. "I understand your desire to overcome this Joe, but you seem to think that just throwing yourself into the race is going to do it. I disagree. It's like this morning, you need to take baby steps. The actual race will be a step, sure, but let's prepare for that step. Let's move toward that step. Isn't it like what you military guys say. You don't just attack the enemy, you locate and fix the enemy first, then you attack it."

"Where'd you come up with that?"

She held up the sheaf of papers. "See, this stuff can be helpful, can't it?"

Another sigh from my side of the little room.

"Second," she went on, "we know your tell."

I opened my eyes. "What?"

"Your tell," she said again. "Whenever you're about to..." She struggled to find the right word.

"Freak out?" I said. "It's Mike's favorite term."

She smiled but said, "Have difficulty" she finished. "You grind your teeth."

"What?"

"Yeah, you didn't know that? You grind your teeth and purse your lip. This morning by our car I could hear you from across the street."

"No, you didn't."

"You're missing the point," she said. "Now that we know your tell we can use it to our advantage. The next time you find yourself grinding your teeth relax your jaw, it should help you relax in the situation as well."

Another sigh. I was saved from more lecturing by my phone; an unknown number this time.

"Hello?"

"Hey, instructor!" Bates' voice. "You made it."

"Of course I did," I said suddenly weary. "Why not?"

"Oh nothing," he said. "I saw Max and he told me you missed the train."

"He did?"

"Yeah, that's why I called."

"Nope," I said. "I made it."

"Well, I also wanted to tell you, we're going to have a meeting in Gentry's cabin. Fifteen minutes. You in?"

I looked up at the door. I didn't want to leave the little cabin that I'd made my ersatz home. I remembered my nose and felt that it wasn't the time yet for the questions that would inevitably come from seeing the team. I remembered Horne and thought of his new partner Max, and thought I'd rather steer clear of both of them for the time. Then I looked across the cabin at Kathy and thought about the baby steps, her project, and her lectures.

"I'll be there," I said.

CHAPTER 24

The meeting in Gentry's sleeper was as much a blur as the scenery outside the window. I remember bickering between everyone about the teams, some sarcastic remarks from Totten, loud reprimands from Kay, Bates' voice, strained and tense as he tried to find a solution agreeable to everyone, and Gentry's final dismissal, sounding less like a lawyer and more like a judge asking a jury to be re-sequestered and come back with better results.

Beyond those few impressions, I didn't pay attention. Later, comfortably back in the cabin, Kathy wanted to discuss it and that was how I got a lot of the details and filled in the gaps.

It boiled down to Gentry and Rochester not being happy with the teams. Luther had come up with the teams. Now that he wasn't involved, there was a faction on the weaker team leading a charge for a change. Each team had to have four members, and each team had to have at least one female. According to Kathy, Rochester wanted to make the teams more even, to have two strong teams instead of one super strong team and one weaker team as Luther had arranged.

"You were there," Kathy said. "I'm surprised you didn't speak up."

I waved my hand dismissively. "I don't care about the teams. I'm not trying to win the race, I'm just trying to survive."

I knew her feelings about Luther. Telling her how worried Luther was about the team's safety, about his paranoia around Horne, this would only add fuel to her views of him.

"I know that," she went on, "but what about those people on the weaker team, they might not even finish the race. They shouldn't have to pay for a race then have the cards stacked against them."

"As long as everyone finishes safely, I don't care." I leaned back and shut my eyes.

Despite my laissez-faire attitude, I admitted to myself that she had a good argument. Like so many other things at AFC, it was just the members making something out of nothing. I've dealt with them long enough to know that if I gave them an inch, they would take a mile. It would be best to just keep the teams as they were. Had Luther been at the meeting, he would have said something that sounded like an order and they would have followed it. Looking back, I should have done the same, but I'd been in no position to say anything. I had just wanted out of the room.

Still, Kathy was right, I should have spoken up. The group was in the midst of a leadership vacuum, and the argument about the teams would continue and ultimately no one would be satisfied. It was a bad way to start a race. If the opportunity for me to stand up and lead came again, I promised myself, I'd step in and fill the void.

"Are you even listening?" Kathy looked across the compartment. Her posture and tone indicated that I'd spaced out again. "What's wrong with you? It's like you aren't paying attention."

I shrugged. I tried to play it off, but I was looking at her hair tucked behind her ears. Had I always found that so alluring or was it only now because we were alone in the train compartment, and I remembered watching her blue-jeaned ass as we walked to the team meeting. Was being a horn dog a side effect of the agoraphobia baby steps, I wondered.

"Was it hard being at the meeting? Was it the crowd?" she asked."I thought you were only afraid of open spaces with crowds."

"I'm just smoked," I said.

"So it wasn't the crowd," she said. She sounded like a clinician instead of a friend. "You just zoned out, not catatonic like at the station."

I rolled my eyes when she said catatonic. "I was fine."

Kathy continued as if I had not said anything. "Were you thinking about having a panic attack? Is that it?"

"I was just tired," I said.

"Tired?" she asked. "Not like at the station?"

I shook my head, tired of the argument and completely confused. What was she even asking? What was she getting at?

"I didn't sleep much last night since I was packing," I heard the frustration in my own voice and knew that she had to hear it too. "I'm just drained from getting on board and dealing with it all. Can't we just drop it for now?"

"Sure," she said. "But that's good right?"

When I didn't answer she went on.

"Actually, from a clinical standpoint, it's great!" There was a lift to her voice. "You aren't afraid of new things, we determined that at the platform, and it's not crowds per se. Just open spaces, that's what we can deduce." Now she was an excited clinician. Like a researcher on the verge of a discovery.

"So?" I opened my eyes just for a moment.

"So," she explained. "It means we're getting closer to identifying the problem."

I didn't respond but leaned back to relax my head against the couch. I really was tired of everything, tired of my teammates, tired of the trip, and a bit tired of Kathy's constant diagnoses. She saw the reaction and replied with a sigh of her own. A sigh that told me she'd been looking forward to a deeper more comprehensive session, but a sigh that held undertones of resignation that there wouldn't be more.

For my part I kept my eyes closed and allowed my mind to take a break. I must have dozed off because when I opened my eyes Kathy was sitting across from me on the couch. She was painting toenails with pale pink nail polish, her hair wrapped in a towel. She had changed into a purple, silk robe with drawings of dragons on it. I could tell by the humidity, the smell of shampoo in the little compartment, the tiny strands of wet hair that dangled beneath the towel that she'd taken a shower. I stalled in my reaction if only because I'd never seen Kathy in such a feminine or vulnerable attitude. It was like seeing a cat expose its belly for a strange dog or a horse stand up and walk on its hind legs.

I watched as she screwed the top back on her jar of nail polish then she rearranged her feet to let the right one dry. After so many years of having nothing but a working relationship, seeing Kathy's legs reminded me of the times we had hung out as kids, swimming during summer breaks, hanging out watching movies. A whole history between us revealed itself, a forgotten history, it all came back slowly as I watched her sitting delicately on the couch.

Kathy looked up and saw me staring. "What?" she asked.

I wanted to say something, but nothing came out. I liked the little sleeping berth for the closeness and security, but now, with Kathy across the way, wearing nothing but the robe, her legs exposed up to her thigh, I realized that there were disadvantages to such intimate spaces. All I could think about was kissing her legs and that was not going to make things easier for the duration of the trip, or for our working relationship.

Finally, I spoke, "Where'd you get that robe?"

"It's a Kimono, I brought it."

"You brought a kimono?"

"Yeah, I brought a bag with me," she spoke as if it was natural to bring bags to see people off. "My contingency bag."

"What are you doing wearing it?"

"I felt like a shower," her voice was defensive. "What's the big deal?"

"Who brings a Kimono to a race in the desert?"

"I'm not racing," she countered.

"Can't you put more on?"

She tilted her head quizzically, then she hiked up the robe

to her waist. I flinched.

Laughing, Kathy said, "It's okay, prude, I'm wearing shorts and a shirt underneath. You're safe."

"Why the hell do you have a robe?" I asked again.

"You never know when you might need one," she winked at me. "And it's a good thing I packed it. Isn't that your motto? Semper Paratus? Be prepared."

"That's the Boy Scouts," I said. "Semper Fidelis is Always Faithful." I saw too late that it had been sarcasm.

I sat up, frustrated even after what was just a short conversation. What followed was ten more minutes of watching Kathy paint her toes. Ostensibly I looked out the window and watched the ménage of oak, grasses, and rows of cotton streak by as we chugged through central Texas. Every now and then she moved and her kimono slipped and exposed her leg.

When we were young, going to school together, Kathy had always come off as serious. Even when we were forced to play together, there was no relaxation, no wonderment, nothing like a regular kid. She was always serious. Four years older, when I was a child she had been so mature she was untouchable. This, her sitting on the couch, painting her toenails a light pink, was not the Kathy I knew. It was definitely a Kathy I wanted to know more of.

I decided that this could be a mistake.

CHAPTER 25

It was the dogs. Those dogs we had seen all morning. Maybe they had picked up the scent of the platoon, or maybe us specifically. They must have been following us hoping for a handout, or to pick up something we might leave behind. That was the only answer. Wilson and I ran into them while moving towards Johnson and the rest of the platoon. We were only three hundred meters out when we startled them.

We were running in a crouch, weapons in front of us, cradled loosely but ready for whatever might show up in front of us. Our objective was to get back to the platoon as fast as possible, but somewhere out there were three vehicles filled with armed men, possibly approaching the platoon. If we didn't get to them it was imperative that we at least re-establish communications.

We were dodging scrub brush and squat trees, moving quickly, moving southeast, always moving towards the platoon. Just as we came up out of a small depression, there was movement to our left. I fell to the ground with the weapon up and let my finger linger on the trigger.

A nano-second passed where I was sure I was going to pull the trigger.

There was movement in front of me. We were alone between two elements of Marines. We were cut off and there were potential hostiles nearby and getting closer.

Movement again and I felt the muscles in my fingers tense. Just a mote more pressure and my M4 rifle would fire a round through the brush at that movement at almost 3000 feet per second. I had twenty-nine more rounds that could follow it. there were eight more magazines in my vest all with thirty rounds. Whoever was in front of us moving through the brush was on the wrong end of over two hundred rounds about to come at them very, very quickly.

That's when I saw the dog.

It was the black one.

He was the movement I had seen.

When he saw me he bolted in the opposite direction. All I saw was his tail and his hind leg as he retreated, but I saw the blood trailing down his leg and knew he had been shot.

"Contact?" It was Wilson, behind me, still in the depression, asking if we were about to shoot. He was also in the prone, weapon up, whispering.

"Just those dogs again," I whispered back. "I almost shot one."

"So we're clear?"

"Yeah," I said as I raised myself up. "I think so."

In a crouch, Wilson came up next to me.

"Holy shit."

I didn't need to ask him what he meant. I could hear it in his voice. He knew as well as I that had I shot the dog we would have had the immediate attention of all three vehicles right on us. Johnson, despite my worries, probably had followed SOP and taken the platoon off the road and was now in a hasty ambush position with no desire to take on anything till I got back. Had I shot, the men in the vehicles, their disposition as friend or enemy still not certain, Johnson would have known that something was wrong. Johnson would have thought we were in contact. A shit storm would have ensued. A confusing shit storm with no radio contact.

Wilson had said it all in that one word, all of it right there, packed in there with his racing breath, thin, tight lips and distrusting eyes, everything that I felt too. We were in a bad position that had the potential to be devastating and I had almost made it worse. My heart was racing so that it felt like it would burst out of my chest, the only thing I could hear was my loud breath sounds, it rang in my ears and I was sure it was loud enough to be heard miles away. I looked back and saw everything I felt, all the fear, worry, and problems in his own eyes. It was seeing him, waiting for me to make the next call that pulled me out of it.

"Ready?" I asked. Even the sound of my voice helped.

He nodded and I saw some steel return to him as well.

Before he could move, I held up my hand stopping him. I could see over some of the brush, and just through the limbs and leaves, I could see the black dog. He was looking back at me, considering me, hesitating. Behind him, I could see the rest of his pack. They were stopped, ears up, heads craned as if looking for an avenue for retreat.

"What's wrong?" Wilson again.

"They've stopped," I whispered.

"The technicals?"

"No," I whispered. "The dogs."

CHAPTER 26

This was all a mistake. Kathy being here, sharing the same room; could she help? Maybe. Could she make things worse at the same time? That seemed like it was happening already. When I planned this trip, my thought had been to collect details to create a small canyon country-style station for the expansion to my railroad while solidifying my position with Luther and AFC, all while getting over my problem with spaces. It was an ambitious plan.

Then there were Kathy's legs. Her hair behind her ears. The silly smile she flashed when she saw me looking at her. The one that forced me to look out the window. Then suddenly I wondered if rolling pasture land might be a more apropos extension for my closet than a desert. Something nondescript, wind-swept stunted oaks, small hillocks with wildflowers.

Legs again, back to the window.

Why not a second level, a shelf beneath my layout, a large, bustling station at one end with a hill country scene sweeping across it?

Hands and fingers that suddenly I found irritable. Back to the window again.

How long would it take to capture the disparity of going from a large teeming, chaotic city-station like Dallas' to one that was far less busy like Waco's which we just crossed?

Legs again and now they were in the shower in my mind. I stood up and grabbed my bag.

"What's wrong?" Kathy looked up.

"I don't think this is going to work."

"What?" She sighed, exasperation evident. "What's not going to work? The room?"

"It's too small."

"You can't be afraid of both open spaces and confined ones." She forced a chuckle. She went back to her toes. "Make up your mind."

"I'm thinking I'll go ask Ahmed if there are any other compartments."

"Good luck. It's a madhouse up there." She looked up again. "Sit down and relax. I'm just painting my nails and I needed a shower. Quit making a big deal out of a little thing."

I sat. I looked out the window and avoided the thigh that showed up with what seemed like every movement.

"I did some reading before I took my shower," Kathy said suddenly. "What?"

She held up the race flyers. "Six major events over three days," she said. "They have a packing list. Do you have all this?" She pointed at the packing list with her little nail polish brush.

"I've got everything I need."

"You have everything you need?"

This time I recognized the sarcasm immediately.

"Sure."

"You amaze me," she said. "For someone who is so detail-oriented with his models, you sure don't set yourself up for success in your own life."

I exhaled, letting her know that it had nothing to do with boredom. This time it couldn't be mistaken for anything but derision.

She went on despite it. "You have all this climbing gear that they list here? I didn't see it with your pack."

"I have a rope."

"You have a rope?" Her voice was mocking.

"I'll be fine."

It was her turn to sigh.

"What?" I asked.

"I'm just surprised." She abandoned the nail polish and leaned back, the kimono falling back dangerously to show the edge of her running shorts. "I mean they give a suggested packing list in the rule book and it sure doesn't sound like you're close to meeting it."

"It's only a suggested packing list." I enunciated the word suggested.

"You really think you're going to finish with this attitude?"

"Finish, yes, but that's not the real reason I'm here anyway, remember? I'm here to get out and be normal again. I'm here to represent AFC. I'm here to watch Horne."

Whoops. She leaned forward when she heard this.

"Who's Horne?"

I sighed. "Luther thinks this guy Horne, is trying to ruin him. He thinks he's behind the two murders. I'm here to look after everyone and make sure that Horne doesn't do anything to them."

I saw on her face that she was trying not to laugh.

"I know what you're thinking and you can save it," I said. "I know it sounds silly to send me to watch these people and protect them when I can hardly watch after myself, but there it is."

I knew I sounded ridiculous, but now that I was saying it, I just couldn't stop. "Luther said he'll sell me the business if I do this. We're making a deal so I can own AFC, and this is part of the deal. Now you know the whole story. Go ahead let it out, laugh all you want."

She sobered up quickly. "I'm not going to laugh, Joe. At least now it makes more sense."

I looked up and saw that she was serious.

"I mean I could see you doing this to try to be normal again," she stumbled over the word normal but drove on after getting it out. "And I know now that you have a passion for trains, but knowing about this deal with Luther kinda makes everything make more sense. You know your dad is off his rocker, right? I mean this guy Horne probably has nothing to do with the murders."

"He was dating Georgia." Again my voice was harsher than I intended. "He's pissed at me cause he thinks I'm part of the reason she was killed."

Understanding broke across her face like an incoming tidal wave. She pointed at my nose. "He did that?"

"He got lucky."

"Still," she went on. "I knew your family when we were growing up. I heard the things my parents said about him. I've heard the things you've said about him. He's crazy, Joe. I mean he's off-kilter. You can't believe this guy Horne would kill two people just because Luther says it."

"I know that," I stood up, grabbed my bag and walked to the door to leave. I stopped when I realized that the compartment, even with a confrontational Kathy was better than anything outside. The milling people, the loud conversations, the chaos of a crowd, just like the station in Dallas, it would all be the same but it would be tighter, more confined, worse. I hesitated, my hand on the door handle.

I heard Kathy breathe in as if to speak, just as a knock came from the other side of the door. It stopped us both.

"Instructor?" From the salutation, it was obvious whoever it was was a teammate, but the voice didn't sound familiar.

I opened the door to peak out. In the dark hallway outside the compartment, I saw a blond girl, hair in a ponytail, large eyes looking back at me.

"I'm sorry if I'm interrupting," she said as if she knew me. "But I was hoping we could talk some about the race and the teams."

"Who are you?"

"I'm Emily," she said. "We met at the meeting this morning. The one in Gentry's room."

There was nothing, no memory of meeting her. She was as much a part of the blur from the meeting with Gentry as the subject matter. She was cute but had a manner of speech that turned every phrase into a question as if she wasn't sure of herself or of the answer.

"Okay."

"Can I come in?"

Kathy, looked up as she came in and smiled a smile of recognition. She threw the kimono back over her legs and sat up to make space for Emily.

"I'm sorry, are you two busy?"

"Just relaxing," Kathy spoke up and waved at the couch. "Have a seat."

Emily was clearly confused at seeing Kathy so I introduced her as my boss, but the revelation that my employer was painting her toes while wearing a Kimono in my train compartment only garnered greater looks of perplexity from her.

"I can come back," she said.

"Don't worry about it," Kathy was reassuring and I could see curiosity in her eyes as if she had a good guess as to why Emily was there. "What's up?"

"Well, I was talking to Bates, and he said we should talk to you about it. We've been looking for you ever since the meeting. We had to ask a porter to track you down."

Kathy waved at her as if it was nothing.

"I mean, I know I'm new to this group, and I'm only a replacement."

It was at this point that the haze around meeting her at Gentry's lifted in my mind. Staccato memories of Bates introducing me to Emily, followed by a surreptitious whisper from Bates about her being there in Georgia's place all came back. It was like a flash flood that came quickly and left almost as fast, leaving just that memory behind. I tried not to show any emotion as it all came back to me, but the startled look that appeared across her face made me realize I had failed.

"I know, I know," she tried to interpret my look. "Bates told me that I shouldn't say anything, but it just seems like it's so unfair."

"What?"

Her brow furrowed. "The teams." She said it as if I should

know.

"She's here to talk about changing the teams." Kathy sounded like a school teacher lecturing a slow student.

"Yeah, I don't think it's fair to have all the strongest racers on one team and let the other team struggle."

"We were just talking about that a little while ago," Kathy said. "I think it's silly too."

Emily turned to face her, they looked like two friends who had suddenly bonded over a new subject. I listened to them rattle thoughts back and forth and come to their own conclusions without seeming to care what I or other team members might think. It was typical Kathy. Latch onto a subject then drive it home to the finish line picking up as many compatriots along the way. She did this with business meetings, with customers, with me, with everyone. Half the reason she was on the trip, making ads and marketing material for the race organizer, was a part of how she worked.

The familiar, out-of-body feeling that I accomplished in Gentry's compartment came back as I watched them talk. My mind rolled away, and my eyes turned toward the window, back to the landscape. It was like turning off the world to watch television after a hard day at work, completely natural and utterly banal. I contributed nothing and heard even less. I let my mind take in the colors and textures and wonder how to model them when I got home.

It was some moments later that I saw Kathy standing up, trying to get my attention.

"What?" I said. "Sorry, I wasn't listening."

"We think you should change the teams," Kathy spoke for the two of them. Emily smiled proudly next to her. I felt my face flush.

"I don't know if you really have a voice in the decision," I said to Kathy. I could feel my temper beginning to flare.

Kathy's strong-arming me was slow at first, but I knew she would pick it up and she expected to win. I saw the glint in Emily's eyes. It meant she expected Kathy to win the argument. It was not a good first, second, or third impression to make with a new teammate.

"Hell, you probably have even less basis for this argument than anyone on this train." It came out like a snap.

"What's that mean, no basis?" Kathy said.

"You aren't racing," I ticked the point off on my finger and went on to several more fingers. "You aren't on the teams and you don't race. Hell, you don't even work out."

"I run," she said as if that one fact dispelled the others that I'd made. "I've run several marathons, a couple of dozen half marathons and even did a few triathlons the last few years."

My smile vanished and I felt the corners of my lips turn down.

"Just cause I don't wear it on my sleeve like you guys, just cause I don't go making a spectacle of myself in the park doesn't mean I'm not a runner. Hell, I ran track in college, Joe."

"But you're not on the team, Kathy," I countered.

"I am," Emily's voice wasn't as loud as Kathy's.

Instead of letting Emily's argument speak for their side, Kathy rushed in with another. "I might not be on the team, but I can understand the argument Emily is making. Luther's basically writing off one team to have one that is elite. You're going to have one team that is competitive and one that may not finish."

"So?" I asked.

"So that's not fair." Kathy continued to plead the case.

Emily watched silently.

"I think you should have two decent teams." Kathy tucked her hair behind her ear again. I noticed.

"How is this any of your business?" I stood.

"It's her business," Kathy pointed at Emily. Emily's eyes widened as if she didn't want to be put in the middle of the fight.

"No, you're butting your nose into something that is none of your business." I raised my voice to equal hers. "Why do you have to insinuate yourself into every single thing, and always on the side against Luther?" I knew as I said it that I would regret it. "You have to make everything around you into the way you want it. You have to own everything you see."

Kathy's lips pursed into a thin line.

"This is my job, these are my teammates," I went on, not caring about her anger. "She's only here for the race." I pointed at Emily. "I have to keep on good terms with the full-timers and most of them either don't give a damn about the teams or want to keep them the way they are. I'm here to look after them, not to piss them off, and not to let my guest piss them off and completely take over."

Kathy's face blossomed into a shade of red I hadn't seen since we were kids. I was saved from further argument by another knock on the door. This time the voice that came through from the other side was distinctly Totten's.

"Hey, Joe! You in there?"

I opened the door. Totten and Kay were outside.

"We want to talk about the teams." As he said it he looked behind me and saw Emily on the couch. He bulled his way into the room as if claiming uncharted territory and planting a flag. Without waiting they all dove into an argument about the teams. Emily and Kathy on one side, Kay and Totten on the other.

My shoulders slumped as I stood in the doorway and watched. Had I known there would be this much controversy prior to the start of the race I might have reconsidered going. I looked back. Emily and Kathy were both standing now, going toe to toe with Totten. My plan to be a leader and try to fix things had not gone well.

I peeked out into the corridor. Diminutive, always positive Bates was there. He gave a shrug, then came over and gave me a pat on the shoulder as if we were nothing more than pawns in a larger game that we couldn't control. Loud voiced arguments took over the room, a sequel I was sure, to the meeting I couldn't remember in Gentry's berth. I stood in the doorway and felt the rolling sensation again. This time, unlike the last two times when I'd just let it occur, I embraced it wholeheartedly.

I shut the door behind me and walked quickly down the corridor to find some place to relax.

CHAPTER 27

The train arrived in Alpine, Texas at ten till six that night, and ten minutes after that the station was barren except for the race workers. All the passengers had moved en masse off the train as soon as the train came to a stop. It was like opening day of a going out of the business sale at a discount running shoe warehouse. The train was deserted in seconds.

I watched the crowd board buses at the far end of the parking lot and head off toward the park. I was content to stay in my little berth and watch them move off, happy I wasn't a part of the throng, sad that I hadn't made as much progress as I hoped, worried that I'd been too harsh with Kathy. I didn't give a thought to how I'd catch up to the racers. A report to Luther came to mind; "started with fifteen but couldn't get off the train so the teams proceeded without me." I banged my head against the window with a thud.

After leaving Bates, Emily, Kathy, Totten, and Kay in my compartment I'd gone to the next passenger car and gone downstairs. Not the most honorable retreat but I stayed out of sight and watched the scenery go by through the little window.

After a few minutes I heard the distinctive voice of Totten and Kay as they walked by upstairs, then a few minutes later other familiar voices. I stayed in that little hole for another half hour then found my way back to my compartment. Kathy was gone. For the rest of the long trip through the canyon country of West Texas, I stared out the window and wondered how I would model the same scenery in my bedroom. It was nice to not have to worry about the race, the teams, Kathy, calming to focus on the layout and its future.

In Alpine, after everyone left, I tried to stay on the train for as long as I could, but Ahmed forced me out of the compartment on his final sweep. He apologized before telling me I had to get off, but I think by then he knew the problem was larger than a jealous husband. He promised to hold me a cabin for the return trip. I didn't ask for it, but I gave him a twenty as a down payment.

While I worked on how to get off the train, my phone beeped that I had a text message waiting. I checked it and saw Mike's text, nothing profound, just two words. "Call me." I read it and vacillated about whether to call him or wait to place the call. I thought about writing to tell him to come to pick me up, but just as it was still a germ of an idea before it could register in my mind what a pathetic thought it was, his second text came. "I mean if you actually made it. Or did you run home to your bed?" It was just what I needed.

This kicked me into action. Even from the far side of Texas, Mike was able to say the exact right thing to piss me off.

The platform was open and the evening sky swept across the flat landscape in a million hues from light blue above to deepening purple on the horizon. The bright white lights of the halogen lamps on the platform shone down making everything appear antiseptic. My mind was a hurricane, I was hyperaware of everything around me. Down at the end of the platform, I saw baggage handlers unloading the racer's bikes.

Kathy was on a bench near the station reading a pamphlet. She looked up as Ahmed urged me off the train with more apologies. I took the step off the train but waited on the concrete at the foot of the steps. Leaving the safety of the train was almost as hard as getting on in Dallas. The train felt safe now. It felt like that one step, the one that got me from the flat, diamond plate steel to the dull, gray concrete of the station platform was all I could muster. I stood, stock still as race volunteers, bikes, and train workers moved around me.

Kathy must have seen my hesitation. She stood up and came over, took my arm and pulled me across the platform, leading me away from the train in the same way that she led me on. She didn't say anything about our argument, she just helped me down the platform toward the station.

I wanted to tell her I didn't need help but felt that it would be a useless sentiment now. She knew I needed the help, I knew I needed the help, who would I be fooling now? It wasn't until she helped me across the platform that I heard my teeth gnashing and remembered what she had said. I forced my jaw to unclench.

She saw me look down at the paper she had been reading. "Race rules," she said. "The buses already left. I got us a ride on one of the vans." Behind her, I saw the bikes being loaded into a row of white vans.

"Thanks."

She nodded. "Actually it didn't take you as long as I thought for you to get off the train."

"I'm not as bad when it's dark outside. Why, how long did you think it would take?"

"I was going to give you thirty minutes then come in and see how you were doing." She turned to look up at me. "It only took you twenty-three."

"You timed it?"

"Sure." She smiled. "Baby steps, right? You're making progress."

Despite Kathy, my mind was still a scramble of activity.

I felt like I was outside looking in. My mind took in the wind rippling through the brown leaves of the scrub brush that dotted the station's grounds. I looked at and tried to judge the angle of the concrete wall that encircled the end of the platform. Those worn boards that camouflaged the station's garbage dumpsters, why were some old and others were new? Why wouldn't they have just replaced them all?

I was moving in a million different directions, hardly concentrating on any one thing for longer than a millisecond.

Then my eyes fell on the dumpster again and stayed there studying it.

"What's that?" I pointed to the garbage dumpster. It took a bit of coaxing, but I finally got Kathy interested enough to walk over with me. What I had seen was a glint of highly polished metal. It was incongruous with the dirty, muddy, dull dumpster next to it. When we got there, we saw a very new, very sleek road bike standing upside down in the dumpster.

"That's the race number for your team," Kathy pointed as we pulled it out.

"Why would they throw it away?"

"They didn't," she said. "Someone, probably one of them threw it here." She nodded toward the baggage handlers. "Someone's trying to sabotage the team."

"You think?"

She nodded and I saw that she was zeroed in on the workers, already walking toward them.

"Horne probably put them up to it." She shot me a doubtful glance. "Let's just put it back."

She didn't stop.

We took the bike over to the baggage handlers and as we watched them put it into the waiting trucks, she asked them all who had put it in the dumpster. None of them fessed up. It was a poor way to try to decipher who the culprit was, but she wouldn't be dissuaded. She harangued them for several more moments, till the supervisor came up and talked to her. He reassured us that it was none of his men and said he'd make personally sure that all the bikes made it to the race. Kathy looked at him dubiously, but there wasn't much we could do. We got into the van and had to wait a few minutes for the final few bikes to be loaded. Then the baggage throwers and other race volunteers who had to get to the park loaded in with us. Kathy and I found ourselves shoved into the back row of benches for the two-hour ride to Lajitas, the little resort town just west of Big Bend State Park.

The sky was a deep black outside and the van was blessedly

quiet and blacked out except for the faint green glow that emanated from the dashboard. All of the workers in the seats in front of us seemed too tired to talk much, and we saw several of them take the opportunity to curl up wherever they could find room for a nap. They were all young, high schoolers, probably volunteering to help improve their chances of getting into college.

Kathy and I watched the landscape race by. Like on the train, I felt at ease. I could feel that things were coming easier for me. Sure it was darker and the platform less crowded in Alpine than in Dallas, but getting off the train and to the van had been monumentally easier than getting on the train. What had been almost paralyzing in Dallas, had been hard but not impossible in Alpine. I could feel myself loosening up the further we drove, and I knew that I had to say something to Kathy for helping. The further we went the more absent the apology seemed.

"Thanks for all your help, Kathy. And I'm sorry about what I said back in the train."

"Don't worry about it," she said. "And I haven't done all that much. You've done all the heavy lifting. Back at the station, you were basically surrounded by chaos and confusion but you handled it. There were baggage handlers everywhere, race officials running around, you had no idea how you were going to get where you needed to go, this is the big leagues. You're out of your comfort zone and you're handling it."

"I don't have a problem with chaos or confusion." I didn't mean to sound like I was mimicking her, but it came out that way.

She went on as if it was another session. "Since we aren't using the vague terminology of condition," She added air quotes above her head as she continued to whisper. "Let's call it what it is, agoraphobia."

"Fear of open spaces." I kept my voice hushed so no one in the other seats could hear us.

"There's more to it than that. It's all in the root word."

"Phobia? Fear of?"

"Not that, the first word. It's Greek for the market place. It's a fear of public places. That," she hooked her thumb back toward the station, "was like a hardcore public place and you handled it great! Think about everything you've accomplished. You got on a train full of people, took it all the way to Alpine Texas, and now you're here, on a van to Big Bend. That's remarkable, Joe. Even you have to admit that."

I shrugged, but she had a point. I knew that she was trying to instill a feeling of accomplishment in me, but I preferred the looseness I felt earlier, that feeling I had had when she had been wearing the kimono. Now there was nothing but a puzzle of emotions that refused to come together. The rest of the ride we finished in silence. The desert passed by outside with the only spots we could see were the two white triangles of light from the headlights on the road in front of us.

Eventually, those white lights shone on a couple of adobe buildings and the van swung into a parking lot filled with other vans and busses. Beyond them, arrayed in a splatter pattern in the desert, were what looked like dozens and dozens of tents. Within the halo of the lights we saw people moving back and forth from the tents to the town carrying plates and drinks, smiles all around, a hive of activity, a party attitude infused everything that we could see. Racers, like parents picking up kids from camp, swarmed toward the trucks that had followed our van, eager to get to their bikes.

The Lajitas Hotel, sign shining brightly in the night, was filled to bursting. People were spilling out onto the road and into the adjacent parking lot. The lot was lined with mesquite trees that were nothing more than black silhouettes against the night sky. A gargantuan barbecue mounted on a trailer had been set up and several fire pits ringed it. A few dozen halogen lights helped light the area, and the low, incessant thrum of generators provided power and competed with the noise of the racers, the sound of tents being set up, people eating and the ringing of crickets in the background. Tables filled with food and dozens and dozens of hay bales for people to use as chairs sat around the trailer and the campfires.

As we exited the van, Kathy grabbed my arm and pulled me toward the tables.

"I think I'd feel better if I could get my gear and my tent." I pulled back from her.

"Nope," she said. "You haven't eaten at all today. I've been watching. You need food."

"I don't know about this." She disregarded me and pulled me straight toward the crowd.

CHAPTER 28

It was the same pack of dogs. The same ones we had been seeing all day. I kept my eyes on Blackie. He stared back at me.

"So?" Wilson again.

"Something's wrong," I answered. I crouched down lower but kept my eyes on Blackie. I saw him quiver. I watched a moment more and that's when he jumped. It was the type of jump that an animal makes when it's not sure what is happening or what to do. The type of jump a deer makes when it knows that there's a hunter in the woods and it's trying to figure out where he is. Somewhere off to our front, I could hear the low thrum of the vehicles followed by the crunch of tires on rocks.

He looked ready to bolt, but he didn't. I could see the whites around his eyes, the panic was creeping in. He was wounded and felt trapped. The village wasn't safe for him, I was in his original line of retreat, the vehicles were in front of him, why didn't he turn and go back the other way? Did he know Marlberg and Lamb were back there? Could he smell them? Was his wounded leg causing him to make poor decisions? Shock perhaps? The other dogs followed his lead and stayed where they were. I sensed that there were only a few more seconds before his jumpiness turned to flight.

We were locked on each other's eyes, he was probably wondering the same things about me that I wondered about him when the bullet hit him and he fell backward.

The sound of the shot cracked through the area just as I wondered why he had thrown himself backward, his legs kicking the air. The rest of the pack, bolted, panicked, flew away from him and ran right towards us.

"Shit!" Me this time, still a whisper.

Wilson didn't have time to get his question out before I pushed him back into the little depression.

"They're coming back."

Wilson was confused but his training took over. He rolled over on his stomach and took up a hasty fighting position next to me, using the rise of the depression as a rest for his rifle. It was one of those moments in life when I could see the outcome, it was inevitable, but there was nothing I could do to stop it. It felt like all those times as a kid when Luther would come home drunk and we both knew, Mike and me, that he'd end up hitting one of us but we were powerless to stop it. It unfolded slowly in my mind but played out quickly in front of mine and Wilson's eyes.

We heard the roar of the motor as the little, overloaded truck left the road and came through the brush to look at Blackie, perhaps to finish him off. Could they see him struggling to get up too, I wondered.

The three remaining dogs ran up on me and Wilson, just as I had run upon their leader moments before. The results were the same.

They turned and bolted back the way they'd come. One of the trucks was at Blackie now. A man leaned out of the back, his rifle poised to shoot Blackie in the head when the retreating dogs caught his eyes. He swept around, his rifle going off as he shot at the remains of the pack.

The dogs veered away quickly, rounds from the men in the trucks kicking up dirt around them as they ran. I could see their paws digging into the desert sand, their tails down, their haunches low. They might all get down the hill, out of the kill zone, I thought. They might draw the men down the hill after them, draw all the men, all the trucks back away from not just me and Wilson, but Johnson and the platoon as well.

There was that chance. Even as I thought if I knew it wouldn't happen.

The brindled mutt went down just ten yards from where Wilson and I were huddled. "Get Lamb on the radio," I whispered to Wilson without taking my eyes off the men in the truck. "Tell them we're in contact."

CHAPTER 29

I set my mind to try to relax, allow my training from the Marines to kick in. Square breathing. I'd considered it on the drive down and was sorry I hadn't had the wherewithal to think about it in Dallas when I boarded the train. It was a technique I had learned in a sniper class; breathe in, count to four, breath out, count to four, repeat. It calmed me down when I was a Marine, slowed the heart-rate, and helped me shoot. Nothing said it couldn't do the same in this situation. I could feel my heart race as we moved toward the banquet tables, and my back teeth hurt as I pressed them together.

"In, one, two, three, four." I thought to myself. "Hold, one, two, three, four."

It was like wading into the ocean. First, the water hit my ankles, then with each subsequent step, the waterline moved further up until it was at my chest. The only things that kept the party from being worse than the platform from that morning were that it was nighttime, I was better with the cover of night, and I had a record of accomplishment from that day. It was worse because we were out in the open and I knew it. No, overhead cover, no promise of a train to keep my mind occupied.

"In, one, two, three, four. Hold, one, two, three, four." I felt Kathy grab my hand protectively. She let her fingers intertwine into mine and it made me think again of her hair around her ears, that kimono, the smell of lavender from the shower. It was a nice way to distract my mind.

As we hit the outskirts of the crowd, I felt the strain in

my jaw muscles as I clinched. I willed myself to relax even as the people swarmed around us. For a moment the idea that other racers would begin crawling over me like bees in a hive seemed close to reality. Despite the breathing and despite her hand, my thoughts sped up and whipped around inside my head.

"In, one, two, three, four. Out, one, two, three, four."

"Okay?" It was Kathy. Her voice concerned as she handed me a plate.

I nodded and took the plate, moving down the buffet line taking food like an automaton, doing something with my hands. All the time my mind busy counting to four.

At one point, Kathy's hand gave my shoulder and upper arm a firm squeeze of reassurance. It was that that made me realize how hard the next few days were going to be.

"Don't worry," she said. "No one is noticing anything out of place. You look like you're doing fine."

What would I do had she not been there this morning? What about at the station? Now here? Worse, what would I do tomorrow during the race? How much more would I have to lean on Kathy for her help and insight? How would I handle the race without her there? I had no answers. Just considering how much of a crutch I'd made of her had me worried.

"So this is good news," she said. "Now we're one more step toward figuring you out. You have no problem with crowds, and open spaces at night are good." She looked over at me for confirmation.

"I can handle them if it's dark." The pain in my jaw lent less credence to the statement.

"Right, so now we just need to figure out how and why you are able to deal with these things and try to transfer that to daylight instances as well."

"And all before race time tomorrow. Not a problem." I failed to sound light and witty as I intended, instead it was acerbic and earned me a baleful glance from Kathy.

We sat on hay bales near the team, and I tried to eat barbecue while balancing the paper plates on my knees without looking too uncomfortable. I saw one or two of my teammates eyeing me strangely. Gentry sat next to his wife, Sherry. Where he was long and lean, she was diminutive, short and plump, proof that opposites do attract. Seated next to them was Mr. Rochester, and Rochester's friend, Michael.

Next to them was Bates, he smiled as he saw me look over at him, ingratiating or knowing, I couldn't tell which. All of them except Sherry were obvious athletes, lean and primed, even Michael who I had been told was only there for moral support. Emily sat next to the new teammate, Clark. Both of them looked slightly uncomfortable, like new kids coming to a school in mid-semester.

On a hay bale just slightly outside the circle sat Kay and Totten, engaged in their own quiet conversation. For anyone who knew them, it wasn't at all odd that they didn't feel compelled to include others. It was almost expected.

"So, what's the plan with the teams?" It was Emily. I looked up as her voice cut through everyone's conversations. She threw it out there like a challenge. I looked across the flames and saw a mischievous but resolute look in her eye. Immediately after asking the question she looked across at Kathy, a look that made me wonder how much they had discussed this after their argument with Totten on the train.

"What's what plan?" Gentry asked.

"The plan is to keep the teams as they are!" It was Totten, he was not happy to revisit the question.

"Well, Dave," Emily said, "Everyone except you, and Kay want to change the teams."

"Bullshit," Totten said it offhandedly and went back to his dinner as if that closed down all further argument.

"Really?" Kathy looked over at Emily. It was as if she took the baton for the argument from her. "Cause I've spoken to just about everyone on the teams, and there's a clear majority for changing the teams."

Gentry's brows peaked when she said it. Totten saw the

wavering flicker in Gentry's eyes as well, he flinched then said, "Doesn't matter, it's settled."

"Wait a sec," Gentry looked over the group. "Raise your hands if you would like to see a change-up in the teams." Several hands shot up, a clear majority.

"I'd at least like to discuss it a bit," Clark said. "Without everyone going nuts again."

I kept my hand down. The only two, whose hands were down, were Totten's and Kay's.

Gentry looked around at the group. He focused on Kathy and Emily whose hands were raised. "You two don't count, you can put your hands down."

"She counts," Kathy pointed at Emily.

"You don't!" Totten yelled. I thought for a moment he was going to jump over the fire to get to her. He clearly saw her as the instigator. "And she's only a replacement!" Totten pointed back at Emily.

"I'm a part of the team and should have as much voice in them as anyone else," Emily stuck up for herself.

A slew of loud voices reverberated around the little group and I saw several people on other teams sitting near us look in our direction. Most of the arguments were against Totten and Kay but they stuck to their arguments. In the middle of the commotion, Kathy punched me. She angled her eyebrows toward the center of the teams in an obvious gesture for me to get involved.

I decided to stay put. Round three of my decision to lead the team was not going well.

Finally, Gentry stood and got everyone quiet enough so that he could talk. "Okay, okay," Gentry said as he set his paper plate on the ground at his feet. "Let's talk about it reasonably. What are the thoughts?" he started to work around the circle one at a time eliciting viewpoints for and against.

Over just the past day, Gentry had become a different person to me. He was far more a product of group rule than I had expected. Prior to the trip, I would have guessed that he was independent in his leadership. He was tall, had a commanding voice plus he had a military bearing and demeanor that initially I mistook for effective leadership. Instead, he played toward the majority rule, every decision was founded on the basis of those around him, good or bad. He would have been successful if not for this attitude.

Clark spoke at his turn. "As I said," he stuttered. "I mean this is something we were never asked about. Luther just made the teams. I'd like to know if we can change them and how it might make a better showing for both groups." It was the common argument for the anti-Totten faction.

Gentry sighed. "I'm not sure if we can change them."

"You can," All eyes turned toward Kathy.

Totten attacked, "How the hell would you know?"

"I asked."

"Why don't you mind your own damn business?"

Totten's voice rose and seemed to echo across the field.

"Knock it off, Totten." I stood up.

For a moment his anger peaked, but I saw Kay grab his arm. He sat down heavily and waited, his face red.

Gentry held up his hand. "Alright, I'll double-check that. But what I want to know is why, and to what end."

"Yeah," Totten spoke up from his hay bale. "We have a team that could win. Me, Bates, Joe and Kay, we can take this thing."

"Yeah, but our team might not finish," Emily spoke up.

"Alright, alright." Gentry held up his hands to stop the conversation again. "Look, for the moment we have a strong team and a weaker," he looked over at Emily, and Rochester, "albeit still strong enough. I think it's prudent to leave it as is. I mean obviously, Luther had something in mind when he made these teams. It's his business we're representing." He looked over to me for re-enforcement and for the final word.

Before I could speak, Totten broke in, "Yeah, he probably wants the publicity that comes from a win."

"Assuming you actually do win." Kathy again.

Totten looked at her with eyes that threw daggers.

"I know Luther, and I'm a small business owner," she explained. "Personally any business owner would rather have the good publicity that comes with two teams finishing in the top ten rather than the bad publicity that would come with a team that didn't even finish."It was Gentry who spoke up.

"For now, unless something else comes up, we're going to keep it as is." Gentry's hands came up and then down as if he was banging a gavel, then he looked over at me. "You agree?"

All of their eyes turned my way.

"Sounds good to me."

I saw a few grimaces from the folks who had their hands up before, but Totten smiled and clapped his hands in support. The jab I got from Kathy this time was far harder and had a different intention than the first one.

"There you go," Totten said. "So let's forget about the whole ridiculous idea." He stood up with his empty plate in a manner that intonated he was as through with the conversation as he was with his dinner. He walked off and Kay followed.

Silently, the rest of the group looked around. An awkwardness built up among the teammates until finally, Clark, his face betraying some bemusement, got up and sauntered in the direction Totten and Kay had gone.

The first to speak was Emily. She turned toward Kathy and said in a voice that was intentionally louder than a whisper. "Still doesn't seem quite settled to me." For her part, she walked over toward Gentry and tried to discuss it more.

"Why didn't you say something?" Kathy leaned toward me.

"Cause I didn't want this," I waved toward the team, all of whom were talking about the teams.

"At least this is better than before."

"Better? How is this better?" I asked.

"At least they're talking about it now."

"Talking about it? They're about to take one another's heads off."

"These people haven't been happy about the teams from the moment I met them, Joe," she whispered. "It was the first thing I heard about."

"That was only this morning," I said.

She plowed on as if I hadn't spoken. "None of them on the second team were happy. They thought they were being set up to fail."

"Yeah, but how's that good?" I asked. "I mean before at least they were resigned to their fates. Now, they're trying to change it and it doesn't look like they're going to be successful, how's that good for morale?"

Kathy studied me for a moment, her face showing that she was disappointed in my reasoning. "It's always better if people have a choice, Joe. Now, they feel like they have a voice, they are a part of the decision, they're a part of the larger team. Prior to this, they were just an addendum, just a team that was tagging along, like a trailer on a truck."

"Yeah," I answered. "But what if they don't get the change?"

"At least now they're a part of the discussion. There can be greater buy-in afterward. It's just like a business deal. Business to business, B2B, Joe. Everyone should get a say-so. It's healthier, it builds a better relationship."

"We're not trying to build relationships, Kathy." My whisper was just a sigh. "You're missing the point of this group. It's a military-style fitness group. They're supposed to follow orders."

"You aren't even giving them any orders to follow," she countered. "Why do you think I kept prodding you to get up? They all wanted you to say something."

I was going to argue but our conversation was interrupted by a loud crash near the barbecue pit and several shouts. Gentry jumped up and stalked off toward the shouts; Bates, Emily, and several others followed.

Kathy stood up and looked down at me expectantly. When I didn't get up she said. "Come on, let's go see what's up."

I hesitated, but in the end, it wasn't Kathy who forced me to get up, it was Bates. He ran back to our circle, frantic.

"Totten and Horne are fighting!" he yelled at me as if it was incumbent on me to referee and put a stop to all fights. I obliged and ran toward the crowd.

There was already a crowd around the barbecue pits. I squirmed my way through the throng, driven both by Kathy and Bates behind me and the concern for protecting my teammates from Horne.

When I broke through I saw several people trying to hold Totten and Horne apart. Horne, by far the larger of the two, flung people off of him like he was tearing off clothes, throwing them into a corner for next week's wash. Totten looked as mad as I had ever seen him, his face purple, yelling curses. At that moment Horne broke free of the people trying to hold him back and lunged toward Totten. I saw fear flash across Totten's face as he realized that with his arms pinioned by racers trying to break up the fight he would be defenseless. I cringed as I dived for Horne. I flung my body at his legs.

It wasn't until he was airborne on top of me that I realized what a bad position I would be in when he landed, directly under him and almost as defenseless as Totten.

Horne fell on me and his entire weight crushed down on my ribcage. With Totten out of reach, Horne looked down, saw me, and without missing a beat slammed his fist into my side. I struggled to free myself but there were more people now most of them were working to restrain Horne, pushing him down on the ground. I was trapped between Horne and the gravel parking lot until more people came and got him under control.

At one point, his face sweaty and contorted by anger, his arms finally held behind him by a mass of people, Horne looked me in the eye, his nose just inches from mine. "I'm going to kill you for this."

I was surprised by the lack of emotion in his voice. I would have expected yelling, a shout of revenge, rage, anger or vehemence. The cold, almost detached, unemotional words were colder than any shout could have been. A chill ran up my spine. Finally, he was lifted off his feet and led away.

CHAPTER 30

Kathy was there immediately. "Are you okay?"

"Yeah." I stood up. My left side a mass of painful knots. A sharp pain lanced across my sternum as I stretched my chest.

The concern in Kathy's eyes grew when she saw me wince. "No, you're not." She grabbed Bates and made him support me on my left while she snaked under my right arm. Holding me up she led me away from the crowd toward the hotel. Piled up against the back wall of the hotel were several unused bales of hay. She angled toward them.

The parking lot which before had supported cocktail party-like noises, loud voices, and excited conversations punctuated by laughter was now filled with whispers from different corners, and uneasy, hushed discussions. I sat heavily on the hay bale, Kathy next to me.

Eventually, someone, a race official I suppose, brought a plastic bag filled with ice. Long conversations ensued and eventually the race director Tony was fetched. The description of events went on for far too long, I listened half-heartedly, nodded when I was supposed to, and nodded goodbye to him when he gave me a smile and a pat on the shoulder. Emily showed up at some point, and I saw her take Bates and Kathy away. I was fine with it. I closed my eyes and leaned back against the wall, happy with the solidity behind me.

The crowd dissipated and a sense of calm overtook me.

Slowly the noises in front of me disappeared and moved off toward the campgrounds. I was alone with the pain in my ribs. A rough end to a rough day and I almost smiled as I thought how it was bookended by being hit by Horne. Eventually, the halogen lights around the parking lot went off and I was shrouded in comfortable darkness. That's when I allowed myself a smile.

The always beaming Max materialized. "How are you doing, man?"

I shrugged. "Been better."

A smile played on his lips. "I saw what happened to you, sorry I couldn't help out more."

I waved my hand in a dismissive gesture. Even that hurt.

"If it makes any difference, they were the ones who started it," he said.

"Who?"

"Kay and Totten," he said and sat next to me. "It was weird. I mean he got in Horne's face, then she started screaming at him for no reason."

I looked up. "Like what?"

"What was she saying?" he asked. "I'm not really sure. I just heard a bunch of stuff about Georgia. Then he just went off."

"Horne went off on Totten?"

"No, he was mad at Kay," he said. "They had to call the paramedics."

I turned to look at him. "He hit her?"

"Smacked her right in the jaw," he said. "Fucking dropped her. She flipped right over the table."

"Kay?" My voice was louder than I'd wanted it to be. "Yeah, he decked her," he continued. "That's when Totten stepped in. He gave Horne a few whacks and Horne took off after him. That's about when you showed up." He looked over at me. "Are you okay? I mean, anything broken? You need a doctor?"

My stomach hurt, but that was nothing compared to the guilt that draped across me. I might not have been fond of Kay, but to hear that she'd been hit so hard by Horne made my stomach turn and an anger blossom in my gut. It was no longer just about protecting my teammates from Horne, I had failed at that. Now, I would actively have to work to stop him.

Once, when I was young, Luther had allowed us a family dog, a mutt we named Julius. Luther assigned me the task of training him. Sadly, even after several weeks of my working with him, sitting, heeling, all of the basic tricks were still completely foreign to him. What's worse he showed a complete loathing to learn. One day I got so fed up with him that I threw a bat at him. I did it out of desperation and frustration. He'd been fifty meters or more away at the time I threw the bat. There was no way the bat would hit him. With each revolution, however, I saw it getting closer and closer to Julius.

The yelps he made for after the bat hit his head and cracked his skull only lasted a few minutes but stayed in my mind ever since. Had I wanted to forget that moment I wouldn't have been able to. The guilt was unbearable and didn't end when he was put to sleep. What I felt when I heard about Kay was the same feeling of guilt and incompetence I'd felt that day with Julius. It went down to the bone.

When I didn't speak anymore Max decided to wander off. I was silently grateful. It was better to be alone with my guilt. Eventually, Kathy came back. I could tell she was mad. I've seen her mad before when a project was late when a model didn't come out right when I hadn't done what she had asked. Her strident pace, her chin down, her hands balled into fists, all the earmarks of an extremely pissed boss.

"What's up?"

"I don't want to talk about it." She looked around furtively, anxiously as she spoke, as if she was looking for a way to get out. It felt like we had switched positions.

"Come on, let's go get your tent. Plus we need to get your bags, let's go." She didn't wait for me but just stormed off towards the luggage.

Emily and Bates were back and watched Kathy's retreat.

"What's up with her?" I asked.

"We volunteered her to fill in for Kay," Bates said.

"Kay's out of the race?"

"Yeah, I spoke to the paramedic. Her jaw is banged up, and

she dislocated her shoulder when she fell. She's going to need a splint so there's no way she can ride or climb."

"So you asked Kathy?"

"Who else could we ask?" Emily now, still watching Kathy.

"The only other person we could ask would be Cheryl," Bates cut in. "She'd never keep up."

"What about Rochester's friend, Michael?"

"Michael?" Bates said with a bit of a laugh. "We need a female. Michael hardly qualifies."

"Kathy doesn't have any of the gear?"

"She'll use Kay's," Bates again. "And there's no one else. Kathy herself said that she'd run a couple of marathons and triathlons. She'll be fine."

"The good news is that it frees us up to level out the teams," Emily said. "Without Kay, the elite team is no longer elite. When it was made it was Totten, Kay, Bates, and Luther. Luther's gone and so's Kay. Even Gentry admitted that there's no way they could win. He's agreed to change the teams up to make them both more competitive."

Emily was distracted by something and looked over toward the tents. "I think she's waving at you," she said to me.

She was right. Kathy holding two bicycles and my two bags stood at the edge of the tents. She looked angrier than I've ever seen her.

I hurried over to her. "I hope you're happy," she said.

"Me?"

"I didn't come here to race."

"At least you got your wish," I said. "They're going to change up the teams."

"Hardly a comfort."

She strode through the hundreds of tents the grass becoming more and more green and manicured as we walked. The campgrounds were on the resort's golf course. We found an open area and Kathy dropped the bags. She placed the bicycles on the ground and plopped down on the ground to wait. She didn't need to say anything. She was in no mood to help me pitch the tent.

Even in the dark, I could see that her face was set, her knees up to her chest, her arms crossed. I found my flashlight in my ruck, flipped it on and went to work, thankful that the deep dark sky, black trees around us, and silence in the campgrounds allowed me some anonymity and feeling of security. No people, no problem. Heaven.

When I unzipped the door to the tent Kathy jumped up, grabbed her bag and crawled inside. For a moment I wondered what I should do. It was her yell, "If you don't come in now, I'm zipping up and leaving you out there!" that made my decision for me.

"I can't believe Emily did that to me," Kathy spoke as I found a spot to sit inside the tent. She was sitting just as she had been outside, steaming. With the flashlight beam reflecting off the interior of the tent, her hair pulled back behind her ears, I saw that she was on the verge of tears.

"What?"

"She ambushed me," Kathy seemed mad and disappointed at the same time. "By the time I got there, everyone knew my race history. They acted like I was some sort of superstar, some kind of savior, I couldn't say no."

"I don't understand what the problem is?" I said. "Just go out there and race. All they want you to do is keep up. You are their savior."

The look that she gave me seemed to suggest she was holding back the words go to hell. Eventually, she dropped it and began to shift around and unpack her gear.

Bates calling our names from outside the tent stopped us both. We peeked outside and saw him and Emily with more gear and two more bikes. It was Kay's stuff. They'd gotten Totten's permission for Kathy to use it. Kathy didn't even speak to them. They sensed her disappointment and didn't hang around. I did hear an almost silent, sarcastic quip from Kathy as they left about the absurdity of getting familiar with strange equipment in the middle of the night before a two-day race. I agreed with her.

I tried to help her as best I could. We tested and fit her backpack, checked inside the pack to see what Kay had given her; a rope, carabiners, climbing gloves, bike helmet, biking shoes, just about everything. She barely spoke. I checked out her bike and finally, with the campground around us almost dead silent, we ducked into the tent again.

"I'm still not sure why you're so mad," I said. "I mean you said yourself you've run some marathons. This is just a bit more."

"Jogged a marathon, Joe." She hissed. "I didn't run it. And there's no way I'm going to be able to do this."

"You'll be fine," I said. "It's a team race. The stronger racers will be able to help you through the harder parts. You'll be fine."

With the flashlight creating an amber hue inside the red tent, I saw her turn and fix her stare on me. "You've set me up for failure here, Joe, and I don't appreciate it." Tears welled on her eyelids.

"I didn't do anything."

"I'm only here because of you." She looked like she would have left had we not been stranded in the middle of the desert. "And what's worse is that now the rest of these people are expecting me to do it. Now, I can't drop out with all of them needing me to run it. I'm not ready for this. I don't like not being ready." She switched off the light as if she were slamming a door.

CHAPTER 31

She took a long time to get herself settled and bumped against me several times. The train berth had been a palace compared to the room inside the tent. She pushed me out of the way to get to her bag and I brushed up against her flank. The sounds of her changing clothes, something that I might have thought intriguing in the train, was now nerve-racking in the close confines of the tent.

"Don't get any ideas," she said suddenly. She huffed loudly as she curled up next to me. "Some great friends you got here, Joe."

"Quit blaming me. I'm only here because I want to buy Luther out of his business. They aren't my friends."

"I thought you were here to protect your team? To try to stop anyone else from being killed or hurt." Her voice came out as if she was mocking what I said earlier. "I thought that was Luther's mission for you. Good job with that this evening."

She enunciated the word mission as if it was something ridiculous. The nylon rustle of the sleeping bag we'd unzipped to use as a blanket told me that she'd pulled it up.

It was tempting to argue, but she was right and it would be best to not provoke her more. "At least we can pretty much agree that Luther was right about Horne."

"You think he killed Georgia and Bridget?" Even though she was whispering, we were laying so close together that it sounded like she was yelling.

"The guy that threw Kay across a table and broke her shoulder?" I asked. "The one who has pummeled me twice in one day? You don't think he had anything to do with the murders?"

"That's exactly what I mean," she said. "Is he an asshole? Yes. Is he violent? Yes. But he's also a hot head and from what I've heard about Georgia's murder it was planned. He's too much a product of his emotions to plan and execute either Georgia's or Bridget's murder if you ask me."

"You don't know anything about him?" I countered. "You only met him today."

"You know he was dating Georgia, right?"

"Yeah," I said.

"So, if he was mad at her, why didn't he just hit her like he did Kay. Murder doesn't fit." Kathy said. Her voice was calmer now. She moved and I felt the bare skin of her leg against mine. I pulled away. Another rustle of the sleeping bag and we were as far away from one another as the tent would allow. Still, I could smell the lavender of her hair and it reminded me again of that shower.

"Contrary to what you've been doing," she started, "hiding out from crowds, I've been out talking to the other team members, hearing from them and about them. Hell, I probably know more about them than you do."

"You've been around them for one day," I repeated.

"Yeah, but you don't know them at all," she said.

"There's a lot going on that you don't know. A lot of mixed emotions. It reminds me of why I went into business for myself." She sat up with a swish of nylon. I felt her leg again.

"I worked lots of jobs and I was always amazed by the amount of screwing around in the office. The manager was screwing the intern. His wife would come by, and I think she was messing around with the accountant. Flings would start up like forest fires, then burn out after a flare-up. It was crazy. It was horrible for business."

Not knowing what else to say I gave a bored sounding, "Humpf."

"It's just like that here with your friends." She continued

her voice reaching a higher pitch. "I mean Georgia and Horne, Georgia and Max. Georgia and a couple of others."

It was my turn to sit up, "Georgia and Max?"

"See, I know more than you."

I decided it would be best to not mention Georgia and Luther as Mike had brought up that morning. "Any others?"

She paused. "I'm not sure yet, but I've heard the gossip already. I'll find out."

"I think you're over-analyzing," I said. "I think you're making this too difficult. Horne's a jerk. He's violent, abusive, and he's linked to Georgia. Not much more to it."

My argument died there. Just behind that thought was the argument I had that morning, that I wasn't there to figure out who killed Georgia, I was supposed to be watching Horne and stopping him from hurting the other team members. Thoughts of Kay and Julius bounced around in my head. I would have rather had an angry and sulky Kathy in the tent than a confrontational Kathy.

The pause lasted a long while and eventually I turned on my side, away from Kathy. I tried to find a comfortable position but was half on half of the little sleeping mat. I gave up and just moved closer to the wall of the tent, abandoning the mat for Kathy to use.

Finally, softer now, Kathy finished my sentence for me, throwing my words back in my face, "I thought we were here to keep your friend's safe."

"I am."

"Sounds more like you're keeping them safe from Horne. That's not the same thing. Not if Horne didn't kill Georgia."

A long pause, then, "If Horne didn't kill Georgia or Bridget, there might be someone else here who did, and they're even more dangerous since you aren't looking for them."

For a moment, silence reigned in the little tent again.

Then, the now-familiar nylon rustle as Kathy shot up abruptly. "That's the question, Joe," she said. "What's the relationship between Bridget and Georgia."

"Why?"

"Cause they're the only two people who have been murdered at AFC, if you can link them both to Horne, then you have your answer. But if you find out they're linked to someone else?" She let the question hang.

"Sounds pretty weak."

"And how does this bike in the dumpster fit in?" she said. "Why do that? Horne wouldn't have any motivation to do that."

I rolled over and let her figure it out on her own. Still, she had a point, worse, each move made me think of other things. It had been awkward hanging out with my freshly showered boss in a small train berth for several hours, but sharing a small tent and a small sleeping bag was far worse. It was an exercise in wondering what she was thinking, trying to avoid touching her, hearing the sounds of her breathing; worse still, it was filled with my absurd thoughts and wondering if she was thinking the same things about me.

My cell phone rang and I felt compelled to at least see who was trying to call before I disregarded it and went to sleep. It was my brother. I decided to take it. I unzipped the tent and stepped outside into the cool night to talk.

"How's the desert?" he asked.

"Fine."

"Lots of people?"

"Yeah."

"How are you handling it?"

It was a moment of true concern. Rare for Mike. "Fine, I guess."

He paused for a moment then plowed on. "So, have you seen anything, heard anything?"

"I think Luther might have been right about Horne," I said. "It's only been the first day and already he's decked me, gotten into a fight with one of our teammates and punched one of the girls so hard that she flew into a table and dislocated her shoulder."

"Holy cow!" he said. "Is she going to press charges?"

It was a typical Mike comment. "I don't know, but she's out of the race and Kathy is going to be taking her place."

"Kathy?" He asked. "My Kathy?"

"Kathy, my boss," I said.

"What's she doing there?"

"She came to help me, I guess. Now she's going to race."

"Kathy?" He asked again. "That's going to be a fiasco."

"Not really, she'll be fine." I had my doubts about that, but I didn't want Mike to feel that Kathy was setting herself up for failure. I don't know why I wanted that, but it just felt right to take her side against him.

"Are you doing her?" Another typical Mike comment.

"No, Mike, she's my boss."

"You better not be," he said.

"Why not?" Again that odd feeling about being protective of and attracted to Kathy.

"Forget it. So you think Horne is our guy?"

"Could be," I said. "It might be worthwhile to see if the second victim, Bridget, had any connection to Georgia or Horne." Kathy's comment from before popped out of my mouth as if it was my own.

"Yeah, I already thought of that," he said. "We wondered the same thing. I'll let you know if we find anything."

"Okay." "Anything else?"

"Yeah," I said. "Check into a couple of other folks for me. Horne's latest victim, Kay. I think her first name is Donna. She's dating another client, Jon Totten."

"Okay."

"And one more thing, just cause it might be interesting. Max Ring. He's a former client who works out with Horne now. He might be involved somehow. The word is that he was sleeping with Georgia too."

"Got it," he said. "That it?"

"I think so."

His sign off was as abrupt as his salutation. "Keep safe."

That was it. I didn't even have time to close the phone before I heard the click of his phone. I crawled back into the tent and heard the ubiquitous nylon rustle and realized that Kathy was still awake. I decided against discussing Mike's call with her and thankfully, she didn't ask. I grabbed a long sleeve shirt and tried to use it as a blanket. I knew I'd be up all night if I tried to share the sleeping bag and had to worry about brushing up against Kathy's leg all night. Better just to avoid the problem as much as possible.

CHAPTER 32

The morning was a long time coming. No more legs brushed against mine even though I had jumped awake with each rustle. Would our business relationship be different after sharing a tent? I doubted it. That kimono and the lavender would always pop to mind whenever I saw her I felt sure. I got one reprieve when another text message came in. It was from Luther. A simple eight-word message, "What the hell are you doing! Stop Horne!"

I guessed it was supposed to inspire me to call him, even though it didn't expressly say so. I decided against calling him. Instead, I wondered who ratted on me; Totten? Doubtful. Tony, the race director? Possible but doubtful. He would have more on his mind than contacting Luther. Mike? Not a chance. Gentry? He was the most likely candidate.

I was already awake when the alarm on my watch went off. I felt as though I'd never truly closed my eyes. It was a bad way to start a long, two-day race.

With a heaviness wrapped around my head, I flipped on the little flashlight. Kathy rolled over and grumbled.

"Too early!" she complained. "What time is it?"

"Four-thirty." I got on my knees and began to pack some of our gear inside our bags.

"Four-thirty!" her voice was loud in the little tent. "We have over an hour!" She curled up into a ball and rolled over in the sleeping bag to block out the light.

"We need to pack, take down the tent, check on the others. Plus we should get something to eat."

Kathy rolled over and glared. "I've decided I'm not doing the race."

"Too late," I said. "Let's go."

I slipped on my shoes and socks and unzipped the tent.

The whisper of the zipper and the cool desert air produced more disapproving groans from Kathy. She would race. Her refusal was noncommittal and lackadaisical. After a night of getting used to the idea, by now she would have had time to embrace the idea. She might not embrace it enthusiastically, but she would be there. I knew Kathy well enough to know that she would race. Once she stepped into something, she stepped into it all the way. Projects that others would pass on, once she took hold, she'd work to the very end.

People were moving all around the tents, most moving as if in slow motion, the heaviness of a campground waking up. I stretched my back and arms and felt the pain in my chest, which I had felt most of the night, spike back. The nose was just a general discomfort now, still tender, but not as bad as before. The ribs felt better as soon as the stretch was over. Despite the lack of sleep, despite the impending rigors that would come with the race and the pains I already felt, despite the problems with Totten, Kay, Luther, and Horne, it felt good to be away from the city, getting ready for a race, working with a group of people toward a common goal. It was good to feel normal, even if I knew that feeling would evaporate when the sun rose and the day was full on us.

"I'm about to drop the tent with you in it," I warned Kathy.

Her response; another dismissive groan. She crawled out of the tent and rolled into a sitting position on the turf of the golf course. She dragged her shoes over to her and began to lace them on. I watched her as she worked.

"What?" She saw me watching and stood up abruptly.

"Why do you keep looking at me?"

"Nothing," I said. "I'm glad you're here."

"Ugh, I hate morning people."

"I'm in my element."

"Well, you better find a way to stay in your element because your problems are going to have to take a backseat. I can't help you anymore. I've got bigger problems to worry about now."

"What's that mean?"

She looked at me as if I had missed a part of the conversation. "This race Joe," she said. "I'm going to die."

"You'll be fine." It was Emily. She materialized from behind the tent that was being struck next to our own. She wore tight-fitting running pants, a long sleeve, light sweatshirt zipped to her throat, running shoes and a ponytail.

"I don't know," Kathy said. "I mean, just the first leg sounds tough."

Emily's smile grew as she saw that Kathy's hostility had dissipated during the night.

Emily bent down and began to help me with the tent. It must have shamed Kathy because she jumped up to help as well. We were done in no time and left with all of our gear and the bikes back toward the hotel and the starting line. Around us, like mass migration, other racers followed with the same loads balanced on their backs or being wheeled next to them.

"Where's Bates?" I asked. "You guys already ready?"

"Oh yeah," Emily said. "Pretty much the whole team is over there waiting on you two. Totten's already pissed about how slow you are."

Kathy sighed loud enough for both of us to hear.

Emily leaned closer to her to say, "Don't let him get to you, he's an ass. Just concentrate on putting one foot in front of the other."

We crossed the little road that separated the golf course from the parking lot and saw the rest of our team. The halogen lights were back on and the white swaths of light cut through the darkness. Scaffolding had been erected over the main street during the night and a starting banner hung from it. Several teams were milling around the starting line all of them packed, ready and amped to get moving. They looked like sled dogs about to be released. Had they been wearing harnesses and traces they would be lunging against them in anticipation.

Michael, Rochester's friend, took my tent from my arms before I even got to him. "I'll go put this in the trailer with all the other stuff." He rushed off down the street with my tent.

"He's excited," Rochester said. "He gets like that when he's put in charge of something."

Emily and Bates followed him and took mine and Kathy's bikes, two each. I watched as they loaded them all into different trailers, bound for different points along the racecourse.

"Mike's in charge of our team's gear," Gentry explained. "I figured we had Mike and Cheryl here, why not put them to work as our pit crew? Plus, Kay is still here, she's going to be helping too since she can't race."

Rochester continued. "Don't even worry about your bikes being in the right place or the tent, food or anything, Mike's on it."

Rochester beamed and I wondered if he had placed the idea for Michael leading the support team in Gentry's head. It was a good idea. We would have enough to worry about with the race, Horne and all the different events; not having to tote my gear to and from the race trailers and constantly worry about it would be a bit of relief.

I looked over Gentry's shoulder and saw Totten and Kay standing together. Kay's arm was in her pocket, no sling holding it in place. Both of them were whispering to one another as they looked around at the other teams, judging them as a finicky chef might look at cattle at a meat market. Kay looked rough, just the way you'd expect a lady to look after Horne had hit her and threw her across a picnic table, but completely disabled? Not really. What were they up to?

"Here!" It was Totten. His shout was followed by a candy bar that flew through the dark right at my head. Had I not been looking it would have hit me. I had to dodge to catch it. "You should eat something so you have the energy for the run."

He threw another candy bar at Kathy. She snatched it out of

the air.

Gentry sounding rehearsed, as if the rest of the team had already had his briefing, said, "The first event is a run. We have to take our backpacks. It's an unknown distance, but based on what I've heard from some of the other teams, it's probably no more than five or six miles."

"Okay."

"I thought we'd even out the teams so I have Emily, Bates, and Rochester. You'll be with Totten, Clark, and Kathy.

That way we have two strong team members on each team." he nodded at me looking for confirmation.

"Sounds good to me." I liked the idea of having Kathy on my team.

Gentry went away to tell the others about the new teams and as he did Kathy came up next to me. "How are you handling it?"

It wasn't until she had asked that I remembered that I was supposed to be stressed out by my agoraphobia. The sky might have lightened, but I hadn't noticed. The halogen lights still dominated the area. I'd been lost in the run-up and preparation for the race, too excited to worry. With Kathy's question, it all tumbled back to mind. Everything that I'd forgotten to be worried about was now at the forefront of my thoughts. Not oppressive or dominating, not yet, but like an all-day cloudy sky, I'd forgotten about the chance of rain until the drops on my face reminded me there was a chance of thunderstorms.

I didn't have time to respond because Tony started speaking on a bullhorn. He stood near the starting line and race volunteers began herding the teams into lines. AFC's first team, my team, was corralled and positioned nearer to the starting line than Gentry's. People milled around everywhere, some with packs on, some with packs off, racers, well-wishers, everyone everywhere. I felt the anxiety approaching, but the concerns and worries about what the race would bring kept it at bay. It all floated through my consciousness.

Kathy appeared in front of me, she looked more nervous than I. I bent down and gave her a kiss on the cheek. She looked up, surprise written on her face.

"For luck," I told her. "And because I'm glad you're here."

Tony fired the starter's pistol for the first team to go, and the other teams waiting to be released moved a step closer to the line. Our team, fifth in line, took a final look at our backpacks. The surrounding crowd of watchers got larger with each passing moment and as each team was sent on its way. My conscious caught up with my mind after the third team trotted off and disappeared into the gray morning haze of the desert.

"How many teams have left?" Gentry stood next to me watching.

"That was the third."

"When do we go?" Kathy asked.

"Two more teams till you go," he said.

"And we leave right after?" Emily asked

He shook his head. "Horne's team is sandwiched between ours."

"You're kidding," I asked.

He shook his head. "That's how the draw came out. Ya'll go first," he looked at me and Kathy. "Then Horne's team, then we go."

My mind went back to the baggage handlers and the bike in the dumpster. Had Horne arranged this too? How much had it cost him to get placed between our teams? Why would he want to do that? What would he gain? Or had it all just been bad luck? Kathy shrugged her shoulders in a helpless gesture. Not only that, why hadn't he been kicked out of the race? Everyone saw what he did to Kay.

I looked around and between the crowd around me and saw Max and Horne surrounded by their own team behind us. My shoulders slumped when I saw Horne smiling back at me. What did he have in mind now? Max, just next to him, looked happy and excited. Their energy and enthusiasm were there for all to see. They looked rested, ready and eager, the complete opposite of AFC's teams.

CHAPTER 33

Just as I'd thought, the technical had come up to inspect the second dog. The truck had come to within just a few feet of where Wilson and I were huddled. The berm was there, but it wasn't enough to keep us from being seen. It was when our discovery was inevitable that I'd stood up, weapon at the ready and said one of the few Arabic phrases I knew, "Don't move."

Whether they had understood me or not I didn't know, but all three of them opened up immediately. Wilson's covering fire had dropped two while I found my way back beneath the safety of the berm. I fired as I retreated and hit the driver. I watched him fall, still alive, and shifted my fire to one of the several guys in the back of the truck who was firing down at us. I fell down into the prone. His fire peppered the top of the berm where I'd been standing only moments before. Wilson took that moment to drop him as well. We could hear them yelling as they tried to crawl for safety.

"How many are left?" I yelled to Wilson.

"I hit two, maybe three."

"I hit one, but he's not out. There were five, to begin with. Make sure they don't come around to our flank!"

Our unit had seen combat in Fallujah prior to my coming on board. Marlberg, Lamb, Johnson most of my platoon were battle-tested. Lamb had seen some of the worst close-quarters battles that the Marines had encountered in Iraq. Me, nothing but long-distance ambushes where the shots were so sporadic and so far away that no one ever figures out where it's coming from. In each of those engagements there had been some return fire, lots of confusion, no casualties, and no final outcome other than our picking up and continuing on with the mission.

I have heard that combat focuses the mind, but at that moment everything was cloudy. When bullets were being fired back-and-forth confusion is quick and deep, like jumping headfirst into a cold, black lake, and not being able to figure out which way is up.

My ears stopped hearing, a long low ring dominated everything. I saw movement everywhere. My actions were automatic and it was only afterward that I remembered reloading, grabbing another frag, and taking stock of my position.

I peeked over the berm, my rifle pointed toward the vehicle. I saw three moving in the brush. They were on the ground, one was obviously wounded. He was dragging himself along with just one hand.

Ever since Vietnam, the military has been bemoaning the poor stopping power of the M-16's round. I thought about this as I watched the three Iraqi's crawl back toward the cover of their vehicle. All three were still alive despite having several rounds in them. I forced these thoughts away and trained my rifle on the center mass of the closest Iraqi. He was crawling toward his weapon. There it was, on the ground, just inches from his hand. I shot. He stopped moving.

A burst of machine-gun fire decimated the top of the berm and sprayed chunks of dirt and rock all over. I felt the sting of the pebbles as they peppered my face. It was the second technical. Had they heard the gunfight and come running or had they come when they saw the dogs, maybe wanting some target practice as well, either way, they were coming in force.

CHAPTER 34

Max saw me and started over. He waved as he came over, his hand outstretched. "Good luck." His voice was genuine and his eyes were friendly. It was the type of formality that Max was prone to.

"I still can't believe you're racing with that jack-ass," I nodded toward Horne who was out of earshot.

"Horne?"

"Don't play stupid." His passive-aggressive demeanor was suddenly as irritating as his smile. What was actually hidden behind his eyes and an easy manner; an ulterior motive? How much of a friend was he really? I was out of ideas about the best way to protect the teams from Horne. The attack on Kay proved that I needed help, needed some reinforcements. Where were Max's loyalties?

"Your friend is targeting us."

Max stepped back as if caught off guard. "Look, man, I was just coming over to say good luck, I didn't want to get into an argument."

"He ambushed me and almost broke my nose on that first morning on the train."

"Come on, Joe..." Max tried to cut me off, but I ticked items off on my fingers.

"I think he tried to sabotage our gear in Alpine."

"I have no idea..." His hands came up defensively.

I pressed on. "He cold-cocked Kay and almost broke her shoulder, not to mention tried to kick Totten's ass."

"Now, hold on!" Max's voice was loud. He looked left and

right and pulled me away from the starting line, away from the teams. "That wasn't his fault, Joe. You should know that."

"He punched Kay in the face." I couldn't keep the incredulity out of my voice but kept it a low whisper like his. How could he defend Horne hitting Kay?

"Look, man," Max's whispers were sibilant. "You know I like you but Kay and Totten," he let his voice trail off.

"He dislocated her shoulder!" I was astounded. There were layers of disappointment and I couldn't keep that feeling out of my tone. My shoulders sagged under the weight of hearing him defend Horne. I had thought for a moment I might be able to turn him to be my confidant, hearing his excuses made me realize it was impossible. Or was it that someone I had hoped would be a friend, wasn't what I had thought.

Max's head tilted as he looked at me. "Did you hear what she said to him?"

I looked back at him, not sure what he meant. "Who?"

Max's voice rose as the starter's pistol went off behind us, the teams in line shifted, and the crowd around us maneuvered closer for a better look. The smile was gone.

"Hell, if she'd said the same thing to me, I probably would have hauled off and smacked her too."

"Are you talking about Kay?" My mind was muddled trying to keep up with him with the surging crowd.

"Yes, Kay," Max said. "She told Horne that Georgia got what she deserved. Dude, something's wrong with her, man. Her and Totten."

"Yeah, something's wrong," I said. "Their friend was murdered last week."

Max grabbed me by the shoulder and pulled me further away, deeper into the growing crowd and noise.

"You don't know these guys, Joe," he said. "You're on the outside looking in. Why do you think I left? You think I like Horne? He's just a better alternative than what Luther has going on. And Georgia wasn't the person you think. She was screwing everyone."

"Including you," I fired back.

"I'm not going to deny it." His face showed none of the shock that I'd expected. "And as soon as I found out that she was a part of all of that I ditched her."

"But not Horne?"

"Horne liked her more than I did," he said. "I guess he thought he could have something more with her. She was more interested in just having fun. She was the focal point of everything wrong in that group, in the whole clique."

"You're not making any sense," I said. "What clique? What the hell are you talking about?"

"All of them, man."

"And Bridget?" I asked. "Was she a part of this clique?"

"Who?" He looked as if he just realized we were having separate conversations.

The starter's pistol fired and a small cheer went up near the starting line. Max looked over his shoulder. "All I'm saying is that there are more problems with your friends than you know, Joe. The exterior might look healthy, but the inside is rotten." He waved his hand and turned abruptly as if he was tired of talking to me.

I watched him stride back to his team. I could see a glowering Horne looking over him, the focus of his stare me. What did Max and Horne know that I didn't? More importantly, how could I get Max to tell me more?

Step one would be to find someone who could tell me if what he said about the fight and about everyone was true. Rochester was nearby during the fight. I made a mental note to ask him about it. Maybe he had heard something that Kay had said. Comparing it with Max's story might lead to more clarity.

Kathy, who had watched me talking to Max came over. "We're next," she said. "You okay?"

"Yeah."

"What'd he say?"

"He was telling me about the fight last night," I said. "He's convinced Horne had nothing to do with Georgia's death."

"That's it?"

"He seems to think there's a lot more going on with AFC than I know."

"I told you." Her voice sounded like a mom's, accusing and knowing.

"I mean I knew there were problems, but I'm beginning to think it runs deeper than I thought."

What Mike had told me about Luther bounced around my head. I couldn't tell that to Kathy, but also, was that something that Max was withholding? Would he know if Luther had been seeing Georgia?

"I agree," she said. "Hardly seems like a business you should be buying."

Tony's booming voice through the bullhorn cut off any chance for me to say more.

"Team number seven, AFC." His voice carried through the morning. "You have five minutes until you start." I turned back to continue talking to Kathy, but she was gone.

I looked down at my watch and realized the five minutes he'd just given us would run out quickly. I checked the team. Clark was on his knees making last-minute checks of his backpack. Totten stood over him looking upset. I watched Totten turn and whisper something to Kay and give her a peck on the cheek.

I swung my pack onto my back and felt the tug of the weight on my back. There was nervousness inside me now that I felt the load. Would I'd be able to make it all day with it? Somewhere beneath those nerves, there was also a sense of nostalgia. The last time I carried a ruck had been in the Marines. The memories of all the training I'd done with my ruck imbued me with a small sense of confidence. I hoped it would be enough to counteract the problems I expected would come with the day. If I could survive eight weeks of boot camp and the Marine Officer Training Course I should be able to survive a three-day race.

One of the ways I made it through boot camp was by competing with others. On long forced marches, where the ruck's straps started to dig into the shoulders when the neck muscles started to strain to hold up the helmet when the arms got tired of holding the sixteen-pound weapon, and the soles of the feet turned into something that felt more like ground meat than feet, I would look up along the long line of Marines that stretched out in front and realize that that Marine at the front of the line had made it up to that curve in the road, why couldn't I? I'd force myself to get to that point where I'd seen that Marine then look up again. He'd made it to that next curve I'd think, at least do as much as he has. It would go on like that for the whole of the march, a never-ending challenge to beat that man at the front. I imagined that the other Marines did the same thing and wondered if we inspired some crazy type of mass hysteria.

I looked around and my eyes landed on Kathy's pack, on the ground waiting for her to muscle it up. She'd have it the worst out of the bunch. Totten was in fantastic shape, what he couldn't muscle through he'd complete using the anger that he held in reserve. Clark? Although new, and a bit of an unknown, he seemed strong on the run last week. He'd be fine. Not exceptional, but steady. I watched as Clark nearly stumbled as he swung his own backpack onto his shoulders and realized that no matter how bad I or Totten or Clark thought our races were going, Kathy would be worst off of us all.

As I considered all this, I heard Tony's voice through the bullhorn again. "Two minutes to start, Team seven." I looked around for Kathy but didn't see her.

Clark waddled over next to Totten, their toes right behind the starting line. Totten waved at me to join them.

Instead of walking over to them I looked back down at Kathy's backpack.

Gentry was next to me. "What's wrong?"

"Kathy's not here."

Totten, impatient now. "Let's go!"

"Where's Kathy?" Gentry yelled to him.

"Are you fucking kidding me?" Totten's voice silenced the crowd around the starting line. All of a sudden Kathy's absence had become a public affair.

"Did she know the start time?" Gentry asked me.

"I don't know." I scanned the crowd.

"Does she know when you start?" Rochester rephrased the question. It was no more helpful than having Gentry ask it.

"I guess. She was just here a few minutes ago."

Gentry ran over to Emily who was sitting on her backpack, waiting for her team to start. I heard him quiz her on the same questions. A slow shake of the head from Emily was the only answer. Rochester ran off, bustled his way through the small crowd by the hotel, and ducked inside, presumably to look for Kathy.

Tony picked that moment to saunter back over to our group. "Team seven!" his voice boomed again. "One minute to start." He checked his watch and strolled lackadaisically back toward the starting banner. He looked as though he knew we were panicking and was enjoying our problems.

"Get Emily to race with us," Totten yelled at me. His toady, Kay, was next to him. When he mentioned Emily she flinched.

"I'm not racing with you." Emily didn't even move.

"We have to have a female," Totten continued. "You come with us and it will give our team more time to find Kathy." He waved at her to come over.

"I'm not racing with you!" Emily again.

"Why don't we just switch the teams," Gentry said.

"We'll go first you guys come to start in our slot."

"Thirty seconds," Tony again.

"No!" Totten screamed. He pointed at Emily. "Get your stuff! You have to race with us." There was panic in his face.

There was anger in Kay's.

"To hell with that," Emily said. "There is no way I'm going on your team." She pointed back at him. Totten's face turned into a mass of anger and frustration. For a second I thought I should step between them.

"Let's just switch positions with the other team," Clark spoke up, his hand was on Totten's shoulder, trying to help him to accept this other option. Gentry already had his pack on and looked more than eager to start for us. "Ten seconds," Tony's voice filled the area.

"I'm here," it was Kathy's voice. She came running toward the starting line just as Tony began his count down from five.

"I can't fucking believe this!" Totten threw up his hands. "Where the hell have you been?" He turned and stomped back toward the starting line without waiting for an answer.

The starter's pistol fired. I jumped reflexively.

Tony smiled like a Cheshire cat. Totten and Clark looked back at me, their start ruined, disappointment evident. "Go!" I yelled at them.

"Hurry up!" Totten yelled as he started running down the street.

"Let's go," I said to Kathy. I picked up her pack and started jogging next to her. "We'll put this on as we run."

She ran but looked at me with a bemused look. "It will only take a few seconds."

"Just run. Totten's about to have an aneurism." I held the pack up so she could slip her arms through. She shrugged it on then tightened it across her shoulders. I helped her strap the waist belt on to stabilize it all while we ran and bumped down the road, the crowd roaring around us.

"Where the hell were you?"

"There was one last thing I wanted to do."

"What?"

"I'll tell you in a bit." She winked at me as if I should have known what she meant.

CHAPTER 35

Running that first leg was easier than I had expected. The morning air provided a slight chill and the desert sand that made up the roadbed was soft beneath our feet. Small green chem lights in the middle of the road, placed every fifty to one hundred meters marked our route. Once we were away from the lights of the town and I recovered my night vision the chem lights became easy to spot. Each neon green marker gave a goal for me to focus on, a faux finish line, just like looking up and seeing that Marine at the front of the line. I would make it to that next chem light, then I would look for the next, on and on and on it went.

The night clung to the desert as if it didn't want to leave. Off to the east, there was a thin band of dark orange that marked the coming daylight. I realized I wasn't just racing the other teams, but I was trying to beat the oncoming daylight. I looked up and saw the canyon that cuts through the park. I knew the Rio Grande River would be at the bottom. The second leg of the race would be onboard a raft as we floated down the Santa Elena canyon. If I could make it to those rocks before full light came on and caught me in the open, I'd be okay. After the rafting event? Who knew, there would be time to worry about the daylight later. Every few steps I looked to see how much larger the band of color was; the first half mile, burnt umber; now, a dull apricot.

Despite the sunrise, I found a distinct comfort in having my ruck on my back. A nostalgia for when I used to live under a ruck; that familiar bounce on my back, the secure feeling of the waist belt against my hips, the tug of the straps on my shoulders. My baggy trousers slapped my legs with each step, the flop sweat that started to flow on my forehead, each step brought back another small memory about my Corps life. Later I knew my neck and shoulders would be sore, there would be hot spots on my lower back and spine, but while running it was exhilarating.

Every few minutes I looked back and saw the still jogging form of Kathy. I had started running alongside her but she quickly told me to run ahead. She obviously wanted to focus on the run in her own way and did not want me around to influence her running. Her head was down, her legs looked strong, her pace determined. Ahead of me, only a few meters or so were Totten and Clark, still gray silhouettes coming to life and color with the brightening day. Every now and then I saw Clark turn to find me. Each time I gave him a thumbs up and a wave to keep going.

Finally, just as the eastern sky had become a peach color when the sun was on the edge of cresting the horizon, the road dipped downward and wrapped around a few mesquite covered hills along the river bank. It was not the majestic canyon walls I had hoped for, but it was some cover, better than the flat desert landscape near the town. I quickened my pace and caught up with Totten and Clark just as the road wrapped around a large hill. Below us, in the river, we saw another team, already in their rafts, floating downstream.

"Rafts." It was Clark. He was pointing down toward the river at another team already on the rafting portion.

Hearing Clark's loud voice, I almost grabbed him and told him to shut up. I caught myself before I did. We were in Big Bend, not Iraq. On patrol, nothing was said above a whisper, ever. The strength of Clark's voice made me realize how quiet everything around us had been during the run. It shattered the bit of peace I had been enjoying but also shattered the environment I had been building around myself, the one that had been slowly transporting me back to my time in combat.

He stopped to watch and I caught up. Together watched the rafters bump down the river, craning our heads, tracking them. I looked back and saw Kathy almost three hundred meters or more behind us.

"Should we wait for her?" he asked.

"No," I answered. "We'll run up ahead and get things squared away for when she gets there. It will make the transition faster."

Clark looked worried. Kathy was very far back. I knew what he was thinking. It didn't feel right leaving her back there to struggle on alone. Thoughts of the road guards I'd left on our run popped to mind. Would she be the next Georgia? Out here where there was no danger?

"You wait here," I said to him. "Help her stay motivated. Totten and I will run ahead to get things ready for the raft."

"Give us your pack," I added. "You can take hers. That should speed things up."

Totten looked irritated, but at least he wasn't arguing. We took the backpack and Clark jogged back, not the type to just wait.

Despite the increased load, I felt Totten pick up his pace. I countered and we were soon pushing one another down the road, the pack held between us like a tether.

"This is bullshit," Totten said as we ran. "There's no way we can make the top ten with her. We'll be lucky to finish."

"Way to stay positive," I said. "It's only the first event."

"What's the point?" Totten continued. "If we have no chance, why do it? We should have blown up the second team and just had one team of bad-asses. We might have won if we'd done that."

It was pointless arguing with him, he was a creature of competition. Maybe there was some thought for Kay from time to time, but if there wasn't a chance to beat someone or to beat everyone, he wouldn't want to be a part of it. I thought for a moment about Max, about hoping he could be an ally rather than an adversary. If there was no chance to beat every other team, maybe Totten could be inspired to beat just one team.

"How about we focus on just beating Horne?" I asked. He didn't answer, but I caught a flicker of enthusiasm across his face. His pace quickened and three bends later we saw dozens of large yellow rafts beached on a gravel bar with two race officials standing nearby. A quarter-mile more and the first leg would be over. We could see the team that had started ahead of us just pushing off into the river.

"If it wasn't for Kathy, we could have passed that team," Totten said.

"It's not like we had a lot of choices," I said. "I thought we were going to focus on Horne."

He grumbled some more but kept pace all the way to the rafts. We rounded the last turn and were met by bright pink ribbons stretched between trees and stakes that led us off the road and down to the river.

Without hesitating, Totten jumped down the embankment and trudged through the sand of the riverbank. I followed along behind holding the pack by myself.

The race officials came toward us and I saw Ahmed. His face lit up. "You're Team Seven right, man?" he called to me.

Ahmed was out of his conductor uniform and now wore rugged khakis, hiking boots, a bright volunteer t-shirt, and a wide-brimmed hat. He was smiling and excited.

"Who were you expecting?" I asked. "What are you doing here?"

"This is my post today, anything for a buck," Ahmed said.

I pointed at his shirt. "Your shirt says, Volunteer."

"And your ticket said Coach as I recall," he laughed loudly back at me.

"Can we hurry up?" Totten was short, but he was in race mode.

Ahmed looked down at the boat next to him. "This is your boat." He slapped it and moved out of the way.

Totten threw his gear into the raft and started to move it toward the water. "Where's the rest of your team?" It was the second race volunteer who had come forward. The opposite of Ahmed, his face was covered in doubt. "You have to race as a team."

"They're on the way," Totten barely paused or looked up as he spoke.

"The rules say all teams must navigate each obstacle as a unit."

"This is a transition right?" Totten fired back.

I heard the two of them lock horns over whether getting into boats qualified as an obstacle or a transition and I turned to speak to Ahmed.

"Have the teams gotten mixed up already?"

"Teams Two and Four both came in ahead of One and Three."

"Really?"

Ahmed nodded.

"By the way," I said. "My friend from the station, the one who smacked me. Big guy. Huge. He's behind us. Keep an eye on him for me will ya? Let me know if you see him doing anything out of the ordinary."

Ahmed nodded, "Like what?"

I leaned in as I spoke, "I don't know, just anything. I think he tried to lose one of our bikes back in Alpine. Just keep an eye out."

He gave me a thumbs-up sign and I hustled over to the raft to help Totten make the raft ready. The three backpacks were lashed down in the bottom of the raft, Totten then grabbed the paddles and placed one in each corner of the raft, two in the front, and two in the back. He got behind the raft ready to push, I moved to the front to pull it into the river and guide it in. I moved into the water and felt the chilly Rio Grande water soak my shoes and socks and move up legs.

The race volunteer yelled when he saw Totten place the raft in the water, "You can't leave without your whole team."

"Wouldn't dream of it," Totten pointed to the road where Kathy and Clark were coming down to the beach. Kathy looked winded, Clark, steadfast with Kathy's pack on his shoulders. Totten waved them on and shouted what sounded like critiques rather than words of encouragement. Neither of them stopped but rather fell into the boat, and before they were completely upright Totten and I heaved the raft into the water.

CHAPTER 36

The water moved the raft along quickly. Everything was chaos those first few seconds. Kathy struggled to find a seat, Totten barked orders that no one listened to, Clark fought to find his own position in the raft, I tried to paddle and make sense of what was going on, all the while the raft was bumped and buoyed down the river.

Just moments before, we had been jogging, everything had felt calm and steady, but now in the middle of the river, we were at the mercy of the water and the currents. Eventually though, like a cowboy allowing a bucking horse to tire beneath him we fell into a rhythm with the waves and movement until we could all manage. After those first few frantic moments of paddling, we established a pattern and settled in. Kathy, sitting to my left at the front of the raft, leaned over and asked, "How are you feeling?"

"I'm doing great actually," I said. "You?"

"My knees are blocks of concrete." She paused then continued. "I guess this means if your mind is occupied enough on workouts, the agoraphobia takes a back seat."

"Or maybe it's occupied with worries about you and the team?"

She shrugged. "Either way, it's a baby step."

Each of us sat on the gunwale of the raft, one to each corner. Kathy and I in the front, Totten, and Clark the back. Kathy held the paddle and tried to keep time, but her paddles were not as strong and I felt sure she was trying to save her strength.

Totten yelled from the back of the raft about white water in our path. The muddy brown water swirled and eddied around us as the raft traversed the center part of the river and as a group, we moved the raft around the first little obstacle. It wasn't enough for Totten who yelled that next time we need to do it better.

"Chill out Totten," I said. "We're all trying hard. Getting mad isn't going to help." I felt sure he wanted to say something in reply, but thankfully he remained quiet.

It wasn't long before we saw the next team on the road above us. They were immediately recognizable. There was the tall, broad figure of Horne and the dark, tanned skin and jet black hair of Max. I felt a jolt of heat through the pit of my stomach as I saw Horne out front.

"What's wrong?" I looked over at Kathy and wondered whether I really broadcasted my emotions so readily or if she was able to interpret me better because of the last few days. She followed my eyes and saw Horne.

"I don't like having him so close to the teams."

"We'll be fine," Kathy responded. "Besides, there's not much you can do about him now. Focus on the race."

"Sounds like something I'd say to you," I said.

"Because it's good advice." She punctuated the statement with a wink.

Things began to slow down for everyone then. The river slowed to a meander, our paddling picked up some in response. I was worried that now that the first transition was over, the first run falling further and further behind us, that my agoraphobia would return. I turned and looked around. Looking for an escape? Maybe, but it helped me stay in place because I saw for the first time, actually saw rather than just perceived, the walls of the canyon moving by smoothly.

Those walls became a focal point. The sun was still too low to crest the tops of the walls. The shadows at their base were deep and touched the water's surface. I studied the striations in the cliff walls, the different shades of gray and black that made the rocks look like they had captured the motion of the river's waves and translated that into stone. I let them close in comfortably around me and took them like a junkie being guided through a difficult trip. I realized that this might be the best place to be in all of Big Bend for someone with my condition.

I turned and saw Totten still struggling against the current, paddling hard.

"You can let up Totten," I yelled to him.

He looked back. "You're tired already?"

"No, but paddling forward isn't doing anything. Just rest a bit and we can save our strength for when we get out of the current."

"So this is your plan?" he said sarcastically. "To not paddle and let the river do all the work."

Clark chimed in. "It makes sense Dave. We'll be better rested for the other events, and really, a bit of forward paddling here and there isn't going to do as much as staying as close to the current as possible."

For a moment he looked like Totten was about to argue but again, strangely, he relented.

Kathy asked, "Shouldn't we take off our shoes, mine are getting soaked."

I avoided the sarcastic eye roll I felt sure Totten performed and said, "Keep your shoes on. You'll want them on in case you fall out." She didn't look convinced. "Don't worry about them being wet," I continued. "We'll tie them to the outside of our packs when we ride this afternoon."

"What about my socks?"

Totten heard the question and fired back. "Are you kidding me! Sock changes! What is this kindergarten?"

"Would you knock it off Totten?" I said.

"There's a lot of running, and I'd rather not do it on blisters," Kathy didn't even turn around as she spoke.

"This is fucking ridiculous." Totten again.

"No," I said, facing him. "This is a team. Get used to it."

I heard his now-familiar grumble and he went back to paddling needlessly, his frustration evident with each stroke of the paddle. Eventually, the rest of us joined him just to have something to do to break the silence and after a few minutes, one by one, Totten included, we all pulled ours paddles up and coasted with the current.

Gradually the walls of the canyon rose. I found myself concentrating on the currents and eddies near the base of the walls and thought about how to model them. Next, I studied the rock walls that overhung the banks and thought about last year when I had tried to create the same look on my layout. I realized how many details I missed.

"You're thinking about your layout aren't you?" Kathy asked.

"Yeah."

"You get a real pensive look when you do that," she said. "I still can't wait to see how we can take your modeling to a whole new level."

I turned. "You know, I probably won't be able to work with you as much if I buy Luther out."

"Why not?"

"I'm going to have to do more," I said. "I won't have as much time."

She shook her head.

"What?" I asked.

"He's not going to sell to you, Joe. He likes to string people along," she said. "Besides what I'm offering fits with your particular lifestyle. How do you think you'll be able to run AFC even if he does let you buy him out?"

"What do you think I'm doing here?" It was the same argument we'd had back on the train and I was tired of making the same points. "Sure Luther needs me to be here to watch his team, but I'm also here to try to get better," I said it all under my breath so that Clark and Totten couldn't hear.

"Despite that, all I'm saying, Joe is that things aren't always what they seem," she said. "People aren't what they seem. You know your father better than I. Do you really think he's going to go out of his way to sell the company to you?" I tried to interrupt, but she stopped me and went on. "If there's one thing I've learned in business, it's that people always have ulterior motives, especially in business deals."

"People don't always have ulterior motives," I answered not sure what other arguments to make but realizing I sounded juvenile as I said it.

"Sure they do," she said. "And you can bet that Luther's got one. He's probably counting on your agoraphobia to stop you from following through with the deal."

"I have a contract." I hated the petulant sound of my voice as it came out.

Kathy shook her head. "Contracts don't mean as much as you think, Joe."

It was the shake of the head that bothered me the most. So many people have run down Luther in front of me for so many years that it failed to bother me. It was that superior shake of the head that got me mad.

"You obviously have a larger point you want to make. What is it?" Her face hardened and her eyes sparkled as she weighed what to say. I helped her along. "I'm a big boy, Kathy. What are you trying to get at?"

"Stop trying to please your father." It came out low but I looked back to see if Totten and Clark had heard her. "The whole reason you're here is to get some sort of validation from Luther. Just about everything you do, you do try and get him to tell you 'Good job.' It's not going to happen. I've been watching you for most of your life and it's not going to happen."

I eked out a tepid, "That's not true," before Kathy went on.

"This whole life you have is designed around getting his approval," she hissed. "You're one of the best model builders in the city, probably the state. I don't even have to market you, companies hire us because of you, Joe, but you treat that aspect of your life like nothing more than a hobby. Hell, you keep some of your best stuff hidden away in your bedroom. Instead of promoting and fine-tuning that craft you've built this other world where you only go out in the dark to work with your father who refuses to acknowledge you exist. Hell, did you even want to join the Marines or was that the only way to get your daddy's approval?"

"Go to hell, Kathy." The skin around my eyes tightened against my temples as I stared back.

"I'm serious," she sped on in a hushed voice. "It's getting worse. I've been offering you a full-time job for the past six months, instead, you work for him and he keeps rolling over you. You're his lap dog and he takes advantage of your loyalty. It's what he does. Don't expect him to change just because you have some contract with him."

I didn't respond. I focused on paddling. Suddenly I felt like what I thought Totten must have felt. Not paddling for any specific reason, but just needing something to do. Doing anything to avoid Kathy and avoid having the same argument again. I guess Kathy realized she'd said too much. I expected some sort of apology but all I heard was the soft sounds of her paddling as well. Clark must have noticed he was the only one not paddling and soon I heard his paddle dip into the water with ours. The boat was quiet for a long while, the only sounds being the lapping of the water against the rubber and nylon fabric, the splash of our paddles and the occasional order barked out by Totten as he maneuvered us around obstacles.

After an hour of paddling, Totten yelled, "Given any thought to the next event?"

"All it said was 'River Crossing,'" I said.

"No, shit, but have you thought about how we're going to do that, particularly with the new girl on the team," he paused as if considering what to say next. Typical for him he let it fly. "Especially since she can't pull her weight like Kay can."

"Up yours, Totten," Kathy said.

He chuckled. "Just stating the facts."

"Despite your overwhelming support," I said. "You have a

good point."

"At least with Kay I knew that we'd be able to tackle whatever they threw at us," he said.

"I meant that we need to think about what might be coming up." Actually, I was glad he brought it up. The truth was I hadn't given the next event much thought. I had been more concerned with starting the race than I had been with planning for each event, succumbed to my own bit of tunnel vision.

"We need to start thinking about it," Totten said again.

"It's obviously coming up." I looked back at him and saw him gesturing toward the top of the canyon walls.

I followed his finger and saw a couple of people looking down. From so far away they looked like little more than silhouettes, or a little head peeking over the lip of the wall. I realized that I hadn't looked up once throughout the entire float. At any point, someone could have been up there looking down at us. A sense of panic flew through me as I realized how easy it would be for someone to hide up there and pick us off. Then, just as on the run, I remembered that this was not combat, and although Horne was a potential danger, he was far behind us on his own raft, unable to cause any harm from that avenue. Despite the reassuring thought, I reminded myself to be more cautious, to think outside the box and to try to think more tactically.

We swung around another sweeping bend and we saw several more people looking down. The onlookers were getting denser with each passing bend we took downriver.

"It's gotta be coming up. We need some sort of plan." Totten again.

The growing number of spectators had to mean he was right, but without knowing more than the title of the obstacle it was difficult to know what to do.

Everyone was looking at me. It was as if they expected some sort of holy writ to be passed onto them from a higher being through me and whatever plan I could dream up. Nothing came. Then I saw the look of resignation that so often settled in Totten's eyes simmer up. He turned toward Clark for advice. I thought back through training, troop leading procedures that I had been drilled on but had forgotten as soon as made it out of the Marines. The only thing that came to me was the motto we used for entering buildings as a team.

"Slow is smooth, smooth is fast," I said quickly, mostly in an effort to keep Totten's attention. It worked, but he looked at me expecting more. The look of resignation turned to disdain as if I had just said a nursery rhyme.

"What's that mean?" Clark asked.

"Transitions are key," I said. "Whenever I ran triathlons the smart racers were the ones who made the best use of transitions. We can make up more time in transitions than we could ever hope to make up during the actual events. As long as we handle the transitions well, we can eat up time where other teams might be goofing off."

"So?" Totten asked.

"So, this obstacle is probably one long transition. We most likely get our road bikes after. We do it just like the last one. Divide and conquer. Totten and I will manage the packs, Clark and Kathy run ahead to scout and come up with a plan then help the others through as much of the obstacle as possible. But don't speed through it. Move with a purpose, but don't rush and make mistakes."

"I like it," Kathy said.

"It won't take two of us to come up with the plan and guide the others, I can do it myself," Totten said. "Better to have three help with the packs."

"It would be better if the three strongest helped with the packs," Kathy countered.

"And how many river crossings have you done?" he asked her.

"Knock it off," I said. "I probably have the most experience, but still we will play it by ear. If it's a long transition, just come back and help, if not stick to what we go."

Kathy gave me a sidelong, questioning glance, the same look I had gotten around the campfire the night before. Despite Kathy's problems with Totten, I just didn't want him around. In Dallas, his attitude was problematic and difficult but was gone when the group went home. Out here, around him for twenty- four hours it was as much a burden as the race itself.

Kathy leaned over and spoke lowly. "I’m a little worried about this next one," she said. "This is going to be way over my head."

I looked up and saw more and more people, dozens now, looking down at us from the lip of the canyon walls.

"Don’t worry, it can’t be too hard. What's the worst they can do?"

CHAPTER 37

Wilson's death impacted me not because of the loss of one of my Marines, nor due to the acknowledgment that a young life had been snuffed out in a foreign land, not even because of the blood and flesh that hit me in the side of my face. It wasn't till I turned to snatch up the hand-held receiver and saw that the RPG that had killed him had also sliced the mic cord in two that I truly felt his loss. It was a disjoint and coldly impassionate way to see his death, but with a group of enemy forces shooting and out of contact with both parts of my platoon, as I scrambled on the ground to pull pieces of the radio together, it was all that came to my mind.

When that second technical showed up, Wilson let loose with several rounds at its grill. The windshield became a spider web of cracks and by the time I turned my weapon on it the little, dust-colored truck was stopped and the men were diving out.

Together we fired at the men. When he stopped firing to reload, I picked up his slack and redoubled my own shooting. We were outnumbered, but we were determined to not be outgunned. The way to win any engagement, be it small arms ambush or the D-day landing is to overwhelm the enemy with fire. I had reloaded two times and the fight was less than two minutes old. I had fired over sixty rounds in that short space of time. Wilson had several empty magazines on the ground near him. That meant that the two of us had fired over one hundred rounds at the three enemy soldiers downrange.

I looked over at Wilson. His mouth was moving, but I heard

nothing. He was yelling at me but my ears were ringing so loudly I couldn't hear what he was saying. It looked like he was saying "flank." He pointed behind me and I realized he must have seen someone running to get up on our right. I pivoted to check our flank. As I did, I saw his head fly back unnaturally out of the corner of my eye.

We've had several KIA's in our platoon. All of them came as a result of IEDs. We were able to find identifiable body parts for only one of those Marines. The other two had been obliterated. Each time I'd been surprised by the size of the explosion and the damage it caused. What happened to Wilson was far more shocking and left me stunned and on my back due to the concussion. It was only later that I realized it was an RPG round, a rocket-propelled grenade.

Six pounds of explosives hit Wilson's in the neck going over one hundred miles an hour. It blew apart the top quarter of his body. Wilson's chest, his right arm, his back and shoulder all seemed to vaporize in front of me. I felt the spray of blood across my face and hands as well as the sting of sand and dirt and rocks pelting me as I fell back.

I may have blacked out. It seemed like I lost some time, seconds maybe, but when I started to move I was working on autopilot. I fired a few rounds over the berm just to let anyone there know I was still there. Next, I pulled what was left of Wilson down further into the wadi to a more defensible position. His rucksack with the radio dragged was still up by the berm. I ran back to get it and then dragged it along.

I shot some more, trying to aim as best I could at suspected enemy positions, but really it was just nuisance shooting, just shooting down range to make them think twice about assaulting my position too quickly. I stopped once I had Wilson's body and myself behind a larger berm. The ringing faded and eventually, I started to hear the pops and zings of the enemy's bullets flying overhead.

I looked down at Wilson's ruck. Lamb and Marlberg would have heard the shooting by now. They needed an update. That was when I saw the severed cord to the radio. That was when I felt Wilson's loss the most.

All RTO's pack a spare mic at the bottom of their rucks. Had Wilson been there he could have gotten it, replaced the damaged one, then gotten Lamb or Marlberg on the line. With the technical's machine gun spraying rounds at my little hasty fighting position, and the enemy maneuvering to get to my flank, the spare receiver was as inaccessible to me as the moon.

To buy myself some time, I snagged a fresh frag grenade from Wilson's ruck, pulled the pin, saw with some satisfaction the handle flip up and away, and hurled it over my head toward where I thought the technical might be. The resulting explosion gave me a momentary morale lift. I hunkered down to figure out my next move. Still, I realized that my situation had gone from worse to fucked up. along with communications, I had just lost any chance for fire superiority.

CHAPTER 38

The obstacle came into view slowly as we rounded the next bend. First, the only thing we could see was a large steel tower anchored to the far side of the canyon. There was a thick black rope that sprouted from the top of the tower and spread out in two directions, one downriver, and one upriver. As we came further around the bend and followed the rope's path with our eyes, the extent of the obstacle became evident.

"I don't get it," Kathy said. "We have to climb those towers?"

"Climb em then crawl across those ropes," I said.

"I can't do that!" Kathy's voice sounded as upset as it had the night before when she'd been trapped into racing.

"It won't be that hard," I tried. As I said it, I knew that it was harder than I had expected. What had I expected? A cable bridge? A floating pontoon bridge? Crawling across two lengths of ropes, first to the far side of the river then back again was definitely more than I had expected. For me, it seemed challenging, for Kathy it must have seemed impossible.

Totten spoke up from the back and said, "Paddle that way." He pointed toward the near side shore where we saw several other rafts and a few race volunteers waving us in.

It went just like we planned. Totten was out of the boat and sprinting as soon as we touched the beach. Kathy looked nervous but followed on behind him. By the time she reached the first race volunteer Clark and I were already dragging the raft further up onto the sand bar and were beginning to unleash the rucksacks. After all of Totten's backbiting and vitriol, it was invigorating to see everyone work together. It was as if we were all part of a vicious circle, each of us feeding off the others.

"Just take a pack and go," I told Clark as I unleashed the packs. "Don't worry about whether or not it's yours." I grabbed two for myself and took off up the beach toward Totten and Kathy.

Totten was deep in conversation with the race volunteer, his eyes darting to the tower and the cables, pointing this way and that as he questioned him. The volunteer handed him one of the large green duffel bags that stood at his feet then Totten looked back toward us. He gave a wave to hurry us along and took off for the first tower. Kathy waited till we caught up then took a handle of one of the bags to share the load with Clark. We chugged along after him as fast as we could with our packs on our back.

"It's exactly what we thought," Kathy said. "Totten has run ahead to get things started."

We looked up again and we saw him standing at the base of the tower pulling on a climbing harness.

"We need our climbing harnesses, two carabineers for each person and we need to put on our bike helmets." He dived for his backpack and began rummaging through it. We all did likewise. I had strapped my helmet to the outside of my ruck so it came off with a snap.

"What kind of plan is this?" Clark asked. He had a good point. The race volunteer was standing next to the tower with a clipboard watching us suspiciously.

"Just put on the damn harness and listen," Totten said.

I shook my head. Even when I tried to get him away from the group, his antagonism prevailed.

"Just sketch it all out for us, Totten," I said.

Totten pointed to the tower. "Joe goes first. I'll help everyone get rigged up on the rope on this tower, Joe can do the same on the far side. Clark, you go next and get to the third tower first. Then help everyone down." He said it as if it was the simplest thing in the world and we were silly for not having deduced it by ourselves. "That a good enough plan?"

Kathy rolled her eyes.

"Any special rules we need to know?" I asked.

"We have to stay secured to the rope the whole time."

"That's it?" I asked. Totten nodded.

I looked up and considered. "Don't try to do it with your pack on your back," I said. "Secure it to the cable with some extra carabiners. Tie it to your waist with a rope and just pull it along like a trailer." I spoke as I put on my harness.

"Good point," Totten said. "I'll make sure it's rigged that way. Hurry and get going."

"It will be faster if Kathy only has to climb by herself if someone else takes and pulls her pack."

"I'll take care of it," Totten said again.

Kathy looked nervous to the point of tears, "Pull hand over hand and keep your legs over the cable the whole time. You'll get way too tired if you try and do it like monkey bars. Watch me then do it how I do it. You'll be fine." I leaned in and shook her shoulder for comfort. "It's safe. Just hard. Watch me and go as quick as you can."

I threw my backpack over my shoulders and looked at the little ladder that snaked up the steel tower. Next to me, I heard Kathy moan. She was looking at her climbing harness like a three-year-old would consider a car engine, complete befuddlement. She held it upside down and couldn't figure out which loops were for her legs.

"I don't know if this is going to work," she said.

"Try doing it while keeping your agoraphobia in check," I whispered and forced a smile. "You'll be fine. Just trust your equipment and trust your buddy."

Totten saw me stopping to help Kathy and said, "I'll take care of her, you get to the other side."

I nodded and turned to mount the tower. The excitement of this transition was the same as at the rafts. I didn't even have time to think about Totten, Horne, my problems, or anything. I just enjoyed the opportunity of tackling the obstacle, focusing on the problem and the solution and working as a part of a team. It was invigorating and freeing at the same time; a completely different comfort from the one afforded by the cramped confines of the tent or of the train cabin. It was refreshing, new and out of the ordinary. I was energized on my hand-over-hand, ladder climb up the tower so that I hardly thought, but instead just performed.

A distinct sway rocked me as I stood at the top of the fifty-foot tall tower. The river, fifty feet below, looked so different. In the raft it seemed placid and harmless, now it looked torrential. I looked along the rope. It was probably eleven-millimeter climbing rope, braided and dynamic, which meant it was strong but that it would lengthen underweight. Despite knowing it would easily hold me, all my weight, and probably the rest of the team all at the same time without failing it looked as though it would snap under the weight of a sparrow.

I took a deep breath, slung my rucksack onto the wire and clicked onto the rope with a climbing carabiner. I took another carabiner and fastened it to my climbing harness and then to the rope. Finally, I latched the ruck to my harness so I could tow it along. I looked up at where I would be going. For a moment I froze as I looked out across the muddy brown water that flowed by. I was now a part of the rope. If it snapped or broke, down I'd go. I felt the rope pull violently in my hands as the wind through the canyon hit it.

"In, one, two, three, four." I thought to myself. "Hold, one, two, three, four."

"Let go of the tower, you should glide out to the middle, then just hand over hand the rest of the way." I looked down. Totten was just coming up onto the platform where I stood.

"Yep," I said. "Just getting psyched up."

"Fuck that, just go!" Totten gave me a hard shove and I went down.

CHAPTER 39

I felt my stomach sink as I slid down the rope. It was not a smooth ride. The steel carbineer and the nylon rope strands rubbed against each other and felt like two pieces of sandpaper scratching against one another the whole of the ride down. There was a loud sigh of relief when I came to a stop about thirty feet above the surface of the river. I was at the nadir of the first leg, my weight pulling the rope down.

I grabbed hold of the rope and lifted my legs on top. I was suspended upside down but was able to pull myself toward the far tower using my hands and feet, like a spider crawling up a web. Pulling my own weight plus the rucksack was easier than I had expected and the climb was over much sooner than I expected. It wasn't until I was on the far side of the river, in Mexico, that I realized how fast my heart was beating, how tingly my skin felt, and how much adrenaline had helped me with the climb.

This second tower was a twin of the first, just a few feet shorter. I braced myself on the platform at the top of the second tower and snapped my rucksack to it. By the time I was set and looked back at Totten still on the far tower, helping Clark. Kathy was about to start the long climb up the ladder. As I watched Clark let go of the tower and zipped down the rope toward the river, his own pack trailing behind him.

I looked over at the final tower, the end of the obstacle and saw the team in front of us on the far side of the river. Their last team member was just climbing off the final tower. The whole team was waiting for her. Behind them, I saw a trail that led up the canyon to the next event, the bike ride. That final tower was just a few feet off the ground. No wonder the hand-over-hand climb had seemed easy, the obstacle was downhill most the way.

I looked back at Clark and saw that he was hand-over-hand climbing up the rope as I had. Only a few more feet to go. When he was close enough, I pulled him onto the platform with me.

"That wasn't too hard." He said with a loud sigh of relief.

"Nope." I unclipped his backpack and re-clipped it to the next rope. "And you only have to do it one more time."

I let him transfer the carabiner that was attached to his harness from the first rope to the second then gently pushed him off the tower. He slid down with lots of jerks and stutters, but quickly.

I wondered if any of the other teams had tried to do this without using a carabiner for their packs. It was much easier to pull a suspended backpack than to have to climb with the weight still on the back. Is that what the team in front of us had tried? Had they all tried to go at the same time? That too would have made the climb harder.

I looked back at the first tower and saw Kathy almost to the top level of the tower. A moment of doubt clouded my mind. What if Kathy was right? What if it wasn't Horne who'd murdered Bridget and Georgia? What if it had been Totten?

All it would take would be for him to push her off the tower, miss-rig her carabiner, heck he'd just have to step on her fingers as she climbed. If she fell and died, he'd have committed another murder, if not, he could claim it was just an accident. I watched her intently and felt a deep pang of regret about the entire plan. Why had I let Totten come up with this plan? It left Kathy completely exposed. I should have been more focused. I remembered the embarrassment I felt at not seeing the onlookers on the tops of the cliffs.

I looked up again and saw them all there, standing, watching, a few yelling words of support that no one could hear because of the river noise. I'd forgotten about them again. He wouldn't do anything to Kathy with so many people watching, would he?

As I stood, one hand holding the rope, feeling the vibration as the wind kicked into it, feeling the movement as Totten moved about on his own side of the river, maybe even feeling the vibration of Kathy's climbing up the ladder transferred through the steel of the ladder, through the tower, to the cable, I wondered what I would do if he did something. Would they cancel the race? Would Totten be exposed? Would anyone believe me if I tried to tell them he'd hurt her intentionally? But Totten couldn't have killed Georgia I reminded myself. He was with me most of the time on that run last Monday. If anyone had a good alibi, it was Totten. Despite this though, a report to Luther composed itself in my head as I watched them on the tower; Started with two full teams, lost one on the river crossing, Kathy, so no loss of revenues.

It wasn't until Kathy was clipped to the rope and sliding down toward the river that I realized I had been holding my breath. I reached for her gratefully as she came to the far side, extending out perhaps too far to help her get up those last few feet. She was huffing and puffing as I pulled her onto the tower platform and rigged her onto the next rope.

"How am I doing?" Kathy asked, she grabbed hold of my arm with her hand, and inched her body up right next to mine to support herself on the small platform.

"You're doing great." I grabbed her and pulled her close to me, her chest against mine, her legs intertwined in mind on the small platform.

"Don't get any ideas," she said laughingly.

"Lots of ideas," I said. "Seriously, keep it up. You're doing fine."

She paused, her face just inches from mine. "What's wrong?"

"Nothing," I said. "Why?"

"You seem tense like maybe this is too close." She pressed up even closer.

"I thought you said not to get any ideas."

She patted my ass and gave me a wink. "Seriously, what's wrong? Your agoraphobia kicking in?"

"No, it's not that. It's nothing," I said. "I just got worried seeing you climbing that ladder with Totten above you."

"I was too," she said. "But, I guess he passed the test." Her eyes were bright, both with nerves and excitement at being in the race.

I looked at her as she was about to let go. "What test?"

"That was the perfect chance, if he had wanted someone else dead, that would have been the time. Just four little Indians left." She moved closer and gave me a big kiss on the lips.

"How's that for an idea?" she said. She let go of the tower and fell away down the rope toward the third tower and Clark.

My mind swirled after that kiss and didn't settle until Totten showed up. His transition was quick, and to share the load I took over pulling Kathy's pack along the final rope crawl. I was the last to make it back over to the United States. Kathy was at the base of the tower with Totten when I got there. Totten was helping her take off the harness. He grabbed her pack from me and started to settle it on her shoulders. I looked at the canyon wall behind them and saw the path I'd seen the other team take, switch-backing and snaking its way up.

"Did Clark go on?"

Kathy looked up, "Yeah, he went to go, scout, the next event and try to speed us through that transition as well.

My own harness fell away onto the sand at our feet. A race volunteer came over and started to collect our gear. "Ya'll were the fastest team yet," he said.

"We plan to keep it that way," Totten yelled as he started to run up the path.

Kathy looked at me as if wondering what to do, I motioned to the path. She started jogging the way Totten had gone, I gathered my pack and followed close behind her. When I fell into pace next to her, she looked back.

"You don't want to keep up with Totten?" she asked. "No, I'll keep you company for a bit," I said. "Find out what you meant about four Indians."

"Oh, that was nothing," she said. "I was referencing a book."

"I know that," I said. "But who are the Indians besides Horne and Totten?"

"The way I figure it, it has to be someone who was sleeping around with Georgia," she said. "That leaves Totten, Max, Horne and either Rochester or Gentry."

"How the hell do you come up with that?" I asked.

"Bates." Her voice was matter of fact.

"What's Bates know?"

"That's why I was late for the start, I was talking to him," she said. "I almost had him admitting who else had messed around with Georgia when Rochester found me."

"Totten was with me most of the run when Georgia was murdered," I told her. "He couldn't have done it."

"Good point," she said. "We didn't think of that. But according to Bates, he did have a fling with Georgia."

"Totten? Are you shitting me? Does Kay know that?"

"Are they even an item?"

"I don't know," I said. "It's weird isn't it?"

"Like everything else with this group."

"I'm pretty sure Horne's the guy," I said. " The fact that he was pissed at Georgia, plus he wants to see AFC go under."

She gave me a glare as we climbed and trudged up the path. "That's just your father's paranoia."

"It's the only thing that explains both Georgia and Bridget?"

She paused as we had to navigate a tricky part of the trail. "I'm still trying to figure that connection out. Bates told me all about that."

"Thanks for that by the way," I said. "Your little tête-à-tête with Bates drove Totten bonkers."

This got her attention. "Really?"

"Yeah, he tried to get Emily to switch teams since you weren't there."

"Oh, I bet that made her happy."

"Fit to be tied," I said. "Literally. Totten was yelling at her to get up and join them. Gentry wanted to have the entire teams switch places which only made Totten madder."

"What a jerk off. Probably pissed that his precious Kay wasn't with him." We paused to navigate a boulder. She went on, "I'll grill Bates tonight. He's itching to tell me some more. Only a matter of time. At heart, he's a true gossip. If I had some wine and a couple of hours, it'd be a cinch."

She stopped because we crested the canyon wall and looked out over the expanse of the Big Bend Park spread out like a flat tabletop in front of us. I stopped as soon as I saw it. The sun was up, blindingly intense compared to the light down in the canyon where the walls had offered shade. Kathy paused and looked around when she saw that I had stopped.

She jogged back a few steps.

"The agoraphobia?" she asked. "You're not grinding your teeth."

I shook my head. "I'm fine."

I had expected this moment. I had expected shock, fear, problems, the whole gamut of problems. Why weren't they coming? Had I progressed so much already? Was it Kathy?

Clark came running up with Totten right beside him.

"We need to make a decision," Totten said. He already had his bike helmet on and I saw his and Clark's backpacks were lashed to their bikes behind them. Further on, organized by team, with onlookers crowded round and held back by flagging, there were all the road bikes that had traveled with us on the train, all neatly parked in bike racks made of white, plastic PVC pipes, completely idiosyncratic and out of place in the desert environment. Behind the bikes I saw Michael, waving frantically, with Cheryl and Kay next to him. He was pointing at our bikes and cheering us on. We ran to our bikes as Totten briefed us on the problem.

"There are two ways to go," he said. "Two roads. One is flat and asphalt, but it goes that way," he pointed behind me, away from the up thrusting Chisos Mountain basin that reared up out of the desert just a few miles away. "The other is bumpier, a gravel road, but it heads directly for the basin." He pointed the other way.

"We should take the smoother road," Clark said as he helped Kathy rig her gear.

"We know that that's our campsite tonight," Totten pointed at the mountains again. "It said we're camping in the Basin. We should take the more direct route."

I finished with my ruck and strapped on my helmet as Kathy said, "I vote for smooth."

Totten turned to look at me. "You're in charge," he said. "You make the decision. We go that way we go away from where we're supposed to go. Simply put... We go that way," he pointed again at the mountains, "we get there sooner."

I heard Kathy start to argue, saw her lips moving and could hear her speaking, but I had no idea what she said. Her words weren't resonating; they tumbled toward me and seemed to bounce off before my mind could process them. My eyes lost focus, and instead of seeing her, or the bikes, or the crowds, all I could see was the long, seemingly infinite desert around us. It opened up beyond us in a bleak vista of emptiness. I struggled to move but my feet remained planted into the ground. I willed my eyes to close, to shut out the desert, but my eyelids refused to respond.

This was what I had expected at the crest of the canyon wall. Why the delayed reaction? I felt the tunnel vision coming, but this time it was worse. This time fear was creeping in with it. Fear for the ride, fear that there was no way I would be able to complete this race, fear that a secret that I had kept for so long from my friends would now be exposed and laid bare to them all. It would all be out there but something much worse would follow; ridicule, sympathy, pity.

As if someone else said it, I heard my own voice say, "No, we go the long way."

Silence followed; then the world went black around me.

CHAPTER 40

My mind caught up with my body astride my road bike. I was on the side of the black asphalt road, the rest of my team in front of me, already dismounted, water bottles in hand, ready to use the water coolers on the folding tables that were manned by several race volunteers. A water stop. In front of us were the Chisos Mountains, much closer now, somewhere inside of them was tonight's campgrounds. I looked behind me and could see the lip of the canyon far off in the distance. All around us the terrain was flat, slowly rolling hills all around us.

Totten and Clark threw me strange looks as they tilted their water bottles back. How far had I gone on autopilot? What had happened in-between? I had only blacked out like that one other time that I could remember. It wasn't a good feeling coming back and wondering what happened. Totten and Clark had to know that something was wrong.

"In, one, two, three, four." I thought to myself. "Out, one, two, three, four."

As we left that water break, Kathy was next to me, quietly coaching, motivating, helping me move forward. Her tone, her words, it made me think she had been doing it for a long time now. I didn't really need her there, not anymore. The horizon, the openness, it didn't bother me. I would remember this section of the ride, but why? What was different now? Had the effects of that initial shock of agoraphobia worn off? Did it have something to do with the delayed reaction? It was as if the tide had receded and taken my worries and fears away with it.

I didn't remember changing my shoes or rigging my pack to the bike. I didn't remember starting out. Two hours missing from my memory. It wasn't till later that Kathy told me that I'd acted like a zombie. Instead of these memories, there was nothing. As if my mind had skipped over a damaged area in my memory banks and kept playing out my life on the next useable line.

"You're looking better," Kathy said as she peddled next to me. "Has it passed?"

It felt odd that the motivational outpouring had switched directions. On the run-up and while paddling the raft it had been from me to her, now we were back to where we were at the train station. I felt like I was stuck in a vicious circle, one step forward two steps back.

I looked over at her as we got back on the bikes and started to peddle. "I think so. It just kinda overwhelmed me. Did they notice?"

"Yeah," she said. "I told them you drank too much last night."

"What?" I said. "Now, what are they going to think?"

"Would you rather that they think you're psychotic?" She said psychotic with a smile and almost laughed as she saw my reaction. I was forced to return her smile despite myself.

"Next time tell them that it was a bit of heat exhaustion. That I just needed some fluids."

Totten yelled back at us. "Come on, guys, we need to form a paceline and pick it up. We can still pass that other team."

Kathy saw my confusion. "We saw another team at the water break when we rode up," she said. "Totten didn't want to stop. He wanted to keep riding and pass them, but Clark and I needed a couple of minutes. We won out."

Looking ahead of us I saw another team, way off in front of us. The road we were riding was smooth with just a few splits, cracks and seams. Way off to our left was a long, low, range of mountains. To our right was nothing but open desert. The road dipped gently and meandered left and right as we moved inexorably toward the Basin, the central point in the park.

Before joining the Marines I had raced in a few bike races. I hated them. Bike races are long and dreary. It was impossible to talk to anyone in a paceline. Kathy for her part was pouring sweat, her face a mass of perspiration that fell off her nose. Her clothes were wet, and the few strands of blonde hair that I could see beneath her helmet were dark and clung to her neck. Clark was silent and steady, but I could see a shudder in his knees with each rotation of the pedals. Totten who sported a far superior bicycle rode as if made for it. His bike had fairings on the wheels that made them look like they were made of solid plastic. He also had molded handlebars and a helmet that swooped back over his neck to help the wind flow over his back.

My bike, well Michael's bike, was old and bulky. Every other turn of the crank it let out a grinding noise that made me wonder if this might not be the last mile it could make. It would have been more fun without our damn packs strapped to the bikes. These bikes were road bikes, they weren't made for packs too. Most of the bikes had flat, bike racks, strapped over the back wheel where we had strapped or packs. It made each crank of the pedals harder to have that little bit of extra weight.

We peddled on, through the desert, my mind calm and at peace. I focused on the team in front of us, and with each passing minute, they seemed to grow closer and closer.

Finally, just as I thought my bike might crumble, and my legs were wearing out we began the long slow incline to the Chisos Mountain Basin. Where the road turned and we saw a steep change in incline as the road moved from the flat desert to the mountain base, were several white vehicles. As we pedaled, we saw they were vans. Another water stop? This looked different. That's when I saw several bikes all staged behind the vans. This was the end of the ride. The team in front of us was wavering as they pulled over to the vans.

"Transition coming up," Totten said breathing heavily.

"How are you two doing?" I asked.

"Fine." Clark forced a smile and added a thumbs-up sign.

Kathy turned to look at me and croaked out a tired sounding, "Exhausted."

The vans closer now, I pedaled up next to Totten. Naturally, he took this as a challenge and sped up. We pedaled quickly and outdistanced the other two in no time. They knew what we were doing, scouting the transition. I felt sure they would appreciate not needing to talk or think any more than they had to at that moment. Ahead, Totten and I could make out the team in front transitioning to the next event, another run. Even if Totten and I picked up the pace, left Clark and Kathy even further behind, we couldn't pass that team before the run.

I heard Totten sigh in frustration.

"What's this next event? Just a run?" I asked Totten.

"It's up the Basin Road," he said. "Lots of elevation changes."

I was thinking of asking him if he thought we'd be able to pass them on the run, but I could hear from his tone that he wasn't confident. He squinted ahead and almost yelled as he caught sight of something.

"It's Horne's team!" he yelled.

I looked ahead and saw that he was right. There, running away from the transition with a dark-headed companion that even from a distance was easy to tell was Max, right next to the tall, broad figure of Horne.

"How the hell did they get in front of us?"

"They must have taken the other route." Totten's voice was a growl and his legs churned into the pedals forcing his bike ahead even faster.

I worked to keep up with him. "When we get to the transition, let's redistribute some weight from Kathy's ruck," I said. "We can still pass him."

I saw a glimmer of avarice or was it revenge, glaze his eyes.

The transition was even smoother than the others. By the

time Kathy and Clark arrived, Horne's team was already out of sight, swallowed up on the road behind a switchback in the road. Before she was even off her bike, Totten ran to Kathy and started to unstrap her backpack for her.

"I'll take the load first," he said. "We'll switch off."

Kathy looked confused. "We're redistributing your load," I said. "We want to try to beat that team up there. It's Horne's team."

"Screw that," she said and held tight to the straps of her backpack so he couldn't take it. "I'll pack my own stuff, thanks."

"It will be faster if I take it!" Totten complained.

"Yell all you want, I'm taking it."

"Then you better keep up!" He started to trot up the road.

Kathy shook her head and sat down heavily. "My shoes are still wet," Kathy's voice was slow and weary. Clark took off as soon as he had both shoes on and his backpack in place. Kathy kept working on her own. It was agonizing to watch her and know that the rest of the team and Horne were moving further and further away.

"Your shoes will dry." I could understand her feelings. Anyone who hadn't trained for the race would have found today's events a killer. I felt like taking a long slow seat on the ground too. The only thing that kept me from doing it was that I hoped by standing I could encourage Kathy to hurry. I imagined she was just shy of quitting and we still weren't through with the first day.

Finally, with a heavy sigh and a withering look at me, she stood. Agonizingly slowly we took off after the rest of our team. Clark, up ahead, was just rounding the corner of the first switchback, Totten was already out of sight. Just a few hundred meters into the run and we were in danger of dividing the team.

After just a half-mile were engulfed by the high, rocky slopes of the Chisos Mountains around us. It felt as though we were back in the canyon, but instead of the river beneath us, we were running on an asphalt road and the rocks around towered around us. The rocks, the boulders, the rising mountains, they all provided some small degree of comfort but I felt as if the openness of the ride had dried out the sprout of fear that constantly grew inside me. Being back in the shadows of the mountains, closed in, back in a comfortable environment, kept that fear in even greater check. A realization that my own personal finish line, the one that led to a more normal life, taking over for Luther, finding a future outside the Marines that didn't include hiding in my apartment, could be within reach; it was all just on the verge of my taking it.

Together Kathy and I chugged up the route as quickly as she could. When we rounded the switchback we saw Clark still running, Totten was at the top of the road, several hundred meters away, waiting anxiously, at the bend to the next switchback.

"We need to pick it up," he yelled down at us.

CHAPTER 41

I suppose the only way to describe the emotion I felt when I heard my Marines open fire was pride mixed with fear. Like the thrill that comes with the first time driving a car, a pleasure at finally being in traffic, mixed with a gnawing fear that something could go drastically wrong. I knew it was Johnson and my Marines. The shots came from the direction where we'd left them, the number of weapons I heard come online, the rate of fire, the caliber of weapons, it all screamed that my platoon was in action. Pride lifted my heart when I heard it. Then I heard return fire from several large machine guns. More gun trucks must have been brought in from the village probably when Wilson and I had been discovered.

First, there were the distinct pops of M-4's, the small caliber rounds and the quick staccato cracks, then faster burps of the M-4's machine gun big brother the SAW also came up. When I first heard the large, more resonant sounds of the grenade launchers go off, I jumped up to go fight alongside my Marines. I dropped back to the ground as a hail of bullets from the men in front of me, the dog hunters, saw me and took shots.

I scrambled back into the hollow where Wilson's body lay with more rounds pinging the ground around me. I grunted and cursed loudly as the rounds reverberated and the dirt flew in my face, so close that the tiny snaps of their passing sounded like thunderclaps.

My Marines kept up the fight without me. The enemy in Iraq, although illusory, had not on the whole been admirable. They were quick to turn and run when outnumbered, their firing was hard to pinpoint and usually off-target, their discipline non-existent. There were probably only a couple of men in front of me. In truth, the fact that they were still there, still fighting, they were the first to impress me for their tenacity. I was surprised that they hadn't immediately peeled off to help their buddies.

Carefully I looked up and saw a flash of movement in the trees, perhaps one was running over to see what was happening. I peered up higher and was welcomed by more fire from the truck, shots from my flank, and more cursing that I couldn't keep in. Just my luck to have run into the only two mission-oriented enemies in the area.

Keeping my weapon up, I twisted so I could speak into the Motorola.

"Bravo, one-two. Bravo, one-two. This is Bravo, one-zero. How copy over?" I pressed my ringing ear directly against the speaker but was rewarded with nothing but static.

I tried again.

"Bravo, one-two. Bravo, one-two. This is Bravo, one-zero. How copy over?"

Nothing from the radio, but from their direction I heard my platoon increase their rate of fire.

A fusillade from the guys in front of me followed. The ping and crack of rounds were closer this time, so close that I was forced to scrunch down even more.

I cursed some more.

An RPG flew down and impacted a few meters from the front of my position. Shrapnel and clods of dirt rained down.

Panicked I yelled into the radio. "Bravo, one-two. Bravo, one-two. This is Bravo, one-zero. Can you hear me?"

Silence from the radio, consistent shooting in the distance.

It was that uptick of fighting for my men that inspired me to move out no matter what. If they were in trouble, in a firefight as large as that one sounded, I needed to be there.

I got up determined not to turn back. That determination offered no protection against enemy rounds. Their shots forced me to scramble back into my hole.

I scrunched down next to Wilson's mangled body and tried to develop a plan. The rounds from and at my Marines continued to punctuate the area to my front and made planning frustratingly tough.

"Bravo, one-two. Bravo, one, two. This is Bravo, one, zero. How copy over?"

Nothing.

I no longer had much hope I'd hear a reply, but I hoped they were moving toward me. Maybe their arrival would distract my guards, drive them off, something... anything,...so I could move.

I looked at the radio again, the idea of finding the spare headset creeping back in. My hopes faded quickly. That last RPG had completely destroyed the radio. That meant that Lamb and Marlberg were out. I had no way of getting in contact with them now.

A dash toward the platoon was also out. The two tenacious fellows in front of me were making sure that wasn't an option.

There weren't many other choices left to me. I looked over and saw Wilson's body. I should at least try to move him out of the line of fire.

More shooting, more dirt, more debris, more rounds, another RPG. The desert shook around me as the enemy tried to force me out of my hole. Wilson's body jerked as several rounds impacted. The shelling lasted for what seemed like several hours but had to only be a few minutes of sustained fire. They had to have used several magazines each.

It wasn't until the bullets stopped that I heard someone yelling. Whoever is yelling should really stop, my mind thought.

I realized a second later that it was me. I was yelling and didn't realize it, yelling in frustration, as much as fear. I tried to crawl out of the foxhole and was driven back again.

I grabbed the Motorola again and tried for Johnson. I shouted into the microphone. Still nothing.

I looked over the lip of the berm. I saw movement and fired off some more shots. I had to keep them back.

More rounds followed and instinctively I burrowed down further into my make-shift fighting position. Pieces of Wilson's corpse flew off of him as the next RPG hit. I lost consciousness when that round landed. Had to be no more than a few seconds that I was out because when I came to they were still firing. I got up to try and run and had to dive back down for cover.

In the distance, I heard my platoon fighting on. It took everything in me to not get up and try to run to them again.

Was I running to them to help or just to get out of the ambush I was in? Another blast from an RPG and I was out again.

CHAPTER 42

"Screw him," it was Kathy speaking under her breath.

"We're going as fast as we can," I yelled back up the road.

Eyes wild, Totten pointed up the road, around the switchback. "They're right up there!" His eyes were locked on mine. The truce we had established during the day was in danger of falling apart and we still had another full day of racing tomorrow.

"I can't go any faster, Totten!" Kathy's voice sounded like she was spitting out a rotting bite of fruit.

"Take some of her weight, Joe," Totten yelled back. "We can probably divide up her whole load between the three of us. She's too weak."

Kathy looked up, daggers flew across the thirty meters that separated them. I've dealt with Kathy on enough of my projects to know how she can dig in her heels. Mules would seem pliable compared to a determined Kathy. I saw that look of determination in her eyes that I had been trying to avoid. Convincing her to pick up her pace would be much harder now.

"Take her damn pack, Joe." Totten wasn't done.

"They're right there!" He pointed again, gesturing with his hand like a knifepoint. I could see flecks of spittle fly as he fumed.

"I can make it," Kathy's voice which had been tremulous on the bike was now filled with concrete.

I had seen this same resolution in my own Marines on long foot marches. We had Marines the size of fifteen-year-old girls who could take a pack almost twice their weight and never stop throwing one foot in front of the other until they passed out from exhaustion. Marching with a pack was more mental than physical, but not even Kathy's determination would be enough to get us past Horne. Although she was maintaining a steady gait, legs digging into the asphalt road, marching uphill, it wouldn't be fast enough to beat Horne.

Totten threw up his hands in frustration and ran on, tension swirled in his wake. Clark followed him silently. I was caught halfway between Totten at the front and Kathy at the back. We were all in a bad place. It was never good to have half the team pissed at the other half, but Totten seemed to inspire it. I looked back at Kathy and flashed a reassuring smile that was answered by her own that turned into a grimace. I picked up my own pace and drove myself up the hill, catching up with Clark in just minutes. I gave him a wave to tell him to keep up with me and soon we were in step with Totten.

The road became steeper and the foliage became thicker and taller. Sharp, spiny cacti were intermixed with the mesquite trees. The evening sun turned everything into shades of deep orange, and as we passed beneath the peaks, the sun gave way to shadow where everything lived in violet shades. The trees and the rocks combined with the sinking sun cast a sudden and deep shadow on the area. It would be harder for those teams behind us who would have to run in the dark, but I guess that they had an easier run this morning when we were running in the pre-dawn darkness and they were running in the sunshine.

"Come on, Totten," I began. "You can't insult a member of the team, particularly if you want her to accept your help."

"We can pass Horne," He tried again, his voice almost plaintive, his eyes uphill.

"I want to pass him too," I said. "But if you piss off Kathy, we're not going to get anywhere."

"Look," he said. "I came here to win not to kowtow to my boss. You want to play nice with your girlfriend, fine. But if she's so big on working as a team, go convince her to give up some of her weight so that our team can pass Horne's team. Go back there and tell her to distribute some of her damn weight." Then almost under his breath, he said, "No wonder Luther's firing you."

Clark stepped away from us his eyes darting back and forth.

"What the hell does that mean?" How did he know about mine and Luther's agreement and what did he know that I didn't?

"His email last night, you idiot," he said.

Clark pulled a face, and Totten and I both saw him shake his head slightly.

"What?" I asked Clark.

"He wasn't a part of the email, Totten," Clark said.

"What email?" I asked.

"Your father's dissolving the company," Clark said. "He said that due to Georgia's and Bridget's deaths he was going to have to dissolve AFC but he's going to reform under a new name and in a different locale. He said he'd have a new roster of instructors as well."

"When was this?"

"We all got it last night," Totten broke in.

I stopped.

Clark and Totten looked back at me but strode on, never stopping their pumping legs as they wound around the switchback, not sure if they should go on or wait with me.

Disbelief washed over me. It felt like the blackness that had overtaken me at the edge of the canyon when I felt the world crowding out my consciousness. Unlike then though I was not afraid of blacking out. Instead of confusion or fear, there was nothing but anger. Anger at all of them, every one of them who'd talked to me last night, this morning, all day, without saying anything, anger at my father for not telling me what he was planning, for keeping me out of the loop, anger at Kathy for having told me not to trust him and having been right. More than any of those other feelings I felt angry at myself for having trusted my father when I knew it would end up like this.

Kathy came up behind me as I stood in the road.

"Uh oh," she said.

"Did you know about this thing with my father?"

"Come on," she said with a wave. "We're falling behind."

I grabbed her arm and made her stop.

"No!" My voice was loud and echoed off the rock wall around us. "Did you know about Luther dissolving the company? About this email he sent?"

"What email?"

I studied her face and felt that she was telling the truth, her eyes concerned and empathetic. This was empathy I'd seen before, it was about the race, my condition, and our predicament. She wasn't hiding her thoughts about Luther, or about his plans.

"You were right." I looked up at the road and made a decision. "Give me your pack."

"I told you I can make it."

"I know you can," I said. "I need your pack. I want to pass Horne and our best bet is if we take your pack."

She was on the verge of arguing, but she must have seen something in my eyes, the anger? The resolve? The betrayal? A mixture of all these things? It made sense that that was what she would see, that was what I felt. She handed over her pack and stepped back.

I threw her backpack on top of my own, felt my body bend forward with the extra weight and took off at a trot up the road. "Keep up as best you can."

She nodded silently.

I knew what was driving me on. It was anger. It's not the best motivator to have for racing. Anger is a fire built with gas. It flames up quickly but dies out fast. My concern was whether that flame out would occur before or after we met Horne's team, and which side of the finish line we'd be on.

We came up to Clark and Totten a few minutes after I took Kathy's pack. Instead of slowing down when we got to them,

I sped up. Totten didn't say a word. He just picked up his own pace to meet mine. Clark asked if he could help me with the weight. I gave a shake of my head and told him we would trade later.

Kathy's pack wasn't as heavy as my ruck, but I could feel the extra weight in my lower back. After a couple more switchbacks I could feel it go all the way to my knees. The weight changed my gait. I felt like a man with rickets, bowed legs bending further because of the weight. It wasn't long before Clark came back to ask to help again. This time I didn't argue. Still running I threw the ruck to him. I felt immediately lighter. I didn't look back at Kathy. I knew she would be scowling and I didn't want to lose my focus on my anger.

Totten took Kathy's pack from Clark when we saw Horne's team just in front of us. The switchbacks made it hard to see too far uphill, so it was a surprise when we saw them. They were right in front of us, less than fifty meters away. Fifty meters is a long way in a run, particularly on an uphill run, but knowing that Horne's team was within striking distance had an effect on the whole team. Without a word, we all ran faster, even Kathy.

We were charging, moving with momentum and determination. The goal was within reach and for Totten, even for me, the goal was personal. It wasn't until we were right on them that I wondered how Horne might react. Would he feel humiliated? Cowed? Less aggressive? It didn't seem likely.

Passing Horne could have repercussions I thought at the last moment. He would be more apt to act out. He would want retribution even more than before. Any plans he might have, plans for getting revenge on Luther would definitely be acted on. Just as I realized that passing Horne was a bad idea I realized that there was nothing I could do to rein the team in. At the next switchback, we were even closer to Horne's team. Only a few feet separated us. We saw Horne try to motivate his team, but they were beaten. Their heads were lowered, they had accepted the fact that they would be passed, we were too close to them and they knew it. Even Max looked dazed. At the next switchback, we came up even with them.

Horne turned. "Fuck you, Joe," he said. His voice was loud enough for everyone to hear. He leaned over and grabbed me. I grabbed his forearm and knew we were about to pick up the fight we'd started the night before, the one that ended with me on the ground and him on top. This time Totten and Max jumped in to stop it. Max pulled Horne back and he cursed me the entire time. His voice boomed off the mountains around us.

I gave him a grin that was designed to infuriate. "See ya at the top," I said.

It only made the curses louder.

I tried to think of something more prosaic or insightful but all that came to mind for my report to Luther was; Both teams finished day one. I quit, asshole.

CHAPTER 43

"Holy crap my feet hurt."

Kathy was in the tent with me. It was nice to be back in the tent. Closed up, secure, had it not sounded so pathetic I would have said it was like a womb, never out loud of course, but somehow that thought kept coming up whenever I entered the tent.

We were both sitting on the small matt I had brought, each of us drinking from the bottles of Gatorade that had been our reward for reaching the finish line. Our feet, unclad and de-socked, were airing out outside the tent, jutting out the little tent door, resting on top of my rucksack. Our backs were propped up against Kathy's pack. Down below our campsite, just within sight from our position inside the tent, we could see the finish line. If not for the mountainous surroundings and the rustic nature of our equipment Kathy and I would have looked like a couple watching television from their Lazy Boy sectional couch. We could see dozens of race volunteers, scores of spectators and fans, all grouped within the area cheering as each team came through.

It was rocky everywhere I looked and the few plants were sharp and tough looking. Concrete shelters dotted the area and etched out campgrounds. Several teams of racers were sitting within the shelters prepping their gear for the next day or just relaxing out of the wind. It wasn't as nice as the golf course the night before, but anything that didn't require running rowing or riding was going to be embraced by the racers.

Since we had been watching we had seen most of the teams

cross the finish line and dozens of buses going back and forth up and down the mountain, ferrying more equipment, volunteers and spectators from the parking lots at the base of the mountain to the finish line in the Basin. The buses made it look so easy, the teams looked haggard and worn out. Three more teams were expected.

Here, in the Basin, we were sheltered from the surrounding desert. The wind was the only downside. A Bernoulli Effect launched each gust through the canyon so that the little tent shook and rattled like a sail. It was strong enough so that I had to close my eyes to keep the dust and grit out. If not for the fact that it would have hurt my feet and knees to move, I might have tried to reposition myself to avoid the sand in the eyes. Instead, I just put up with it.

A few minutes ago Kathy had taken my hand in hers and intertwined our fingers. It felt nice. I thought about that kiss from earlier. I considered leaning over and kissing her, but realized that it would hurt too much so I put that thought on hold too.

Slowly, after our finish, the anger about Luther's email ebbed away. By the time I had the tent up I was past caring. Thankfully, everyone remained silent about it. Even Totten, usually so eager to needle, had dropped the subject. The last thing I'd said on the subject had been to Kathy, five teams ago. We'd both used as few words as possible, no conclusions had been reached. Just a general acknowledgment of what I'd found out. She'd nodded sagely in reply and must have understood I didn't want to talk about it.

"Wow, they look spent," Kathy said as she watched the tenth team come through. Was she trying to get me to talk or was she just saying things to pass the time?

She seemed to comment with each passing team. It was like she was looking for something to do or say while we sat together. For my part, I was just happy to be in the tent, surrounded by the mountains with my feet up and my back supported; nowhere to go and nothing to do.

We had missed watching Horne's team's finish. We had been putting our tents up when they came across. I figured we had beaten them by fifteen minutes, maybe more. We had been on hand for every team since. We found ourselves grading each team like judges at a diving competition. The team behind Horne's had come in strong, all of them sprinting up the final hill to the finish line. A few minutes later another team sprinted up the road to the finish line. Kathy said something about one of the members but I didn't really hear her. I saw one of them start to limp and almost fall over as they dropped into the arms of a fan. It looked as if he would forego tomorrow's events if given the opportunity. I nodded as Kathy said something more, but just a nod.

"Hey, Joe!" Kathy leaned over to look at me. "Are you listening to me or are you checking out again?"

"Nope," I said. "I'm fine. Just relaxing."

She leaned back again, nodding as if she'd confirmed something within herself. "I said my feet are killing me. I don't know if I'll be able to make it tomorrow."

She pulled one foot toward her and crossed her legs. She massaged the underside of her foot with her free hand but didn't let go of mine with the other. I watched her leg and her thigh. I couldn't help myself anymore.

"My feet feel like hamburger patties that have been ground one too many times," she said.

"Nice legs."

"They hurt too."

"They look nice."

The campground was rocky and the ground on which we had pitched the tent was as hard as cement on my back. Bates had finished with Emily, Sorrels, and Rochester, then pitched his tent immediately next to ours, Emily next to him. Finally, the entire AFC group had gravitated toward the buffet near the finish line. Ostensibly, if you asked the rest of the team, Kathy and I were guarding the campsite in case other teams wanted to come in and crowd us out, but mostly we were just relaxing.

All around us were other racers. Despite the numbers, the group was quiet, like contented cows focused only on eating or relaxing in the fields. Every now and then laughter or a louder than normal voice would arc above the gentle, low hum of the campground and remind us that the group was larger than the quiescence seemed to imply.

Eventually, Bates and Emily came back from the buffet and handed over large plates of barbecue. Hard work and long workouts always tended to suppress my appetite. Now, with the smell of the food hitting me, there was nothing I could do to resist it.

"They've already started posting the times," Bates said as he and Emily sat down near us and propped their feet up as well. Bates looked spry and light. He looked as if he could run several more miles. His smile, his eyes; all bright and ready in the slowly darkening valley.

"What times?"

"They posted the split times by the restrooms over there." He motioned with his head toward the main trail where I saw a large group of racers.

"How'd we do?" Kathy asked.

"For the most part you were average in each event," he said. "You beat our team on the river crossing, but we edged you guys out on every other event. The difference-maker was that you guys killed us in the transition times. Hell, you had the best transition times of the many teams. You're in third place."

"What about Horne?" I asked.

"He's in fourth. He had you on the bike event, but you caught up in the run."

"What happened with that?" Kathy asked. "Which route did you guys take?"

"We took the road too," Emily said. "Apparently it was twenty miles longer but smoother the whole way."

I thought back to the train platform in Dallas, of meeting Max and seeing his multipurpose bike. "Horne's team took the dirt road?"

"Yep," Bates said. "Based on the results he was the only one who did." A crescendo of cheers and clapping brought all of our eyes around to the finish line. A team slowly pounded its way up the road and finished.

"It almost worked," I said. "He had us beat till the end."

"What do you think happened?" Emily asked. "On the run I mean."

Bates spoke for me, but he said the same thing I would have. "Horne's not a big advocate of planning ahead," he said. "I bet he went all out too fast and killed the rest of the team. That's the way he used to instruct too. His team was probably on the cusp of dying as you passed him."

"You have Totten to thank for that," I said. "He might have had an aneurysm if we hadn't passed him."

Kathy groaned. "Totten sure got you motivated," Kathy said before she chomped down on a mouthful of chicken, her paper plate balanced on her crossed legs. Were my eyes on the plate or the legs?

"If I didn't know Horne was such a jerk," Kathy went on, "I would have almost felt sorry for him today."

"We'll have to be more careful now," I said. "If he was mad before he'll be even madder now."

Kathy looked up at me. "You're still taking this thing with your father seriously?" she asked.

I shrugged. I hadn't thought about it since finding out about Luther's letter to his clients. Watching out for Horne, protecting the clients had become second nature over the last two days. I hadn't considered that the mission would change. As Kathy asked about it, I realized things had changed, but I couldn't figure out how to change the mission to meet that change.

I looked up. Bates and Emily were listening, obviously wondering what we were talking about. We filled them in on Luther's mission to me and the letter that Totten had told me about. Bates nodded as I got to that part.

"Yeah," he said. "I wondered if you knew about that. I guess I didn't really think it was my place to tell you if you didn't already know."

"You know I'd offered to buy Luther out?" I asked.

"No," he said. "But that would have been an improvement. To tell you the truth, if it wasn't for the fact that Horne's group is the only other option, I would have left a while ago. A lot of us would have."

"Really?"

He nodded again and went on. "Yeah, even before Georgia's death people weren't happy. It's gotten too cliquish, too cloying. It's like a soap opera. I just want a good workout, I don't need all the other stuff that's started to come up."

"What stuff?"

"Well, like I was telling Kathy," he said. "There's just a lot going on in the group. It's caused a huge mess."

He raised his hands defensively as he heard his words come out of his mouth. "I don't mean that people can't do what they want with their personal lives, but when it affects the dynamic of the workout," he paused as he tried to think of what to say next, "It just makes things messy."

"I know Georgia and Horne were together," I said in an effort to keep him talking. "But I didn't know she'd had a fling with Totten too."

Bates looked around to see if anyone was nearby. He really didn't need to bother. I hadn't seen Totten or Kay since we'd crossed the finish line. Kay looked more morose and haggard than usual, mad perhaps that she'd come all the way to Big Bend and couldn't race. They'd set up their tent at the edge of our campsite then left. Bates would be able to scream his suspicions and they'd probably be lost in the wind before reaching anyone outside of us.

"More than a fling," Bates leaned forward. "It was a while ago, two or three years at least, but they were very close."

Emily leaned in as well, interest gleaming in her eyes. "Does what's her name know?" she asked. "His girlfriend?"

"Kay," Bates said and nodded. "She knows and she never liked it." We heard cheering and we all looked down the trail toward the finish line. Another team dragged themselves across the threshold and crumbled to a heap among the race volunteers.

"So Horne and Totten," I said. "That hardly seems like a reason to leave AFC."

"Try, Horne, Totten and several others," Bates said. "She was basically using the class as her own dating service. I want a workout, not a soap opera."

"Who else?" Kathy asked quickly.

He looked wary as if he knew he was being asked to divulge too much. Finally, he shook his head.

"Nope," he said. "Probably best if I didn't say much more."

"Bridget, too?" I was desperate for more information and hoped it didn't show on my face or in my tone. "Was she messing around too?"

"Bridget?" He almost laughed. "No. She was like me. Tired of it all."

"Really?"

"Yeah," he said. "She probably hated the controversy more than the others."

"Who else?" Kathy said again.

Both Emily and Bates looked over at her and stared. Were they surprised by how eager Kathy was to know more?

"I just said she wasn't doing anything with anybody," Bates looked suspicious.

"No, no," Kathy said. "I'm back on Georgia. Who else was she sleeping with?"

"I really don't think I should say." His voice had grown hushed, hardly audible above the wind.

"So it's someone on the teams?" Kathy asked.

Bates shook his head.

"You might as well spill it, Bates." Emily this time. "She's not going to stop till she finds out."

He leaned back. "It's nothing, just drop it."

"It might help us figure out what actually happened to Georgia," I said. "And besides I already know about Max. He said Gentry and Rochester were involved with her too. Is that why you don't want to say anything?"

He sighed and looked up and away as if he saw the inevitability of the discussion. "Rochester and Georgia were just good friends. They went out a lot, that's all. Hell, he swings the other way. And yeah, I don't want Michael thinking otherwise."

"And Gentry?"

He nodded and shrugged his shoulders at the same time. It was the type of movement that said he'd suspected it but wasn't sure, maybe also that he didn't care.

"Do you know when?" Kathy asked. "Or how close they were?"

"I don't really know much more than that people thought they were hooking up," Bates said. "And that's all just gossip."

"Did you tell this to the police," I asked.

He shook his head. "Like I said, it's all gossip."

Rochester, Gentry, and Clark appeared at the top of the trail and Bates stopped talking. Behind them were Rochester's partner, Michael and Cheryl Gentry. We all waved and they came over to join us. The primary topics for the whole group were the race times, the split times, and the events for tomorrow. Gentry said there was a rappel in the morning, an off-road bike ride through the desert, another run, and a mystery event. My team, it turned out, would once again be followed immediately by Horne's, just a few seconds behind that team would be the second AFC team.

"Great," I thought, "I still have that to worry about."

Somewhere during all the talking, I saw Totten and Kay come back to the campsite, neither of them looked as fresh as the rest of the team. They didn't slink in, but they didn't let anyone notice them either, no perfunctory wave, no cynical comment, no questions about tomorrow. They just went to their tent and seemed to collapse from the day's strain like all the other racers.

The conversation ranged for a long time, and we heard at least one other team arrive. Finally, someone saw more standings being posted at the bulletin board and the curiosity about what they said was too much for most of them to ignore. Kathy grabbed Bates as he turned to join the others walk down the trail to the posted sheets of race results.

"Does his wife know?" she asked as if there hadn't been a half-hour interlude in their previous conversation.

"Yeah," Emily chorused. "Does Cheryl know about them?"

Bates looked at them as if they'd just asked something monumentally silly, like does the sun rotate around the moon. "Of course not."

I heard their questions and his response, but vacantly. My thoughts were diverted by another team, the last, falling across the finish line. My eyes locked onto a familiar-looking figure wearing cowboy boots that seemed to be watching me from the back of the crowd, my brother Mike.

I squinted to try to look harder at the person through the growing dull gray of dusk. It was Mike for sure. I shook my head as I thought about Mike driving all the way out here. Why? For me? Because of Luther? Because of the case? Georgia and Bridget's killings?

Then, my eyes drifted back, away from him, toward the back of the parking lot. Call it a sixth sense, fate, something, perhaps my eyes focused on this person in the back of the parking lot because it was so familiar, more familiar than my own brother, or maybe because of everyone else out there by the finish line this was the only other person who, like me, was focused on Mike. I would know that stature and form anywhere, even if it was camouflaged in poor fitting clothes as it was now. Even from several hundred meters away and in the desert mountains of West Texas I couldn't help but recognize him.

It was Luther.

CHAPTER 44

Once I had him spotted he was easy to follow. I got up quickly and threw on my shoes. Kathy watched me but didn't say anything. I walked down to the parking lot and tried to stay out of view of both of them. I trailed him behind a small crowd of other fans heading downhill toward the buses. It came to me that had it not been for his watching Mike, I never would have seen him. They obviously weren't there together. Luther had been watching Mike, not traveling with him. Why? Why was he there? Why was Mike in Big Bend?

Worse, why had he lied to me? There wasn't a limp in Luther's walk, not even a slight one. He was fine, why?

I hustled down the trail, past the bulletin board with the standings and all the people crowding around, past the tables with the red and white cross-hatched picnic tablecloth held in place from the blowing wind by the mounds of food still being harvested by incoming racers, past the last team that had just come through the finish line, and all the volunteers following them up the road. It wasn't till I was at the finish line, safely past the tall form of Mike who I'd surreptitiously passed by in a throng of other racers that I found Luther again.

I considered last night's text message. He must have seen the fight, or at the very least been there for the aftermath. He'd had firsthand knowledge that Horne had hurt another one of his clients, he didn't need Bates or Gentry or anyone else to report back to him, he was on site seeing it all himself. Did he send out his message to everyone after that? That made sense. Luther liked to do things himself. He was not the type to ask someone else to do what he could do himself.

I paused as that sentence struck home. Was he the type to ask his son to stand in for him? Two days ago I would have said yes. Now, I understood, he hadn't asked me to come along to help protect the team, he'd asked me to be a decoy. I was only there so he could blend into the background and not be noticed. Observe without being observed. Act without being involved.

How long had he been there, I wondered? Had he been on the cliffs earlier this morning, watching as we cruised down the river? My mind screamed yes. He had been there. He had to have been.

My heart hoped that when I caught up to him, he would tell me he'd just arrived, but I knew that he'd been there the whole time. I closed the distance between us, passing several other people, the wind shooting up the road made everyone's clothes flap loudly. He was in front of a small crowd with me just ten meters behind. Then, at a sharp turn in the road, almost nonchalantly, he ducked into the brush at the side of the road. All the people on the road, so intent on the wind and the walk, didn't notice. I'd been expecting it. Luther had spent time in the Marines as a sniper. He'd feel most at home in the brush, watching from afar. Why had he come out? Just Mike? Had he seen Mike and wanted to know more?

I turned down the small game trail and followed him.

Instinctively, knowing that he was only a few meters ahead, I slowed down, treading lightly. How much light was left? I looked up and around. Thirty minutes? Fifteen? Dusk would be quick here in the mountains. Should I run up ahead and try and find him? Should I continue to slink along until I found his hide site? What would I do if I missed it in the dark?

Instead of making a decision, I looked down and followed the faint outline of his footprints in the soft sand of the trail. Would he watch his back trail? A good sniper would set up a hasty ambush along their own trail to ensure they weren't being followed. I slowed down as this came to mind. My eyes scanned the sides of the trail for any signs. It was a few meters further that I saw a slight break in the brush, an area of the trail that looked unnatural as if someone had tried to disguise tracks. I stopped and knew before he came that he would emerge.

I was thrown to the ground, Luther pinned me easily. I let him. I knew who he was and what was going on. Despite being tackled and wrestled to the ground, for that moment, just that one small moment, I had the upper hand.

The dust settled and I looked up to see Luther's glare. Confusion turned to anger in an instant on Luther's face.

"What the fuck?"

I kept my voice calm. "Who did you expect?"

"Keep down." He hissed as he got off of me. He crouched and pulled me into the brush behind him.

His caution was infectious, or maybe it was the years of obeying his orders, but I followed along. He yanked me behind him away from the trail, staying in a crouch. With each turn through the brush, every second that I watched my father slip through the terrain in a covert crouch, Kathy's words became louder. How many times had she told me he was crazy? How often had she said his paranoia was not normal? This wasn't a war zone. If it was, was Luther the enemy?

I followed him behind a large boulder and climbed up on top of it. From here we could look down on the Basin campground. At my feet was a woolly, brown ghillie suit balled up near his overstuffed rucksack, looking like a sad tumbleweed. Next to it was a tripod-mounted night scope pointing uphill. I shook my head. I knew Luther was serious about things, intent to the point of seeming crazy, but this, watching his son and his customers covertly in the desert, was something I'd never have expected. I was relieved that there wasn't a rifle.

I stood up just as Luther took a tactical kneeling position.

"Get down."

"No."

"Keep your fucking voice down," he said.

"What the hell are you doing here?"

Luther stepped up to me, crouched down like a snake, both hands in front of him ready to fight. "If you don't show some damn field discipline, I'll fucking drop you here and throw you out on the road."

Would he? I studied him, seeing him in a new light. He refused to look away. He probably would. Reluctantly I took a knee and dropped my voice to a whisper.

"What are you doing here?" I said.

"I'm doing what you are supposed to be doing," he said. "Watching over the clients."

I pointed at his knee. "What happened to the ACL?"

"I had to make my absence convincing."

"So I was just a decoy?"

"Of course you were," he said as if it was natural that fathers didn't trust their sons. "This way you could watch them overtly, I could do the same covertly. I'm not giving that bastard another crack at my clients."

The wind swirled through the area and made me squint as it picked up dust and debris and flung it at my face.

He stopped me before I could ask another question. "It was because I went out to make sure it was Mike, wasn't it?"

We both knew he was asking how I saw him.

I nodded.

"What the hell is he doing here?"

For a moment I thought he sounded worried. Why would he be worried about Mike? The answer came immediately. He didn't want police around. Could that really be it? Could he really be that far off the edge? Was there a weapon here that I couldn't see?

I stood up to leave.

"You've lost it." My voice was only a mote louder than a whisper. Not angry anymore, just depressed at what I saw.

"I'm doing what you couldn't," he said. "I saw the way that asshole kicked your ass last night. He almost killed Kay." His voice was loud but some of the volume was lost to the wind.

"You are nuts," I said.

"Shut the fuck up and get down here and listen to me," he waved at me to join him in his kneeling position.

"Nope, I'm through."

"What?" he stood up. "We had a deal, your job is to watch the clients. Just because I'm in a covert over-watch position doesn't change that. If anything it should make your job easier. You should be happy I'm here."

Not sure what to say I shook my head. The email Totten had told me about shot through my thoughts. "No," the words tumbled out slowly despite the fact I wasn't thinking them as I spoke, "I can't trust you, and I don't want anything to do with you."

I turned and walked back down the path.

CHAPTER 45

I felt as if I was watching someone else's life play out in front of me as I walked back to Kathy. Everything I'd found out in the past few moments confirmed what I'd been struggling to repress, Luther was well and truly crazy. What kind of business owner fakes an injury to secretly follow his customers to a race? What kind of father uses his son as a decoy for his perceived enemy? I wanted to wake up and find out that everything over the past few days had been a dream.

I wanted to be at home, in my apartment, back to modeling, back to a life where the hardest decision was how to make a building on my layout look more realistic.

Mike was in the tent when I got there. Dusk had dropped around the campsite, and with the mountains blocking any last rays of the sun, there were only a few minutes left before it would take flashlights and lanterns to see. The wind had increased as the light had deadened. With each gust, the tent bent and wavered like a drunken wavering man. Mike and Kathy were arguing. There was his solid, tall build with the slightly, stooped almost lazy way of standing. He wore his boots which to anyone else would have seemed apropos in West Texas, but in the mountains, and among the racers, they stood out and screamed that he was an outsider to this crowd. They stopped their argument and turned to look at me as I walked up.

"Where'd you go?" Kathy asked, concern, fear, and latent irritation in her voice.

Mike looked surprised. "You seem to be in your element. No

more problem with spaces, eh?"

"I saw Luther." I watched Mike and saw he was not surprised.

Kathy had enough surprise for both of them. "Your dad?"

I nodded.

"Saw Mom early this morning. She said he was probably here," Mike said. "That's one of the reasons I drove out here. She said he left two days ago. Figured he'd be around here somewhere."

I decided not to ask him why he didn't just call or text. It seemed like a long drive just to warn me about Luther. Had he been worried about me? Was it jealousy over Kathy?

"What's he doing here?" Kathy again.

"Being a nut," I said.

Mike nodded his agreement.

"No really."

"Really," I said to her. "He's here to watch the teams. To watch Horne. He's convinced that Horne is going to do something. He's sure he's going to try to kill someone else."

She looked around. "Where is he?"

"Hiding in the brush down the road," I said. "Camping?"

"No," I said. "Hiding." I enunciated the word. "He's got a hide sight, like a sniper, all set up on a rock. A night vision scope, a ghillie suit, everything."

"You don't think he's dangerous?" Kathy said. "I mean I know he's always been paranoid, but do you think all this stuff with the murders and with Horne has made him lose it?"

Mike shook his head, probably a habitual response from years of people asking him if his father was off his rocker. I didn't shake my head. Kathy noticed.

"Joe?"

"I don't know," I said. "I think he's gone off the deep end, but I don't know if he's dangerous."

"Shut up," Mike said. "It's just Luther. This is what he does."

Kathy turned on him and looked to be on the point of arguing. She checked herself, realizing that there were other campers around, and whispered instead.

"Your dad has always walked a thin line between sanity and full out craziness," she said. "We've always thought he was one good push away from going over the edge. Even when we were young my parents made sure to watch out because they thought he was crazy or as close as you can get and still function, and that was twenty years ago."

"He's just intense," Mike tried.

"Intense is fine," she said back, her voice grew with each sentence. "But driving across Texas, faking an injury, hiding out in the woods with a night scope, not telling his sons where he is and what he's doing..."

"Using me as bait," I interrupted.

Kathy turned. She obviously hadn't come to that conclusion yet. More compassion in her eyes now, then she turned back to my brother. She yelled at Mike now, either because of the argument or because of the wind, maybe both. "He's focused all this hatred and intensity onto Horne. Hell, from what Joe and I have discovered, neither of us thinks that Horne had anything to do with either of the murders."

Mike raised his own voice. "He's not crazy. And if it wasn't Horne, who was it?"

I stepped forward. I knew Mike wouldn't do anything to Kathy, but I didn't like his being so close.

"You're the detective," I said. "Detect something. What'd you find out about those names I gave you?"

He turned, his focus dropping away from Kathy.

"Last night?" he stumbled.

"Yeah," I said. "Gentry, Max, Totten. Remember?"

He shook his head as if to clear his thoughts. "Oh, right."

"Yeah," Kathy said mockingly. "Those guys, the people who could also be the killers."

Mike looked around as if finally realizing he was among the very people we wanted to know more about. "Maybe we should talk about this in private?"

Kathy pointed to the tent then led the way inside. Mike sat awkwardly on one side, Kathy and I shared the other. I turned on the little flashlight and gave us some light. We shut the tent flap to keep the swirling, dusty wind out. The tent flexed under the strain of the wind and made the roof seem shorter than it otherwise would be.

Mike looked around the tent with a questioning look. "You're both sleeping here?" he said. "Together?"

"Get over it Mike," Kathy said. "Now, tell us what you found."

He didn't look ready to concede but wasn't sure how else to go on. Instead of saying anything he pulled a little notebook from his back pocket and flipped through it. He extended his legs as if he needed more room and forced them between me and Kathy. Kathy gave his shin a rap with her knuckles and was rewarded with a grunt when he nudged her side too hard with his foot.

"It's too cramped in here," he said.

"Yeah it was hell earlier when we fucked," Kathy said.

"Are you two screwing?" Mike rasped trying to stay quiet. "Seriously, are you two an item?"

"It's none of your business if we were, but let's just go ahead and say sure, if only so you'll shut up," Kathy said. "Just tell us what you found out."

"Jeez, you try and do a brother a favor." He made another show of repositioning and eventually got around to reading.

"First," he said. "Horne. No alibi, tons of potential motive, according to our Daddy." He looked up then went on.

"Nasty break up with one of the victims six months ago. No connection that we've been able to determine to the other, Bridget."

"Right," Kathy interrupted. "But he was also still in love with that first victim."

"Killing someone you love has been known to happen in the past," Mike responded. "He might be the top of Luther's list, but he's not necessarily the top of ours."

"Who is?" I asked.

"I'm getting to that." Mike used his 'I'm the big brother and know better' voice but continued to whisper. "Second, Totten. You wanted me to look into him. I had my guys interview some of his friends and family while I drove up here. We know that he had a fling with one of the victims several years ago, but he had no opportunity. We reviewed the statements of all the witnesses to both murders. He was seen by several of your friends and can be accounted for almost every minute during the run the day Georgia died."

"So he's out?" I asked.

"You might not like him." He must have heard something in my voice. "But, he didn't kill her."

"So what about Max?" I asked.

"Max Trevon," Mike continued the sermon in undertones. "He doesn't have an alibi. He wasn't at workout that morning, in fact, neither was Horne. Apparently, it was just his assistant instructor and a couple of regulars that day. None of them saw Horne or Max."

"Do you think he'd kill Georgia?"

"Possible," Mike said even though I'd been asking Kathy. "But we've gotten nothing on him."

"He had a relationship with Georgia too," Kathy explained for Mike's benefit.

"Regular hussy," Mike said.

"Hey!" It was a perfunctory defense for a victim, but the ensuing silence in the tent proved he had said what we all thought.

Mike eventually went on. "And this guy, Gentry. He was on your run too. His alibi isn't quite as airtight as Totten's, but unless he took her into the woods, killed her with a knife he had beneath his running clothes, then caught back up to the other runners without anyone seeing, he's probably not the guy."

"So we really haven't gotten any closer than the other day?" I asked.

Mike put the notebook back in his pocket and went back to looking at the interior of the tent and moving his legs.

"We know that a couple of people definitely couldn't have done it," Kathy said.

"And we still don't know how Bridget figures into any of this."

Mike swung his eyes up. "She was going to leave."

"What?" I said.

"We talked to her family," he went on. "She was going to leave AFC. Her husband said she wasn't enjoying it anymore. He said that some people weren't as much fun to be around and she was thinking of moving to Horne's workout."

"That's the same thing Bates said," Kathy threw in.

"How far had she gotten?" I asked.

"What's that mean?" there was irritation in his voice. It could have been from the tent roof bending down every few seconds hitting him on the head but to me, it looked like the more he saw of mine and Kathy's sleeping arrangement the madder he got.

"I mean," I spoke slowly. "Had she told Luther she was leaving? Had she signed up for Horne's group yet?"

"Yeah," Kathy threw in, "and why was she leaving?"

"Like I said," his anger becoming more and more evident. "All I have is what I said. She wasn't happy there anymore. She said she didn't like the other members. I don't know what that means, and I guess her husband didn't either."

"Yes but, had she made the change-over yet?" I tried again.

"Why the hell does that matter?" Mike tried to move into another position but was caught short by the low roof of the tent.

"If Horne knew that she was going to change he wouldn't have killed her," I said. "It could be one more thing that could vindicate him, or at the very least prove that the murders weren't connected."

"Well," Mike's voice dripped with brotherly sarcasm. "I don't know, Mr. Amateur Sleuth. we didn't ask her husband that and he didn't say."

"Are you sure?" I asked.

He pointed a trembling finger at me. "Don't tell me how to do my damn job, Joe."

Kathy spoke up now. "Why don't you do your job then, Mike. It's a good question."

The roof blew down and hit his head again. That seemed to be the final straw.

"Both of you go to hell," he said. He stopped and looked around, mentally changing topics, moving on to something else. "Why is this place so small? I thought I was going to be able to sleep here, damn it. I don't see how the hell that's going to work."

"You're not sleeping here," Kathy said.

"Well, where do you expect me to sleep?" Mike's voice was just shy of plaintive.

"Not here," she said.

"You'll cozy up to Joe but not to me? That's pretty fucked up, Kath. Even for you. You don't ditch a guy then go for his younger brother."

"Holy Christ!" Kathy exploded. "Is that really why you're here? Is that what you think? You think I'm trying to get it on with Joe? Hell, even if I was it wouldn't be any of your damn business. I broke up with you years ago, you ass."

"You just said you were fucking him," Mike said.

"I was fucking joking, Mike."

He looked relieved.

Kathy's face changed. "Oh my gosh. You don't think there's still a chance do you?"

"I didn't say anything..."

"Mike we are so over there is no chance of anything ever again." She looked around and started grabbing her gear. "I'm done with this family. Your crazy father is in the woods probably reliving some war. You," she pointed at Mike, " You drive all the way out here out of some messed up sense of jealousy or to rekindle something that was never there. I'm beginning to think whatever incurable psychosis Luther has was passed on to you two at birth!" She grabbed her pack then turned to me.

"Before I thought this crowd and this race was nutso, now I'm not so sure. They might be crazy, but they're not as crazy as you three."

"Kathy, wait," I said as she turned toward the exit.

"No," Outside the tent she looked back at me, her eyes glistened. "I've had enough of crazy. I'm done with all of it." Parting shots are hard when there's no door to slam, but the silence that was left in Kathy's wake was worse than any banging door could have been.

CHAPTER 46

I woke up and saw the world resolve slowly. It was dark. It was night, too dark to see without night vision. More shots from Johnson's direction; mopping up shots, not the loud, intense, violence of before. Had they swept through? Were they reconsolidating? They had to be confused, not sure what to do next.

And where was I? Stuck in a shrub unable to move. In the past few hours, I had survived attack after attack by this little band of the enemy. Off and on, during those times when I was conscious, I heard my platoon. They had done a better job than I. My guess was that Marlberg and Lamb had come down to support them, and turned the battle because, at one point, I heard the distinct burps of our machine gun crews. Why hadn't they come for me? I didn't know. I couldn't figure that out.

Several more RPGs and grenades had landed on my position, and I found that my blackouts came with each successive blast. It had to be a mixture of shock, concussion blasts and blood loss from the shrapnel wound in my thigh that had come at some point during the battle. At some point, low on ammo, I had low crawled out of the little wadi and left Wilson's body behind. I had to retreat into some deep brush fifty meters or more away.

The last thing I remembered was a misfired RPG that completely missed the wadi and impacted within five meters of my position.

The little wadi where Wilson's body was had been a luxury compared to the depression that I crawled to. The little fighting position became my biggest frustration as well as the only thing that kept me alive. Every time I had tried to get up, being forced to dive back. Deciding to try to work back to the Lamb, Marlberg and the guns and being ground back down into the wadi, then being stopped by more rounds. Thinking that it might be worthwhile to check the radio damage, I had almost crawled back to Wilson and the Wadi, but I had been cut off from that too by a fusillade from in front, bullets pinging off the rocks around me. Again and again and again, each time I thought I had a plan I was forced to sit tight and keep the enemy back. Everything I tried was repulsed and rejected until I couldn't think straight.

I came to look forward to the blackouts.

Now it was completely dark.

Were they there? Were they still out there? I hadn't heard any shots for a long while. How long should I wait? Johnson and the platoon had stopped shooting. Were they coming for me? Were they out there looking for me?

I grabbed my night vision goggles. They were next to me. I must have dropped them during the last attack. A theater of green resolved in front of my eyes when I turned them on. I could see everything now. It took a long time, but I got up and took a knee.

More scanning.

I took a step and stopped again. I waited for a shot. I felt sure I would have to dive back down.

Another step. Another pause while I waited to be shot at.

It seemed to take hours to get back to the wadi.

Wilson's body no longer looked like a human body. His ruck and radio too were destroyed. Bullet holes and shrapnel rips permeated everything. I thought about picking up his body but realized I couldn't. It didn't look like there would be anything to hold. I checked my GPS so I could make my way back later. With the coordinates, I'd be able to come back and get Wilson's ruck and his body. Still, it didn't seem right to leave his body behind. Carrying Wilson with me to the platoon would mean moving far more slowly, not being able to see everything, it could prove fatal if I ran into any enemies.

Despite no shots, despite no movement around me, despite the cover and concealment that the darkness provided, I decided to leave Wilson's body and come back later.

Limping, I crouch-walked on, stopping every time I moved, never losing the idea that any moment the attack would come again. I looked back. The wadi was even shallower than I thought it had been. I was surprised I had survived. No wonder they had been so aggressive. It looked like I would be an easy target. I hiked my ruck on my back, crouched, cradled my weapon in front of me, and moved away from the area slowly, crouching, waiting, stepping, and waiting again.

I stopped when I saw the dog.

The dog, the black dog that I'd seen so many times that day, the one I'd seen what felt like eons ago, prior to the fighting, as he marched with his friends toward the village, was in the middle of my route. He was still alive. He didn't move, didn't even lift his head. The only way I knew that he was still alive was that I could see his chest moving up and down. Probably in shock, pain, dying. I moved by him quietly and continued on toward the truck.

As I got nearer, as more and more of it came into view, I slowed down and tried to think of what to do. Should I run up and clear it? Bypass it? They could be using it as cover, did I want to engage them? They might still outnumber me, but I had the advantage of night vision. I stopped when I was about fifty meters away and waited, wondering which course of action I should take.

Fifteen minutes later. I saw him. I saw the rifle first. He was wounded, walking with a limp, and next to him, his buddy was surveying the dark scrub brush around them. His rifle too was up and his eyes were wide. He was looking only a few dozen meters from me but couldn't see me. These were two of the enemy who had kept me from my Marines.

I had a laser on my rifle that was zeroed to fifty meters. If I aimed it directly at his chest, a bright neon green line of light that only I would be able to see would pinpoint exactly where a bullet would enter his body. It's in the night when we Marines can be at our most lethal.

Instead, I waited to see if there were others. I could shoot these two sure, but what if there were more? My shots would bring them running. I could be forced back into the same situation that I had been in for the past few hours. Worse, I wouldn't have any ammunition for a sustained fight.

I didn't turn the laser on.

Silently I waited and let them walk by.

I waited five more minutes than I walked by the truck, going perpendicular to the way the two men had just gone. When I was fifty meters beyond the truck I picked up my pace and hurried toward the road where I'd left my Marines.

CHAPTER 47

I was awake long before dawn. The morning came slowly. Unlike the quick dusk, it seemed to take forever for the Basin to grow light enough to see without a flashlight. I hadn't slept well. The small tent was smaller with Mike in it. Every movement he made kept me awake. Along with my brother's bulk, were the weighty thoughts about Kathy. Should I have followed her out of the tent? I think I should have. I should have followed her. I had spent the entire night thinking about that. She followed me all the way to Big Bend to help me. I should have followed her out of the tent last night. Why hadn't I followed her? I stepped over a snoring Mike and left the little tent.

Kathy was awake as well. I saw her as soon as I unzipped the tent. She was sitting on the picnic bench under one of the shelters, a lantern silhouetting her, eyes staring out into the few wisps of morning mist.

The wind, so rugged the night before, was not even a breeze now. She was wearing her running shorts, a loose-fitting sweatshirt, and flip-flop sandals. With her ponytail, she looked nothing like my Kathy from last week. Had I not seen the transformation, I wouldn't have believed it. She looked over but didn't say anything, instead, she motioned me to come over with her head; a small movement but one that said that yesterday's argument was already forgotten.

"You didn't sleep out here, did you?"

She shook her head. "I slept in Emily's tent."

"What are you doing?"

"I guess I'm worried," she said.

"Don't worry about Mike," I said. "He's a jerk."

She shook her head. "Not Mike," she said. "The race."

"Oh," I felt silly for misinterpreting.

"And don't get me wrong, Joe," Kathy said. "I like you, I like you a lot, more than your brother by a long stretch, but I know we're just friends, and that's fine for now. But I like you, and yes I mean I like you enough to want to see you."

A long silent moment followed, awkward, at least for me. I studied her as she turned her eyes back toward the mountainside, and realized that there was no awkward feeling in her, something was eating at her, but it wasn't what I felt. It looked as if Kathy, perhaps for the first time I'd known her in her adult life, looked hard-pressed to find words. I saved her by backtracking to something she'd just said.

"What about the race?" I asked. "You're doing fine. Today won't be any different."

"I don't know. It has me more worried the more I think about it."

One of the things that Gentry had put out prior to the

The start of the race was that day two started with a climb and rappel. Each team would have a long jog to the southern rim of the Basin, almost 5 miles with packs, then climb to a drop-off and rappel down to the desert floor. I could understand Kathy's difficulty. I had done a lot of climbing in the Marines and even I was a touch nervous about this first event.

"You'll be fine," I tried to sound positive. "They can't make the climb too hard and rappelling is easy. You just let it out to the speed you want to travel."

"I've never done it before." She said. "And I'm so sore this morning. I'm worried that it's going to be too much for me."

They were words that prior to this weekend I would never have thought she would say. She looked at me. I saw in her the same thing I had seen so often during my few months in Iraq. During that time our platoon had been augmented by new Marines, freshly trained recruits, just hours from having stepped off a transport aircraft, so far away from having the confidence the other more battle-hardened Marines in our platoon possessed.

Sure they had their own swagger, the same camouflage all Marines have, buoyed by esprit de corps and the bravado drilled into them by the drill sergeants, but behind that mask was the same uncertainty that I saw in Kathy now. We gave them confidence through constant drills. Drill a Marine enough, acclimate them to a task over and over again, and the chance that they will perform under stress is greater.

"Wait here a second, I'll be right back." I walked over to my pack and grabbed my climbing harness, gloves, and a rope. I came back to Kathy who was no longer looking into the distance but was now actively watching me and engaged in what I was doing. I handed the harness to her.

"Put that on."

She buckled the harness in place while I tied one end of the rope around the picnic bench. I came back and attached a carabiner to the front of her harness.

"Now," I said. "Hold the free end of the rope with your left hand behind your back and put your right hand here as a guide."

She did it and the rope around the bench went taut as I pulled her back by her waist and the rope accepted her body weight.

"Now what?"

"Just walk backward," I said.

She tried to, but the rope held fast.

"See," I said. "You have the brake on. You have to let it out at the waist, otherwise, you won't go. Nothing can go wrong with the brake on."

"So what do I do?"

"Move your left hand out." Her left hand came out tentatively and she stepped backward. The rope shushed through the carabiner as she moved backward.

"Let it out more," I said. "All the way out like this and walk back fast." I moved my hand to show her. She did it and with no friction to stop the rope, it slipped through the carabiner smoothly. I expected her to lose her balance so when she did I jumped forward and caught her before she fell onto the ground. She was lighter than I expected and for a moment I felt proud and somewhat happy to be holding her in my arms.

She lurched forward out of my arms with an angry and embarrassed look.

"Not funny," she said.

I shook my head. "I wasn't trying to be funny. That's just rappelling. You let out the brake too fast."

"Now, I'm really worried," she said. "This rope is supposed to support me, my gear, and take me safely down 600 feet? I lost control right here."

"Don't worry about the rope," I said. "It's the same as the one we used on the river crossing. It could hold the whole team and all our gear at the same time and not break. These climbing ropes only fail if they're cut or damaged. So the rope shouldn't be a concern."

"So now all I have to worry about is going splat at the bottom of the cliff because I can't brake."

"Also not a problem." I walked to the rope and doubled it over so that there were now two lengths of rope going through the carabiner. "Using two ropes is for beginners or heavy loads." I guided her back toward the bench to try the drill again. "Try it now."

She looked hesitant, but she did it again. "I like that more," she said as she walked back slowly. "It's like I have more control."

"Right," I said. "Even if you are in full free fall you'll only go a few feet a second. Make sure when they rig you up that you have two ropes through the rappelling rig."

"You think someone will be there to help?"

"For an event like this," I answered. "They will have to."

"What if they don't have two ropes?"

"They will," I said. "And if they don't, tell them to fix it so you do. They'll do it."

I watched her as I said this. These were similar words and advice that she had given me in the past about models.

As I watched, she tested the rappelling line and harness several more times and eventually the same swagger that I saw return to recruits who had come slumping off of the transports, returned to Kathy as well. She kept at it, trying different maneuvers and postures, constantly drilling for what was to come up that day.

The light had come up during the little class and with it had come a shallow crescendo of activity from the other campers. I saw Gentry make some coffee then come over to try the rappel drill himself. Bates reminded me of a puppy: eager, vibrant, and ready. Emily, flashed a knowing smile at me as I stood by Kathy and tried the rappelling herself. Totten and Kay, despite the eagerness and happiness of almost everyone around them, looked immune to the enthusiasm.

Had they changed or had I? Was I seeing things in Kathy, the fear, the uncertainty, that were new to her, or was it just that I'd never looked for them? Kathy had come to life for me in ways I hadn't expected, but so had my teammates. Gentry wasn't the leader I thought. He was an administrator. He wasn't a second in command during workouts because he was a leader, instead, he enjoyed the minutiae and details.

Bates was fast and fun-loving on runs, but when he wasn't running, he kept everyone at arm's length, as if the lack of a quick pace, a stimulating heart rate, or any of the other aspects of a workout left him stone cold and vacant.

Kay and Totten, who prior to the race only entered my thoughts as two clients, who were only remarkable in their desire to compete and perhaps irritate, had turned into one being on this trip. They were inseparable, two people who acted like one.

And Max, someone I'd thought saw the world in a manner similar to my own, showed me the exact opposite. His views were a complete mystery now. The only person who hadn't changed was Horne.

Throughout the campsite, every head turned as we heard the loud clanging of a dinner bell. Breakfast was being served, and as a group, the teams all started moseying down the trail that led downhill. Kathy grabbed my hand and stopped me as I tried to follow.

She waited till everyone was out of earshot then said, "You know, I thought you'd follow me when I left last night." She paused. "I guess I hoped you'd follow me. When you didn't it kinda made me think."

"I know I should have come to talk to you," I said. "I realize that now."

"You're missing the point." She waved her hand dismissively. "That's not what I mean. I'm not looking for an apology." She paused as if she was considering how to continue. She studied me then seemed to make up her mind.

"It's your agoraphobia," she said as if it was difficult for her to get out of her mouth. "One of the things my friend said when I talked to her about you was that there is usually a focal point, an event, something that triggers the problem. I know you weren't like this as a kid, so I kinda assumed that it happened in the military, the trigger, whatever it was."

She paused to let me say something, but I only gave her a nod. This was the last thing I wanted to talk about. My thoughts about getting out of the apartment were still reverberating through my head. I felt good as if I was making progress, I didn't want whatever Kathy was hinting at to stop that progress.

"Okay," she looked disappointed that I hadn't said anything. "I guess what I'm getting at is that I don't think you are afraid of open spaces. I don't think it's agoraphobia."

CHAPTER 48

"What are you talking about?" I said. "You obviously haven't been paying attention."

"Actually I've been paying a lot of attention, and I doubt I would have figured it out if I hadn't been. I realized it last night when you didn't follow me."

"What does any of this have to do with my not coming after you last night," I said. "I told you I was wrong."

"It's about your decision-making process, Joe."

"You're not making sense."

"Tell me what happened in the Marines, Joe." Her change in topic and tone were abrupt and caught me off guard.

"What?"

"Tell me what happened in the Marines to make you agoraphobic," her voice was low but firm. "I think that's the key to all this."

"I don't want to talk about this."

"Joe, it's like you said when we hit the river crossing, you have to trust your equipment and trust your buddy. I'm your buddy."

She sighed and I could tell that she didn't want to talk about this either. She had the type of look she had when she had to talk about salaries, letting people go, or projects that she had lost. Kathy got excited when she got to talk about new projects or new jobs. This was not the excited Kathy.

Looking at her in the glow from the early sun that still hadn't peeked over the mountain tops, she looked haggard and overwhelmed, but determined at the same time. What did I look like to her I wondered...Scared? Depressed? Worried? Or did I look world-weary too?

I suppose I told her about Iraq because I felt I owed her for my not having followed her out of the tent the night before. Hell, she might have known that I'd feel guilty about that and used it to her advantage, I don't know. Still, I told her about Iraq anyway.

I've told people about that mission on Sakhar before. The first time was the worst. I had to tell Sergeant Lamb why I hadn't returned to the platoon immediately. I told him how I was pinned down, what happened to Wilson, the waiting for the cover of darkness, I knew it sounded weak. It was as if the more I tried to convince him the less sound the arguments became. The second time I told anyone about the mission I was confined to my quarters afterward by the CO. An investigation ensued and I was interviewed several more times.

By the time the investigation was over I'd given up trying to explain myself, or trying to make anyone understand what I felt; I just gave them the bare facts. It was as if I didn't even believe myself. The investigation may have determined I had followed the procedure as best I could and not disobeyed orders, but my CO was not shy about telling me my actions bordered on disgraceful. He was quick to allow me to retreat from my command. I was cycled out of theater, I never saw my Marines again.

I heard from Johnson later. His letter was sharp and pulled no punches. Why had it taken hours for me to get through to the platoon? How had Wilson been so horribly killed yet I survived with only one wound? Why hadn't I done more to save Wilson? It was filled with questions and recriminations. I was through leading Marines after that. Everyone would hear about this, and everything I might try to do would be undermined.

The therapist I was ordered to see was the most understanding of everyone who heard the story, but still, I could see somewhere within him the same revulsion that had been so easy to see in my command staff. A look that said they were confident they would have acted differently, that their decisions would have been better than mine had been. That therapist, also a Marine, had made that initial diagnosis. Back then I never came out of my barracks room, and it was the last time I'd told anyone what happened on the mission. My discharge for psychological reasons had come the next day.

Luther had never asked. I don't know why. I know why my mother never asked. She said she just wanted me to be the way I used to be. She's not good with sensitive subjects, this was way beyond her pay grade. Mike? I don't know what Mike thought about my leaving the Marines. I doubt he gave it more than a few seconds thought. However, how many of his personal problems have I spent time considering?

Kathy heard the whole story, from moving the gun team into position all the way to my being discharged. She sat through it and didn't ask any questions. In every other instance, I was always interrupted and asked to explain myself more, not with Kathy. She just sat passively and listened. When I finished I saw that she was smiling.

"So he said you had agoraphobia?" she asked.

"Who?"

"The therapist."

"Yeah," I said.

"No one else has said that about you?"

I shook my head.

"And you never saw another therapist?"

"I've only been out for eleven months," I said.

"I don't think your agoraphobic," she said.

My eyes narrowed instinctively. I wasn't sure what to say. What does a guy say to someone, their boss no less, their friend, who is so completely wrong in their diagnosis? It was just what I didn't want to happen and the reason I didn't want to talk about this with her.

"What the hell do you know about it? You're a business owner, not a doctor."

Unfazed by the eruption, she went on, "Well, you might be agoraphobic, but I think it has a lot to do with the decisions you make."

I turned to go get breakfast, but she caught up with me. "It's a manifestation of the fact that you don't want to make decisions in your life," she went on. "You enjoy the safe route, the one that is laid out before you. The one that won't lead to," she paused as if choosing her words carefully.

"You can say the word 'problems' Kathy, I just don't like when you say I have a problem."

"I was going to say potentially deadly consequences or something like that."

I shook my head.

"It ties in with your story, Joe. You don't like to make decisions."

"Bullshit." I stopped next to a picnic table. "I make plenty of decisions all the time. Hell, Kathy, I decided to come on this trip. I decided to work for you. I decided to get up. I even decided not to listen to your psychoanalysis and get some breakfast instead. Who could be able to function without making decisions?"

Kathy held up her hands defensively. "Don't get mad, Joe. I'm just pointing out what I've seen. You make plenty of decisions, but you only make the safe ones. The tough ones you leave to others. Totten planned out the transitions and the events, hell you told him to. The team decided which way to go on the bikes. The second you tried you froze. You freeze when you have to make tough decisions. You're just using agoraphobia as an excuse to not make tough decisions."

"I don't think your pop-psychological diagnosis is what I need," I said. "Besides, I decided to take over for Luther. I decided to run his company. The safe decision would have been to leave."

She went on as if I hadn't said anything. "Some people have a Peter Pan complex, you have a Charlie Brown complex. You might make decisions but they're only the same ones you've made before, and they're not the best. Anyone else would have told Luther to take a flying leap months ago, but you keep on working for him. It's like Charlie Brown trying to kick the football Sally's holding. You want to do the right thing by him but your dad keeps pulling that sucker out from in front of you. Yet you refuse to make the tough choice and leave."

"You don't know what you're talking about." I felt like saying more, but I paused. I looked down at my hands, they were gripping the stone picnic tabletop.

"Look," Kathy stepped forward and placed her hand on my shoulder. A couple of other campers walked by. Racers coming back from breakfast. Kathy leaned in and whispered in my ear, "I don't expect this to be an epiphany or anything. There shouldn't be some bright light of revelation or anything like that. It's just something I've noticed, and it makes sense Joe. It's just something to consider."

She followed this with a peck on my cheek and a shoulder squeeze. "And that's something else for you to consider. Mike's right to be jealous." She walked down the path toward the breakfast area.

CHAPTER 49

The start of the race on the second day was much more reserved than the first day's start. Where before there were dozens of fans cheering as each team left, now there were barely a couple of early morning, weary warriors who had found enough enthusiasm to look up from their steaming coffee cups.

I made it down to the starting line with the rest of the teams, congregating with them in the parking lot, just as the second team was sent on its way. Unlike yesterday, when everyone seemed fresh and ready, the team jogged down the dirt path that led to the south rim with a raggedness that looked painful even to the spectators. My legs quivered as I watched them go by. I'd be following the same path in a few moments. It hurt to think about.

I did not speak or even look at Kathy after she returned from breakfast. She was watching the start with the rest of our group, and I was glad that she wasn't trying to approach me. She must have sensed my anger. In the past thirty minutes, I had rousted an exhausted Mike, broke camp, and packed up for the race without uttering a single word to anyone. I don't know if anyone noticed, and I didn't really care; I was just happy that they left me alone and got ready for day two. It had only been a day, but I was tired of my teammates. Actually, I was tired of everyone. Tired of Kathy's therapy and games, tired of Totten's and Kay's arguing and secrets, tired of hearing rules and advice from Gentry, tired of Mike's jealousy and tired of worrying about what Horne or Luther might do next. Why should I care about these people?

Kathy was right, why didn't I just walk away from them all? I didn't need to finish this race. Luther was somewhere around here looking out for the teams, let him do it. There was nothing stopping me from walking down the Basin road and finding the first bus home.

If I thought my legs had hurt the night before it was a shadow of the pain that came that morning. When I strapped on my rucksack and headed down the trail to the starting line there were sharp pains in my knees and ankles. My shoulders too were a fire bed of pain. I cinched the waist belt tighter around my hips and prayed that I could survive the jog. My face, my cheek, and my nose were swollen from yesterday's punch from Horne, and my ribs seared with pain if I twisted my torso too fast. I did not look forward to today's events.

The idea of leaving kicked back up in my mind as I felt my shoulders scream. I considered it. I looked down the winding road that led down from the Basin. Behind me, the third team was sent off with a yell from Tony. I could go down or up. I probably considered the options for too long because eventually the nagging and still unsolved difficulty of Georgia and Bridget surfaced.

That's why I was still here. They were the only things keeping me in the race. If Horne or someone else struck today and another of my friends died would I feel vindicated or guilty? Georgia and Bridget, like Wilson in Iraq, had been killed while under my command. I needed to find out, why. I needed to ensure that no one else was killed because of me.

"How you feel?" it was Bates. I gave him a grunt, but he wasn't going to be put off that easily. "That bad?" he asked.

"I'm fine," I said. "Just mad."

Bates looked confused. It caught my eye since it was such a departure from his normally straight-faced mien.

"Mad at what?"

I turned and pointed at the starting line. Next to the team that was getting ready to depart was Horne's team. "Mad at that, for one." Horne saw me point at him and returned my gesture with a finger gesture of his own. His was obscene.

"He's a jerk," Bates said. "Don't let him bother you." "Can I let them bother me?" I pointed to Totten and Kay. Bates followed my finger and saw Totten and Kay on the border of the small group. It was clear they were still arguing. "That's just the way they are," he said. "You know them, they're inseparable and think with one mind."

"Not right now," I countered. He looked again and saw that she was shaking her head, he was nodding. Bates gave a shrug as if it meant nothing.

"To each his own," he said finally. Totten saw us looking at them and must have thought I was hurrying him up. He finished what he had to say, and Kay walked down the trail toward the south rim as Totten came over and joined our team.

Spectators had a choice of viewing stages for the climbing obstacle. They could watch the climbing portion of the stage from up on top of the South Rim ridge or down below. Up top, they could watch where the contestants had to climb up and over to a rappelling lane. Down below there was a large tent with bleachers set up on the desert floor so people could watch the descents.

Busses were shuttling fans out to the tent from the campgrounds so they could watch the contestants slide down the mountainside. This was where the bulk of the crowd was going to be. Who would want to watch a bunch of bleary-eyed racers limp off down a dusty trail when they could watch them rappel down a mountainside? If I had the choice, I'd have my butt on a bleacher instead of getting ready to run with a backpack.

I looked at the team in front of us as they lined up at the start. They were even more ragged than the first two teams. As bad as they looked what's to stop us from placing? We could pass them. All we had to do was keeping shaving time wherever we could and keep Totten fired up as much as possible. Maybe his inner fire could be enough to carry us over the finish line with a respectable time.

Max came over again. It was the third morning of the trip and it was the third morning he'd come to talk to me. I wondered if the fourth morning would bring yet another visit.

"Your boy was pissed when you passed us," he said.

"Not my boy," I said. "Your boy."

He smiled as if this forgave all previous sins. "Well, he was good and pissed."

"Good."

"I had to calm him down."

"He's an ass," I said.

"He's not involved like you think."

"We'll see."

"I'm serious," he said. "We had a long talk about it last night. He had nothing to do with any of this stuff. You're barking up the wrong tree."

I shrugged.

I guess my lack of response touched a button because he lowered his voice as he threw me a parting shot. "Or your handler has you barking up the wrong tree." He threw me a knowing look.

I knew he meant Luther, but by the time it registered he was already back with his team and the moment to have gotten mad had passed. I looked around for him, probably the hundredth time I'd scanned the area for Luther, but like before I couldn't see him.

I looked down the road, where I knew his sniper hide was situated, but I couldn't see anything that way either. Knowing Luther he'd already picked up and moved. He'd been compromised by me, he wouldn't trust me not to say anything, and that more than anything else, the fact that I knew he wouldn't trust me with his secrets, proved how much my understanding of him had changed.

I didn't even know what I had to get mad about anymore. Max was more right than he knew. Luther was my handler, and he'd treated me like a dog. He'd sent me on this wild goose chase, he gave me the target and the mission. When was the last time I'd made a decision on my own?

Someone slugged my shoulder and I winced at the sharp movement and the digging of the backpack straps. I was no closer to getting used to it. It was Mike. His eyes were smiling, but at the same time, his face was pouty. It was typical for him. A mixture of emotion, but the eyes told me we were okay.

"Hey jackass," he said.

"What's up asshole," I replied. "Thanks for kicking me so much last night. I don't know what I would have done if I'd gotten too much sleep."

"Up yours," he said.

"It's no wonder Kathy dumped you," I said. "She obviously wasn't tough enough to put up with your elbow in her side every night." It was as good a time as any to try to put this behind us.

For a moment I thought he might explode, but then a smile blossomed across his face. "It wasn't my elbow that kept her awake all night," he laughed.

"I hope it was your elbow last night." The full grin grew larger.

"I'm sorry," he said. "I know you like her, hell, I understand why. I just thought I might not have fucked that up as much as I did."

"We're just friends," I said.

"No," he said. "I see how she looks at you."

Tony's booming voice broke into our conversation. "Team nine, you have two minutes to start time."

All of us, Clark, Totten, and Kathy looked up and found one another with our eyes. We shuffled up to the starting point. I saw the same dreariness in their faces that must have been in mine, the same foreboding and pain being masked by subtle false motivation. Tony's voice picked up in the silence of our slow movements.

CHAPTER 50

Our start was glacial. I felt like I was a captain of an oil tanker that had to get revved up to begin any sort of movement. First one foot, then the other, eventually the next. There were a few times when I'd felt worse in the Marines, but this was something I hadn't trained for. I hadn't carried a pack in over a year. By the time we hit the trailhead I was going as fast, I would go. Thankfully, Totten and Clark looked as though they were going full speed as well.

The trail was easy, and that may have been our saving grace. It wound downhill slowly and was graded so that we had no problem with footing. From last night's briefing, we knew that the first event was five miles away. We already had our helmets strapped to the outside of our packs and climbing harnesses strapped next to them. When we got to the climb, we would be that much faster to get ready to go.

We jogged in a line, none of us talking.

"When we get there, who should go first?" It was Totten.

Just as when Bates spoke to me earlier, I didn't want to answer. Clark was just behind me. Let him answer.

"Haven't really thought about it," Clark said.

Totten turned as he ran. "What about you?" He looked at me.

"Doesn't really matter," I said.

"What's your fucking problem," Totten's voice was loud enough to qualify as a yell.

"Nothing," my voice was a notch or two down from his.

"Then get your head out of your ass and start planning."

Clark jumped between. "Why don't you two chill out."

"All I want to do is come up with a plan." Totten again.

"I got a plan," I could hear the sarcasm coming, like an avalanche rolling downhill, no one could stop it. "How bout we run to the end of this trail, then we climb, then we rappel," I said. "How's that for a plan?"

"Fuck you." Totten gave me a shove as we ran. "I'm still trying to win this bitch."

I shoved him back. I wasn't sure which hurt my shoulders more, his shove or the jostling of my pack as I shoved him back. I decided at that instant that if he shoved me again, it wouldn't be worth a shove back.

"Guys!" Clark again. "Why don't you two run up ahead, take a look at what's coming, and get a plan together like we did yesterday."

It was sound advice and I could tell from Totten's face that he saw the same wisdom. Without a word, Totten picked up his pace and I followed along. We left Clark and Kathy behind.

"You're an ass."

"Yeah," I said. "Thanks."

"When we get there, I think you and Kathy should go first, I'll partner up with Clark and come behind."

I shrugged and I suppose he saw it because he didn't bring it up again, not even when we came up to the event. It started at a window in the rock, two vertical rock walls that rose up and framed a panoramic view of the desert hundreds of feet below. There were a couple of people standing by, one or two clapped when they saw us coming. The race volunteer waved and we ran to him.

"Everyone needs to hook up to the safety lines," he pointed to two ropes that were secured in different places along the rock wall. "It runs all the way to the rappelling station. No climbing with a pack on your backs, but you will have to rappel with the pack. At no time, should you unclip from the safety line. When you get to the end, someone will be there to brief you on the next event." He looked around and behind us.

"Hey? Where's the rest of your team?"

"They're on the way," Totten already had a harness on and his safety lanyard out. He had hooked it to the safety line. He took his backpack off and used a carabiner to hook it to the safety line as well. He started to make his way to the side of the rock wall to mount it and begin climbing.

"New plan," he said. "I'll go first and get things ready for the others. You brief them and follow along last."

I shrugged again. Did I not care or was it just becoming a standard response to every question? Or was this what Kathy meant by refusing to make decisions? It didn't feel like it. This just felt like not giving a crap.

"You can't leave without your team," the race volunteer tried to sound stern.

Totten pointed back up the trail where we saw two heads bobbing up the trail, Kathy and Clark. "They're right there." He left without giving the race volunteer time to argue. Instead, the volunteer looked over at me as we watched Totten's hands disappear onto the other side of the climbing wall. I gave him my standard noncommittal shrug. I wondered if by the end of the day my voice would be hoarse from grumbling or my shoulders worn out from shrugs.

Kathy and Clark showed up moments after. They slipped on their helmets and harnesses while I secured their packs to the cables. When they were set, I hooked them both up to the safety line with the line from their harnesses. Clark went first, then Kathy, I came last. I watched Kathy and I was surprised how strong a climber she was. It wasn't a difficult climb, only about fifty meters, but even easy climbs, particularly those that are 500 meters above the desert floor, are by their nature difficult. It never got too dicey and for the most part, it was just a nuisance.

"Don't look down," it was Clark. I looked over at him and saw that he was advising Kathy not me. In either case, it was good advice. I looked down after watching Totten start out and it hadn't provided much comfort to see the way the mountain peeled off down toward the desert floor. It looked like the pictures of the cliffs of Dover that I'd seen, reds and browns instead of white and desert at the bottom instead of waves. The end of the climb came sooner than I expected. The hardest part of the climb had been having to tug a backpack along the safety wire every few steps. Still, my knuckles were stiff and my fingertip pads were scarred and tender. "Great," I thought, "perfect compliment for my feet."

Kathy and I were forced to wait a second on the rock as Clark decoupled from the safety wire and moved toward the rappelling lane. Totten helped him. Behind them I saw more race volunteers and a small crowd of spectators, some of them clapping, others taking pictures. There was only room on the little rock shelf for the safety folks, Totten and Clark so Kathy and I were forced to wait while Clark got rigged up and the race volunteers checked his rigging to make sure it was safe.

Totten yelled at us as he hooked Clark up. "There are two lanes, a steep one and a bunny slope. Choose the steep one, it's not that hard."

Somewhere behind him I heard Kay's voice yelling and cheering on the team. I noticed it because it seemed so out of place. Kay? Cheering? It was like Totten being supportive. It wasn't generally found in nature. I craned my neck and saw her with the small crowd.

"Go, Go, Go! Clark!"

Kathy saw it too and gave me a look that said she thought it was odd too. "What's gotten into her?" Kathy said.

Another shrug.

"Ever going to talk to me?"

"Eventually."

"You aren't really mad?"

"I don't like to be analyzed."

"Well, get over it." She leaned way over and gave me a peck on the cheek. It was awkward as we were both holding onto the rock wall and her backpack was in her way, and for a moment she almost lost her balance. I grabbed her and she finished the little kiss and gave me a wink.

"Thanks, and I've been analyzing you a lot more than that, get used to it."

I didn't have time to say anything as Totten started yelling at her to move up and get rigged up for her rappel. She put on her pack and made sure it was all buckled up correctly. I watched as she got unhooked from the safety line then went through the motions of having Totten rig her up to the rope. He balked when she said she wanted two ropes. As a response, she moved toward the second, less steep rappelling lane.

"Are you fucking kidding me?"

"No."

"You'll be as slow as molasses."

I decided to speak up for her, "It's her first time, Totten. Just do it so I can get off this damn wall!"

He acquiesced and started to run a second rope through her rigging. I saw Kathy look over at me just before she got set to step off the side of the cliff. She gave me a smile, not a hundred-watter, something quite less, but still, it was good to see her try. She dropped out of sight tentatively, but with aplomb. Then Totten was looking at me.

"It's going to take her for fucking ever to get down, so you might have to wait awhile." He scowled. "But you can come up here to wait."

"Give her a break, she's never done it before." He helped me up and off of the rock wall and away from the safety harness. "You'll just have to go faster to make up for her being slow."

He grumbled and together we waited for the radio call that would come from the bottom of the rappel lane telling us she was safely on the ground and the next person could go.

We waited silently, both of us watching the rope jostle back and forth as Kathy went down. Finally, a scratchy sound came from the radio strapped to the safety volunteer behind us and he motioned to us that we could rig up.

"You go next?"

I suppose it was just that I was tired of him and had been

in an argumentative mood all morning that I said, "Why don't you go next? I can bring up the rear."

He turned and for a split second I thought I saw panic, but then he quickly recovered. "No, if that was your plan you should have brought it up before, this is my transition plan and I'm going last."

I gave up and decided it wasn't worth the argument, particularly since I was already rigged up. I took a few tentative steps backward. Kay, still across the ledge with the spectators, yelled and caught my eye.

"Go Instructor! This is the chance to make up some time. Don't use the brakes."

Again a head tilt of confusion. Totten brought me back to reality by telling me to get a move on.

I leaned back and felt the weight in my hands as my body weight was taut against the rappelling rope. My leather gloves felt firm and the rope felt secure. I leaned further back and then took a big step back. I went a few feet down. I pushed hard and away from the rock wall and the rope zinged out of the rappelling rig as if it was covered in grease. It felt good.

I stopped myself after my third bound just to make sure I could. I realized how fast those first hundred meters had gone and decided to take the last few hundred meters in a more controlled manner. It didn't work. The thrill, the weight in my backpack, the desire to be done, it all had me dropping just as quickly on the second portion as the first. I saw several safety volunteers stationed along the way, hanging by their own ropes, they looked to be set out at every hundred meters. There were just quick waves and smiles from each one as I zipped by. Finally, far too quickly, I was on the desert floor. Well, not exactly the floor, but as close to it as I was going to get by rappelling.

The bottom of the rappelling route, the spot where I was standing, surrounded by Clark and some more race volunteers, was a large granite boulder. There were hundreds of them on the floor of the desert. I looked down and across the area. There were the grandstands, the spectators, rows, and rows of vans and buses the fleet they had used to bring us from the train and bring the spectators down to the desert floor.

"Pretty fast, Instructor," it was Clark. He unhooked me from the harness and signaled the volunteer who turned to speak into his radio. Kathy was standing behind us and we all looked up as Totten stepped off from the rock ledge, a small black shape that began to increase in size as the rope shimmied and shook with each of his leaps. For a moment we saw him falter, he swung around in space aimlessly for just a moment, then with a long hard jump, he took the final one hundred or so meters in one long leap. He shook himself away from the rope with Clark's help and we all backed up to give him space.

"What the hell are you all still doing here?" his voice was sharp. "Fucking Horne's team was right there when I left, move! Move! Move!" he waved his arms and we all started jogging down the path that led from the boulders to the desert floor.

He was right. We'd been lost in the moment, watching the rappelling. It's fun to watch, it's like watching human flight, carefree and fast. Except for Totten's one lapse, he would have made the entire length of the rappelling lane in less than a minute.

As we jogged down the trail, I looked up and back to see the next figure stepping back to start the next rappel. It was a large person, had to be Horne. I saw him take a powerful squat and launch himself out away from the rock wall. The rope zipped away violently and I saw him coming to a stop about halfway down the lane. Smooth, technical and simple. But with the hard brake, I saw his body jolt awkwardly then realized why he had lost the rope. He was in freefall. It was as if he'd been a bungee jumper whose line had snapped at the nadir of the jump. I saw his arms flail then heard the crunch of his body hitting the boulder.

CHAPTER 51

We all ran back as one. Although we had only gone a few dozen meters down the trail when Horne fell, by the time we got back to the boulder where we had ended the rappelling lane, there were already two safety volunteers there.

"Wait here," I said to Kathy and Clark. Totten was already hanging back. I edged forward and saw that there was no hope for Horne. His legs were splayed out in a manner that screamed out in its unnaturalness. It was the lack of sound that made the entire scene the most gruesome. Anyone in the position that Horne was in should have been screaming in agony or yelling for help, instead, it was all silent. I heard the scrabble of feet on the rock as the safety guys made their way down to him, I heard them speaking into their radios, but from Horne there was nothing.

I looked around and found the rope that he'd been using to rappel. I found it a few meters away, still attached to him like an umbilical. I picked up the rope and followed it with my hands, away from him, toward the other end. I found it several meters later. I picked it up and looked at it. It was sheared away. Why would Horne cut the rope?

"I thought you said those things don't break." I turned and saw Kathy.

"It didn't break," I stood up and walked over to her, the end of the rope held out. "It was cut."

"He cut it?"

I held it up to her to show her the end of the rope. It was frayed as if it snapped. I pointed to one side of the cross-section of the rope.

"See here," I said. "This has been sliced through. This side snapped due to the weight."

"He only cut through half of it before he fell?" she asked. "Why would he cut it?"

I looked up and around, scanning the area for Luther. "Go see if they can find a knife near Horne, but I don't think he did it."

"You think someone cut it?" Kathy looked around as well as if she might find the culprit nearby. Was she looking for Luther too? She answered my question with her own.

"You think Luther did this?"

"I think Luther is possible of anything right now," I said.

My eyes fell on the group of spectators and like the day before I zeroed in on Luther. He was there, intermingled in the crowd, surveilling as he had done yesterday, finding cover and concealment in the mass of people. As I watched, he stepped away from the stunned crowd. He saw me looking for him. He was setting himself apart from the group so I could see him. Why would he want me to see him now, I wondered?

"He's right over there?" Kathy followed my gaze.

"He's crazy but I don't think he would do this."

It came to me quickly. I should have seen it earlier but the distrust from the day before had blinded me. "He didn't do it. He's letting me know he was down here. He couldn't have cut that rope and made it break just for Horne. He couldn't have done it before he got on the rope, he was down here."

"Then who?"

I thought about that huge leap that Horne had taken just before he fell and thought about where his first bound landed in comparison to the pause that Totten had taken. That pause. What had Totten been doing during that pause?

"I think Totten did."

"Totten? How could he cut it, he was down here with us?"

"He paused during his rappel, about a quarter way down," I said. "I think he cut halfway through the rope."

"But then he might fall, right?" she asked. "Not even Totten is so stupid to risk making himself fall like that." I turned away and considered the rope.

"Horne's heavy," I said. "With his pack on I bet he was three hundred fifty pounds at least."

"Still, what if Horne's weight hadn't been enough?" she asked. "Totten wouldn't risk hurting someone else, would he?"

"Maybe he was counting on Horne taking that huge leap." Even as I said it I knew it sounded like a weak argument.

"There are too many variables," Kathy said. "I don't like Totten either, and sure he might have hated Horne, particularly after what he did to Kay, but not even Totten is so callous that he'd risk someone else dying."

I looked at the rope again. Kathy was right. Luther had a motive to try to hurt Horne, but so did Totten. Totten would want revenge for Kay. I focused on the rope in my hand and saw all the little strands, some cut, some busted, that made up the rope, hundreds, maybe thousands of strands of nylon. If one strand fails, the others are forced to take up the slack. Each of them works together to make a stronger rope, just as Totten and Kay made one another stronger.

"Totten didn't do it alone," I said. "Kay helped him."

"Kay's up there," Kathy whispered.

"You heard her egging us on," I said. "I bet she did the same to Horne. She's aggravating enough to encourage him to put everything he had into that rappel. I bet Totten was telling her to do just that this morning."

"I don't know," Kathy said. "It still seems kinda iffy. What if Horne hadn't gone first?"

I thought a second then said, "I bet that if Horne didn't go first, then one of them would have said something. You saw the way Totten looked up there with us. He saw it was Horne getting hooked up to go. I bet if he saw someone else he would have told the safety guys that he saw a problem with the rope. Or, hell, even Kay could have said something."

She shook her head, but I could tell that I'd given her some things to think about. There was more to it than just Horne. If Totten and Kay were working as a team here, when else might they have worked together. The discussion from the morning before about who could have killed Bridget and Georgia, Mike's comment that Totten couldn't have done it since he couldn't have been in two places at once, Totten and Kay working as a team could. They could be in two places at once. Together they could have killed Georgia and Bridget, but the real question was why? Totten had a motive for wanting to hurt Horne, what was his motive for the other two?

Kathy brought me back from my thoughts with another question. "If what you think is what happened, how can we prove any of it?"

I held up the rope. "Anyone can see that this was cut." She shook her head again. "That's not enough."

I thought for a moment and that's when Luther arrived. He leaped onto the boulder and came up next to me and Kathy as if it was the most natural thing in the world for him to be there.

"It was cut wasn't it?"

"Yeah," I said. "How'd you know?"

"That had to be what that bastard Totten was doing."

"Exactly what we thought," Kathy said, despite being on the same side as Luther I could tell it pained her to have to agree with him. "But how can we prove it?"

"Go see if he has a knife!" Luther's voice was sharp and the tone made it sound as if Kathy and I had been overlooking the most vital aspect in our discussion. He was probably right.

Still holding the rope we walked over to the side of the boulder that was closest to the trail. Below me, further down the trail than before, were Totten and Clark, both with packs off. They looked like they were discussing the accident. I heard Totten say, "It could have been any of us up there."

"Hey, Totten," I yelled down to him. "Do you have a knife on you?" Kathy and Luther standing behind me.

"Course I do," he said. "Why?"

"Cause this has been cut."

"Wasn't me." He tried to turn away. He stopped with his arms out wide and said, "We all saw it, that rope snapped. Hell with that backpack he probably weighed more than three normal people. Add the force of his rappelling..." he shrugged as if that explained it all.

I heard Luther come up from behind me. I expected him to say something but when he didn't I dropped the rope and walked down toward him. "It wasn't too much weight. It was cut." I said again. "Where's your knife?"

Totten turned to face me, he looked over my shoulder and seemed confused. "What are you doing here?"

"We know what you did," Luther's voice growled behind me.

"What?" Totten looked stunned.

For just a moment I felt the indecision on our side.

What if what he said was true? How could we prove that it was Totten? We had all seen Totten pause, but by itself that didn't mean anything.

Luther can say all he wanted that he saw Totten cut the rope, but from the spectator's stand? What could he really see? And our thoughts about Kay might be substantiated, but the volunteers and other spectators who saw her would say that she cheered just as loudly at all the other racers. What could we prove? It was all hearsay. The pause became large and long. Totten flipped his hand at us dismissively and walked further down the trail toward the bleachers. A race volunteer ran up behind Kathy and asked us all to get out of the area and clear out so they could get a stretcher up there. We shuffled out of the way, but for those few moments we were all silent, wondering, waiting, it seemed other-worldly as if none of us had any idea how to continue. There was no course open to us, no course that any of us could see.

Several more EMT's ran by. I felt as if a moment was slipping by, those moments in life when I know I should say something but couldn't. Inevitably the moment passes and the idea comes later. Something I should have thought of was out there, and the longer I looked for it the more nebulous and confused it became. The window of opportunity was closing quickly.

I felt Kathy's hand on my shoulder and it made me think of what she said that morning. Was this one of those moments where earlier I would have done something? What would I have done? Was this a moment that had I not been stuck in Iraq I would know what to do? I looked back down the trail and saw the retreating form of Totten. He was walking further away. Where when we spoke he was only twenty meters from me, now, almost two hundred meters down the trail. Where was he going? More importantly, why?

Finally, without any rationale to bolster it, I made a decision.

CHAPTER 52

I jumped down from the boulder and landed on the trail, a sharp jolt of pain welcomed my feet on the trail, but I disregarded it. The only thing on my mind was catching up with Totten and stopping him from getting away. If he was leaving the area, he had to have a reason. I might not know how to prove it now, but stopping him from getting away was the first step.

I ran past the still standing Clark and he fell in behind me and asked, "Leave him alone, man," he said. "You two have been going at it all morning. He couldn't have done that."

I didn't respond. As usual, his logic was sound. I couldn't prove anything and I was working on nothing but emotion, but somehow I thought it was best not to lose sight of Totten. Instead of stopping me he kept following. The trail broke out of the rocks onto the desert floor and a hundred meters in front of us were the bleachers, the busses just behind them. I saw Totten. He was entering the crowd of spectators as they milled around at the base of the bleachers still shocked by what they had just seen.

I yelled if only because I didn't know what else to do, "Totten!"

He looked back and saw me. He didn't yell back, he didn't stop and wait, instead, he disappeared into the small crowd.

"Where's he going?" Clark asked as we ran after him.

"He's trying to get away."

"Get away where?"

He had a point. Where the hell was he going? We were in

the middle of the desert and there were few access roads back to civilization. There was no planning here, no forethought. Hell, the evidence we had was thin as hell. Where was Totten going and why?

Clark and I followed him into the crowd and quickly got lost. At the moment we lost sight of him he was heading toward the back of the bleachers and the busses. We slid through the crowd as quickly as we could and were among the busses in no time. I remembered the train cars at the station in Dallas. Comfort and stability surrounded me in the steel and glass large buses around us. I was in my element again. Here I could take on Totten no problem. The problem would be finding him.

I only took a moment to enjoy the moment and quickly looked left and right for any sign of Totten.

"Which way?" It was Clark asking, he was a few busses down on my right.

"Don't know," I said still looking back and forth. "You go that way, I'll go this way."

Clark took off to the right, I went left, into the narrow pathway between the fronts of the buses and the backside of the bleachers. On one side the cold comfort of a steel behemoth, the other the steel structure reaching over me. Heaven for just a moment while surrounded by desert. I felt invigorated again. There were a dozen buses out there and even more support vans, all parked behind the grandstands. The spectators were flowing in as well, swarming around us, it was becoming chaos quickly. My moment of solace was evaporating. The general hum of the crowd became louder, race organizers were trying to regain order, instructions were shouted, some folks were following, some not.

I felt a wave of relief as I slid between two buses. I walked down the length of the bus and scanned as much as I could for any sign of Totten. I got to the end and peeked out from between the busses hoping to see Totten. Nothing. I looked back the way I'd come and saw Clark working through the vans and cars in a manner similar to my own. I wondered if I should go back and join him. Why would Totten pick a bus to escape in? A van or car would be much more sensible. I hesitated. The pull of comfort near the busses held me.

A yell from Clark woke me. "Instructor!" His voice rose over the hum and thrum of the crowd. "Over here."

I turned and ran back down the line of busses toward the vans. I pushed through the crowd, shoving people out of my way as I went. I got a couple of mean looks from a couple of them, but another yell from Clark, made me move even quicker. Wilson's last moments flashed in front of me as I ran. My Marine, dying next to me in Iraq, the best RTO I'd seen, always willing, always ready. This was Wilson all over again. Clark, I was determined, would not be the next one to die. He would not be the next Georgia, not the next Bridget, not the next Horne, and definitely not the next Wilson.

I turned toward where I had last saw Clark and there they were, Clark and Totten, fighting, grappling.

Totten looked back and saw me coming a split second before I tackled him. I hit him between his lower back and shoulder blades like a linebacker smacking into the blindside of an unsuspecting quarterback. In that short time between seeing him and hitting him, I'd seen his fist rear back and smack Clark square in the face. At his feet was Ahmed, unmoving and sprawled awkwardly on the ground. We all went down together.

Somewhere among the arms and legs under me, I lost sight and hold of Totten. He was up and running before I knew what was happening. I saw him snatch up his rucksack and run away from the people, away from us, back toward the base of the cliffs and the boulders. "What happened?"

"He was trying to steal this car when I found him," Clark said around a nose that was swelling badly. "I think he knocked that guy out. Took his keys." He pointed at Ahmed. I leaned over and felt Ahmed's neck. By now more people had arrived and thankfully I saw someone calling for a paramedic. Ahmed had a strong pulse. One death at least I had been able to prevent.

Luther and Kathy arrived. "

Where's Totten?" Kathy bent down to try to help Clark, Luther went to Ahmed.

"That way," I pointed back toward the cliffs.

"Should we go get him?" It was Kathy.

I was about to ask, "Where's he going to go?" when I looked down at Ahmed. It had been my taking action that kept him alive. It had been my acting that had helped Clark.

Would Totten have killed him? Probably. He would have killed him as easily as he had killed Georgia, Bridget, and Horne. Would inaction result in another death? I looked up toward the rocks that speckled the area at the base of the cliffs. I saw the motion of Totten as he fled into them and disappeared.

"Come on," I decided.

CHAPTER 53

Kathy and I ran out into the open after Totten. Rather than feeling the absence of the grandstands, the people and the close-parked vehicles all I felt was a desire to stop Totten before anyone else got hurt. It was a hundred-meter sprint to the rocks, so we were there in seconds. As soon as I got to them I regretted not making sure someone was calling the police or the park rangers. Luther was still back there with Ahmed, surely he would tell someone with authority. As soon as I thought this, I discounted it. Luther would be the last to call the police or even a park ranger.

I saw a flash of movement on the little trail we came to and recognized the retreating form of Totten. "Where's he going?" Kathy asked.

"Maybe he thinks he can hide out in the park till he can find another way to get out of here," I said. "Come on."

We followed the little trail that wound its way into the boulders. I imagined that at some point, miles further on and further up, this little trail hit a major hiking trail and probably dropped hikers off at the Basin. Our only chance was to stop Totten before he could get lost in the wilderness of the Chisos Mountains. Eventually, the rangers might find him, but what if they didn't? What if he stumbled across a family of campers?

It was better if we stopped him now than hope for later. The surrounding rocks looked like sentries for the mountains in front of us. Hundreds of them of all sizes, but gradually increasing in size until they became behemoths near the foot of the cliffs.

Scrub brush and trees were all around, some gnarled oaks that had stood through years of desert harshness and had the battle scars to prove it, ocotillo cacti, and mesquite. They found areas of landscape within the rocks and provided tufts of green among the red and yellow rocks. There was no mistaking when the boulders ended and the path started to climb the mountain. We stopped when we came to a first really large boulder and the trail broke off in two directions. I looked for any signs that would tell us which way to go. Nothing. No footprints, no debris, no anything to help us figure out where Totten had gone.

"You go that way, I'll go this way," I said. "Yell if you see him." It wasn't a good plan, but what other options were there? The longer we waited the further away he got. I took the path to the right and padded softly in the dirt around the boulder.

All the time as I worked my way up the path I wondered where Totten thought he might be going. He had a better chance of escape by staying near people, near the crowds, near the vehicles. He had his pack, but how long could he survive out here in the wilderness? A day? Two? Maybe three? This couldn't be a plan, his coming this way must be the result of panic.

It was a gunshot that brought me out of my reverie. It was unmistakable. It echoed off the rock walls around me, but I could tell it wasn't directed at me. It came from Kathy's direction. Not even a moment of frozen hesitation. I turned and took off down the path, this time at a full sprint. I made it back to the bolder where Kathy and I had split in under a minute. Luther was there, his face turned toward the path that Kathy had taken.

"Was that a gun?"

"I think so," I said. "Kathy went that way."

I took off up the path and Luther followed. Behind him, I saw that more people, one of them unmistakably a park ranger, breaking off from the crowd in the parking lot heading in our direction. They seemed to move painfully slowly and I only gave them a glance.

Another shot, this one much closer stopped us. We took cover behind a boulder. It sounded as if the shot had come from just a few meters away, but still, I felt it wasn't aimed at us. I crouched down and slowly peered around the side of the boulder in front of us. Up the path, I saw Kathy. She was up the trail several dozen meters, lying on the ground, cowering behind a small rock. As I watched I saw sand and dust spit up like a minute geyser just a few inches in front of her rock.

I would like to say that I acted quickly. I didn't. I thought of Wilson. I had not made the right decision in Iraq. I should have done so many things differently. It had been echoing through my mind every day since that day he died. It had been spinning through my head each day, always jumping around, ricocheting but never slowing, and I never saw it till I heard the third bullet aimed at Kathy barely missed her and kicked up dirt near her head. It was then that I understood what I had been thinking for the past year; what I should have done back in Iraq was taken the fight to the enemy.

How many people get the chance to relive their greatest mistake in their lives and try again? More than that, how many get the chance to do it again but have a moment of clarity that gives them a chance to relive it differently, successfully? That's what that moment felt like. An epiphany that lasted the length of my hesitation, a millisecond, maybe less.

"What?" Luther asked as I turned and moved past him on the trail.

"Get down and stay down," I whispered. "Yell up that way to Kathy that we're here to help her. Don't let Totten know that I'm coming."

He nodded and I hoped he understood my plan.

I made my way through the brush on the far side of the boulder. I moved quickly but stepped lightly to keep from making too much noise on the broken, uneven terrain. I had no idea where Totten was, but from Kathy's position, I guessed that he would be fifty meters or so uphill. It was a guess that had little foundation and my biggest fear was that I would accidentally move into Totten's field of fire. It was this worry that drove me to veer more to the left, hoping to come up behind him.

I heard Luther calling to Kathy, downhill and to my right. "Kathy!" he yelled. "Are you okay?"

Kathy said something but her voice was less distinct.

Luther yelled again and I knew that my time was limited. "Help is coming, just hold on."

Movement somewhere ahead of me. Was it Totten? Had he heard Luther? Was he worried about more people showing up? Was he getting ready to move? If I moved that way would I run into Totten or some animal, a park critter trying to escape the commotion?

Totten's fourth shot removed all doubt. It was right in front of me, just feet away, just on the other side of the boulder to my left. The boulder was the size of a compact car on its end. No longer caring about the noise I charged up the backside of the rock and got on top. It took just seconds. Once up there I didn't act, I reacted. I saw Totten beneath me on the far side of the boulder, taking a shooter's stance, lining up his sites for another shot.

My jump was not graceful and there was even less grace in the landing. There was no ensuing struggle, and I never heard the fifth shot, the one that hit me. There was an explosion of pain, but that only came as I rolled off the inert Totten, when I hit my side and landed on my hip. I think that was when I yelled. I felt the pain radiate up from the hip. I tried to find comfort but couldn't. With no other alternative, I kept myself still and hoped that something might happen in the next few moments that would help.

I looked around and wondered how long it had been since Big Bend had an Earthquake. The rocks, the trees, Totten, everything around me shook. Just like yelling in Iraq when I was bombarded, it took my mind a second or two longer than it should have to catch up with what my eyes and ears took in. It dawned on me that the shaking was not the world but me. I was struggling to breathe, shuddering so harshly and so quickly that it was making the world tumble around me. I blinked my eyes to stop the movement. I held them shut and tried to embrace the pain in my waist. There was no getting used to it. It was everything all at once, completely commanding the attention of every nerve ending in my body. I don't know if I blacked out, but the next time I opened my eyes Kathy was staring down at me, her face inches from mine.

"Joe!" It took a moment for her voice to register. Then, like before, my conscious caught up.

"Joe!" she said again. "Are you alright?"

I tried to shake my head, but she stopped my head with her hands, one on either side and bent down to give me a kiss on the cheek.

"You're going to be fine," she said. "Just stay awake."

I saw EMT's and race volunteers scurrying around. Luther came into and out of my field of vision. There might have been a second's worth of relief in his eyes, but I couldn't be sure. I remember the bumpy ride on a fabric hammock style stretcher as several people hoisted and carried me toward an ambulance. Then there was the ambulance. It was only then, as an EMT leaned over and said something in a very serious manner before putting a syringe in an IV that I sort of let myself go, allow myself to relax a bit.

The tunnel vision started, and this time I knew I was going to black out.

CHAPTER 54

It took the other racers less than twelve hours to get back to Dallas. It took me a week. The race was canceled after Horne's fall on the rappelling lane and Totten's ensuing escape attempt. He died when I fell on him. His head collided with the side of the rock at about the same time the gun went off. Who knows if that bullet had been on its way to kill Kathy when my upper thigh intersected it, but she seems to think she owes me her life.

Once I was evacuated, once the two crime scenes were cordoned off, Horne's and Totten's, the racers were packed off to the train for a quick return trip and the spectators, those who weren't detained and questioned as witnesses, were allowed to leave. I bet the park returned to normal quickly and our little adventure was given very little thought. No one ever got to finish the Big Bend Adventure race and based on what Kathy told me no one ever would. Tony, the organizer, had told her that he was going back to managing fun runs in the city.

I was questioned in the hospital both in El Paso, then again in Dallas. There was a lot of unraveling to do. I was glad for Mike's help. Without him, I doubt if the police would ever have believed our story. Even I had a hard time believing it all.

At first, I only gave the facts of what I knew. How I had seen the cut end of the rope and suspected Totten. How he ran when I confronted him. How he started to shoot at Kathy and how I jumped on him to stop him. It wasn't till after the third round of questions that I allowed myself the chance to think about why. Plus it was Kathy in the hospital next to me, recovering from her own gunshot wound, a shot to the arm that went in then back out, who helped me piece it all together.

It was from Mike and Kathy, back at my apartment, that I heard about Kay's confession. After Horne and Totten died, she had broken down and confessed. She had killed Georgia. Jealousy. She thought that Georgia was trying to get back together with Totten and she confronted her about it. It came out that she confronted her in that vacant lot with every intention of killing her, the fact that she lured her down the path and had the knife proved that out. Was Georgia trying to rekindle her past relationship with Totten? Was that why Georgia had left Horne? Who knows? Kay thought so. Anyone else who could have shed some light on it wound up dead, Georgia, Totten, and Horne, all gone.

Bridget? She had nothing to do with any of it. She was a product of Totten trying to draw attention away from Kay. Totten had an alibi for Georgia's murder, he was seen by all the others on the run. Kay hadn't been there. According to Kay, after the police interviewed her and Totten, Totten decided that he needed to make it look like someone was trying to target Luther's clients. So on a day when Kay was out with the group, Totten rode down Bridget. She said that he hoped no one would think that two people were involved in the only two murders of the group's existence.

She was also able to tell the police why Totten killed Horne. Kay said she wanted to confess once they came on the trip, but Totten refused to let her. He said that they had to keep appearing normal. It was when Horne shoved Kay that Totten decided to kill him. That too had been a tandem effort. Kay had been a spotter for him on the rappelling lane. Totten cut through half of the rope and zipped down knowing that a much heavier Horne would cause a tremendous amount of stress on the weakened rope. Kay was there to ensure Horne went down the rappelling lane first and to make sure no one else went if it didn't break. How she was supposed to do that without exposing her and Totten who knows, but in the end, they had a pretty good plan.

I found all this out, but it took us a few long days and nights in the hospital to try to come up with a reasonable explanation for what we thought was the biggest mystery.

"Where did he think he was going to go?" Kathy asked for what to me seemed like the thousandth time. She spent an equal amount of time on her laptop and asking questions about Totten.

"I guess he was just trying to get away, escape," Mike said.

"But why?" Kathy again. "Just because of the rope?"

"Panic," Mike said.

Typical for Kathy, she was tenacious, but as they talked, my mind worked. Eventually, some answers came to the surface.

"Where could he go?" Kathy asked. "I mean sure he could disappear into the mountains for a few days, but not forever. He was surrounded by desert. He had to understand that."

"I think you're asking the wrong question," I said. They both looked up at me. "I think what you should be asking is why he panicked."

"What's the difference?" Mike looked puzzled.

"If he was panicking he obviously wasn't thinking straight," I said. "He was just trying to getaway. What made him start panicking?"

"That's easy," Mike said. "It's like you said when you confronted him with the rope and asked him about the knife." "Nope," I said. "That's not when he really started to panic."

Kathy considered for a moment then spoke up. "He's right, it wasn't the knife," she said. "It was Luther."

Mike looked over toward her. "What about him?"

"It was Luther," I said. "It was when he saw Luther that he started to run. He even said, 'What are you doing here.'"

"So?"

"So, I think Totten thought we knew more than we did.

I think he thought Luther was there for him. Like Luther knew he and Kay had killed Bridget and Georgia."

I had been thinking ever since I got to the hospital. Why had he run? Over those long days in the hospital, it had been hazy but, once I got home it had started to congeal. Now, saying it out loud, I could feel the pieces coming together. I felt like a kindergarten teacher trying to explain physics, lots of explanations but little understanding.

"I don't understand," Mike said.

I looked at him. "We know he didn't kill Georgia, Kay admitted that she did it. And we know he killed Bridget to try to throw the police off her track. I bet Totten thought they'd never believe there were two people committing the murders. Since they both had alibis they'd be safe."

"And he was right," Kathy said. "They were insulated from the murders. Mike told us he wasn't a suspect. Neither was Kay."

"Okay," Mike said. "I get all that but that doesn't help your argument that he would panic when he saw Luther?"

"He thought he was safe," I said. "Think about how worried he must have been when after this third murder, Horne's, when he thinks it will have absolutely no bearing on the first two, he sees Luther standing there. You and I knew he was there," I said to Kathy. "I mean Luther came out of nowhere for him. He was probably shocked to see him."

"I knew he was there but still I was shocked when he just came up," Kathy added.

"Right," I said. "Naturally Totten would have thought about AFC and Dallas. Now add to that the fact that he was worried about this third murder. He was amped from having just killed Horne. He probably thought Luther had figured out something about Georgia's and Bridget's deaths."

"Plus didn't Luther say something like 'we know you did it'?"

"Exactly," I said. "Luther was just talking about the rope. Totten probably thought he meant all the murders. It was probably the only thing that made sense when he saw Luther standing there."

It came to me later that night that it was somehow fitting

that Luther's paranoia would lead to Totten's panic and, ultimately, to the solution to the murders at his business.

CHAPTER 55

It was two months before I could walk. Even then I had to use a walker. It was four months before I was able to walk by myself. Jogging and running took the better part of a year. No working for Luther throughout that whole time. After a few weeks, I didn't mind. The longer I went without seeing him and the other team members the easier it was to sever the bond. It was like weaning myself from a drug. Eventually, I started to wonder what it was that I used to like about it so much.

I was able to model almost immediately. Kathy had to help me a lot at first. For that first week or two, she was over every night. With my not being able to move quickly it took me much longer to finish a model on my own. Things that would have been simple like reaching the next table to get a modeling knife was painful and took three times as long. Kathy stood in as my assistant.

She hired me a real assistant on the third week. They showed up early one morning. I tried to keep my disappointment concealed but I'm sure it came out.

"You don't like him?" Kathy asked me as the assistant looked around at the models on my table and got oriented to the work he would help me with.

"He's fine I guess."

"Then why are you so down?" she asked. "Your hip hurting?"

"Yeah," I said, not sure I wanted to discuss the real reason. I felt her hand rub up and down my back gingerly. It was that touch, and not knowing if it were intimacy or friendship, that made me decide to tell her what I really felt.

"Actually my hip is fine," I whispered so that the assistant who was looking at the beginning stages of an oil derrick wouldn't hear. "I'm mad about something."

Kathy turned so she could look me in the eyes.

"What?" she said.

I pointed my finger at the assistant. "I don't need him. I thought I was working fine during the day and then together you and I knocked out a ton at nights."

"I want to sell more of your stuff," she said. She pointed at the assistant. "With Richard, you should be able to get a lot more done."

I knew it was going to sound ridiculous when I said it, but I couldn't stop myself, and at this point didn't want to. "I liked having you come over at nights," I said.

Kathy smiled. "He only works until five. You're not getting rid of your evening assistant." Her hand traveled up and down my back again, this time there was no confusion if the gesture was meant to be friendly or intimate. She followed it up with a slow kiss to my cheek.

I saw Luther and Mom a lot while I convalesced. They came over most Sundays to bring me dinner and a casserole for the week. Kathy always found a way to be absent when Luther was around. I didn't blame her, for the most part, I wished I could have joined her. Dinner was always stilted and awkward. Luther barely spoke, Mom always asked how I was doing. They looked at the models and Luther tried his best not to sound too disdainful. It was almost a full year since the adventure race when I was finally up and running again, that Luther brought up AFC.

"When you think you can come back out?" he asked.

Despite his deep, gravel voice his tone was light and airy as if he thought it would be a nice fun topic of conversation.

We were sitting at my little kitchen table. Mom had just served her lasagna. The steam from our plates wafted in front of our faces. Despite the fact, we had not spoken about AFC for almost a year I knew exactly what he meant.

"Don't think I'm going to," I said.

"You're running okay, right?"

I nodded.

"More salad, Sweetie?" Mom tried to interrupt but Luther went on as if she had not spoken.

"So, then," Luther continued, "when are you coming back out?"

"I'm not."

"Why?"

"I'm doing alright here." I motioned to the models in the living room. There were five or six different models on the tables now. More expensive and more detailed than any that I had been working on a year earlier. Kathy's promotion of my work had made my work her most profitable business line. She was looking for space for me to expand and was thinking of hiring another assistant as well.

"I'm offering you a chance to own a real business," Luther said. "I haven't forgotten our agreement. We can still make that happen."

"Maybe we should talk about this another time." Mom again. I think even she knew there was no stopping the conversation.

"You forgot about that deal last year as I recall," I said. "And I don't want your business anymore."

"What's that mean?" Luther's voice grew rougher and more intense.

"Which part?" I asked. "The part about the deal or not wanting your business?" It felt good to not be afraid of Luther.

Luther considered me for a second; his head tilted to the side. I wondered if he thought it made him look thoughtful. I didn't tell him that it made me think of a puppy. My view of him had started to change during the Sunday dinners and I had my assistant, Richard to thank for it. I remembered how Luther treated me, both as a son and as an employee. I realized how easy it was to mentor, how fulfilling it was to see an employee grow and perform, how proud I was at his accomplishments. Had Luther ever felt these same things for me?

"You're telling me you'd rather sit here and fuck around with these rinky-dink models rather than own your own business."

"I'm making more with my models than I could with AFC," I countered. "Plus Kathy's making me a VP."

Luther leaned back like he was holding aces in a game of poker. "Hell," he said, "I'll make you a VP if that's all you want."

I shook my head and I saw in Luther's eyes that he knew his aces were useless. The rest of the meal was typical Sunday evening, but I kept seeing Luther glance over at me, and every now and then look over at that models as if wondering what secrets were in them that could possibly counter AFC. He could look all he wanted, he would never find it.

###

Thank you for reading my book. I hope you enjoyed reading it as much as I enjoyed writing it. Please take a moment to leave a comment at the site from which you downloaded it. You may also contact me at rgh8373@gmail.com

www.ingramcontent.com/pod-product-compliance
Lightning Source LLC
Chambersburg PA
CBHW071247170626
46809CB00001B/115

9781301821419